The staff of Terrace Vale Police Station have their work cut out. As it is, their clear-up rate is one of the lowest in the Metropolitan Police, and they are still no nearer catching a man they have nicknamed Phantom Flannelfoot, a burglar whose technique once inside the victim's house is decidedly amateur, but whose method of gaining entry without leaving the slightest trace remains a mystery. An elaborate chain of buck-passing leaves the case at the door of Detective Inspector Harry Timberlake, a policeman of unusual background.

Then WPC Sarah Lewis, known at the Terrace Vale nick as the 'Welsh Rarebit', finds the body of Howard Foulds QC with an axe embedded in his skull. He is the first victim of a spate of violent murders, which will make the workload even heavier.

DI Timberlake becomes heavily involved in the Foulds case, but he has problems of his own. His first serious love affair, with the attractive Dr Jenny Long, is somehow making him uneasy and constant work interruptions don't help. At the same time he is becoming increasingly aware of WPC Sarah Lewis's attractions. And for that matter Sarah Lewis's own personal life is far from straightforward, so when she gets an idea of how Phantom Flannelfoot might be operating she decides to devote her energies to her work.

Vengeance

Max Marquis

MACMILLAN
LONDON

First published in 1990 by
MACMILLAN LONDON LIMITED
4 Little Essex Street London WC2R 3LF
and Basingstoke

Associated companies in Auckland, Delhi, Dublin, Gaborone, Hamburg,
Harare, Hong Kong, Johannesburg, Kuala Lumpur, Lagos, Manzini,
Melbourne, Mexico City, Nairobi, New York, Singapore and Tokyo

ISBN 0-333-54306-8

A CIP catalogue record for this book is available from the
British Library

Typeset by Macmillan Production Ltd

Printed and bound in Great Britain by Billing and Sons Ltd, Worcester

Chapter 1

This was the fourth night the man in the car had waited to kill Titus Lloyd and he felt in his bones that this time he would get him. The first night a couple of drunken teenagers, a girl and a boy, had come swaying past. They were giggling and fumbling with each other, making Lloyd cross the road before his usual spot. The next night a newspaper van drove past. Once Lloyd suddenly changed his mind and went back to the station for something he'd forgotten. The man in the car could have waited till he came out again but he'd made up his mind that the slightest variation from his plan would make him scrub the operation. He could always try again later when everything was perfect.

Titus Lloyd was forty-five, medium height, medium colouring, medium build. The only thing that set him slightly out of the ordinary was his railway porter's cap. Maybe it made him even more ordinary. Although Lloyd was a porter at Wallsend Bridge station, he never carried anyone's luggage. He did everything else: sold tickets, collected them, answered the phone, changed faulty light bulbs, took care of all the cleaning and locked up the station at 00.37 a.m. every morning when he was on night shift. Wallsend Bridge station served the southern part of Wallsend, a Thameside area of expensive Edwardian houses and workmen's cottages that had been modernised into 'desirable town residences for executives' who didn't mind living like sardines.

The area was full of media people. Somebody said that if a bomb dropped on Wallsend, most of the BBC, ITV and the TV-commercials studios would go out of business the next day. A lot of people thought that might be a good thing.

There were only two passengers on the last train. Five minutes after they had gone down the road out of sight, Titus Lloyd carefully locked the station's steel trellis gate, checked it, then walked

7

towards the pedestrian crossing twenty yards up the road, away from the man in the car. Even when there was no traffic about, Lloyd always used the pedestrian crossing.

The man in the car started the engine and let the car roll forward slowly. As Lloyd got a third of the way across the road the driver slammed the accelerator to the floorboards and switched the headlights on full.

For a fatal second – literally fatal – Titus Lloyd stopped, frozen by shock, like a rabbit in the middle of a country lane, a perfect target for the ton and a half of car bearing down on him.

The Metropolitan Police Terrace Vale Area runs from the park with its expensive houses and medium-sized hotels in the south to the grimy, half-industrial, half-residential area in the north. The northern boundary is a winding main road which finally joins up with the motorway still further north.

To the east, Terrace Vale almost reaches a fashionable shopping area, managing to take in only the less prosperous side of a street lined with shops that sell electronic spares. The expensive hi-fis and TVs are sold on the other side of the street, in the next Metropolitan Police area. The western boundary is a feeder road to the main ring road, and then a combined British Rail and Underground line. In a triangle formed by the ring road, feeder road and railway, and under a concrete umbrella of a flyover, is a gypsy encampment of expensive cars and shiny caravans, all paid for in cash. An almost permanent pall of smoke hangs over the camp from broken-up cars being burned.

Terrace Vale is as complete a mish-mash of urban living as you could hope – or fear – to find: a few minor embassies and consulates, luxury hotels and seedy boarding houses, expensive private homes and old houses divided and subdivided into cramped bedsitters, plush gambling clubs and dubious clip joints, high-class call-girls and back-of-the-car whores, four-star restaurants and Chinese takeaways, gardens and ghettos . . . There are long-standing residents and overnight transients, international criminals and junkie bag-snatchers: a teeming, multi-racial community in a self-contained area where something is always going on – usually illegal.

In the south-east corner of Terrace Vale, just off the main road, is a building that never sleeps and never closes its doors.

Staffed by a team of men and women, it operates twenty-four hours a day, 365 days a year.

Terrace Vale police station, otherwise known as the nick or the factory, was built in the last century. Someone once said that it had originally been designed as a workhouse but had never been used for that purpose because it was too gloomy. The rooms and offices were large and high-ceilinged and almost impossible to heat, except in summer, when they could do service as a sauna. A week after the rooms were redecorated they always looked dingy again, and the windows seemed to have some strange attraction for dirt and grime. When you were in the place you always felt it was raining outside. A couple of hours in there dented the resistance of the cockiest criminal.

Just across the river, in the more select south-west London area of Wallsend, PC David Harley was patrolling a side street not far from the riverside road. Something caught his eye. After a moment's inspection he called up on his personal radio.

'One-oh-four to Control.'

'Control to one-oh-four,' Sergeant Peasegood replied from Wallsend police station.

'Harley here, Sarge. That hit-and-run last night. The porter killed near the station.'

'Yeah?' Sergeant Peasegood was a man of few words in the morning.

'I think I've found the car. Radiator grille bashed in, nearside headlight smashed, blood on the grille and bumper. It's a Rover 2600, registration . . .' He read off the number from the twisted plate.

'Stand by.' After a moment the radio crackled into life again. 'It's registered to a man in Barnet. Reported it stolen from outside a restaurant.'

'I bet,' Harley smiled cynically.

'It's kosher. He reported it ten days ago. You hang on there until we can come and pick it up. Make sure that nobody touches it.'

Harley switched off his radio. 'I'd never have thought of that,' he said with heavy irony to no one in particular.

Detective Chief Inspector Ted Greening parked his car in the courtyard behind Terrace Vale police station, belched sourly and dug into his pocket for his indigestion tablets. He went in through the back entrance, hoping that no one with bad news would notice him before he got to his office. He was out of luck. The duty sergeant, Sergeant Anthony C. Rumsden, was keeping an ear cocked for the back door. As soon as he heard it click he put his head out into the corridor.

'Ted!' he called. Greening recognised the tone, and briefly considered pretending that he hadn't heard before answering, 'Morning, Tony.'

Sergeant Rumsden preferred to be called Anthony if people addressed him by his Christian name. Tony would do at a pinch, but he reacted badly to being called Tone, or Rummy. The C stood for Chamberlain. Rumsden's father had been a great admirer of Neville Chamberlain and believed that Winston Churchill had given him a raw deal. Locally, Anthony Rumsden Senior had been considered something of an advanced nut case. Sergeant Anthony Rumsden kept his middle name a close secret. If it were found out his life would become impossible, given the coarse and disrespectful minds of most of the Terrace Vale coppers.

'The Chief Super wants to see you soon as you get in.'

Greening swore. 'Any idea what it's about?'

Rumsden shrugged.

In the minute or so that it took Ted Greening to get to Chief Superintendent Liversedge's office he tried to guess what Liversedge had found out about him so he could have a ready answer. The list of possibilities was depressingly long.

Ted Greening was just over fifty, but looked older. He was a glad-hander, back-slapper, knowing winker and dirty storyteller. All he wanted now was a life with no waves. His eye was firmly fixed on his retirement in a couple of years. The pity of it all was that once he was a first-class copper, a successful thief-taker. He had several commendations for his work and his bravery, but the last one was a long time ago. Bernard Liversedge was a superior-class, smoother version of his DCI. He and Greening understood each other.

'Good morning, sir. You wanted to see me?' Until Ted Greening knew what this was all about he was playing safe by calling Liversedge 'sir'.

'Sit down, Mr Greening.'

'Mr Greening.' Not 'Ted'. The signal was clear. *Oh, Christ*, Ted Greening thought.

'The Assistant Commissioner has been on to me. They've started compiling the latest crime statistics.' He shuffled some pieces of paper on his desk. 'Our clear-up rate is one of the worst in the Met. Now, you know I believe in letting each man get on with his own job as much as possible. I don't like to interfere. Delegation of responsibility . . .' He gave a politician's smile.

In other words, *I'm* not taking the can back, the message came through.

Liversedge shuffled his papers again. 'These break-ins . . .' Greening knew exactly which ones he meant. 'Where are you with them?'

'Inspector Timberlake hasn't got any further than the coppers in the other areas,' Greening said, his tension easing. He could pass the buck, too. At the same time he made the point that Terrace Vale wasn't the only area that was struggling. 'Chummy's got all of us completely f— foxed,' he underlined the point. 'According to the collator, he's worked a couple of other areas before coming on to our patch. He was at Wallsend Riverside last. We call him Phantom Flannelfoot.'

'I see,' Liversedge said neutrally. 'What's so special about him?'

'Once he's inside a drum it's obvious he's an amateur. Opens chests of drawers from the top down instead of the bottom up. Takes gear out of the drawers bit by bit instead of dumping everything on the floor or the bed. Doesn't go straight to all the regular hiding places – under the mattress, key on top of the wardrobe. You know. And he's no expert. He's lifted a lot of rubbish and left expensive gear in plain view. Yeah, he's an amateur all right.' He paused. 'But . . .'

'If he's an amateur, he shouldn't be too difficult to find.'

'Ah,' said Greening with a hint of returning confidence. 'The trouble is he gets in like a pro. In fact, more like a sodding magician. Nobody has the faintest idea how he does it. Not a mark, not a scratch on a door or window. Nothing. Not on a single one of the thirty-odd drums he's done that we know about. Forensic have been over the whole lot with bleeding microscopes, ultra-violet and God knows what.'

'No common factor to all the robberies?'

'Not that we can see. No servants, of course; no locksmith,

gas-fitter, carpenter, electrician, meter-reader, window-cleaner, milkman, insurance agent or company, paperboy . . . Nobody's common to more than two of the houses. Maybe three.' Answer that one, Greening thought with some satisfaction. 'Nor doctors,' he added, like a man trumping an ace.

'Fences?'

Greening shook his head. 'The snouts haven't heard a whisper, and none of the stolen gear has turned up. Probably out of the country by now.'

'How much has he stolen?'

'On this patch, and the others, something between four and five hundred grand. Nearer five is my guess. Like I said, he's got everybody right flabbergasted.'

'All the more credit to you when you catch him, then,' Liversedge said with a thin smile. 'You', not 'we', Ted Greening noted.

'I'm sure Inspector Timberlake hasn't lost sight of that.' Greening knew how to duck just as well as his chief superintendent.

Detective Inspector Harry Timberlake, the son of a general labourer and a hospital cleaner, was born in the docklands area of east London. The birth took place at home, the Timberlake's council house, otherwise the parents would have sworn that there had been a mix-up of babies in the hospital.

Harry was a victim of an eruption of long-buried genes which caused a weird regression to some unknown ancestor's physiognomy. He was a complete enigma to Herbert and Daisy Timberlake, for he had virtually no physical resemblance to either of them. The only things he seemed to have inherited were his father's muscularity and his mother's Virgoan nit-picking fastidiousness. As Harry matured he grew increasingly unlike them: Herbert and Daisy Timberlake were pudding-faced ordinary, while the teenage Harry had a face with strong planes and deep-set eyes under thick eyebrows, which gave him a disconcerting, penetrating stare when he turned it on. In profile he looked almost like a roman emperor, although the fashionable long hair of the period disguised it somewhat. Later a street fight against the odds rearranged the shape of his nose and made him look even more intimidating.

While Harry was still a youth his appearance caused a great deal of gossip among the neighbours. For a time his father was constantly having punch-ups with men who made crude jokes about Daisy and the rent-collector or milkman. The comprehensive thumpings that Herbert Timberlake handed out eventually discouraged any more snide remarks – at least in his hearing.

Young Harry's physical appearance was only half the story. He sailed through all examinations. He got seven O levels and three A levels – English, sociology and history. He could have got a fourth in political science if they'd let him take it. When he left school and started looking for a job, without thinking too much about it, Harry joined the police. It was an instinctive decision and not a reasoned one.

For once, Harry Timberlake – sometimes called the whiz-kid or HT, as in 'high tension' – was having a day off. He was owed enough days off to take a Mediterranean cruise, but he enjoyed his work. He was taking this break only because his latest girl-friend, Jenny Long, had presented him with an all-too-believable ultimatum: either he take her out on her day off, or it was goodbye. Definitely and permanently.

Dr Jenny Long was a surgical registrar at St Lawrence's Hospital in west London, a vast Victorian pile that looked as if it had started life as a German railway station. Jenny met Harry when he was taken into Casualty one night with a couple of wounds in his shoulder from a broken bottle. At first she had thought he was a thick macho yobbo who'd been involved in a football ground punch-up. She was pretty sharp with him as she stitched up the cuts. He put her down as a snooty feminist bitch and probably frigid with it. It didn't take long for both of them to realise their mistakes.

With her clothes on Jenny reminded him strongly of the actress Joanna Lumley. Harry didn't know if she looked like her with her clothes off. Harry and Jenny had been lovers for seven months now. It was the longest relationship he'd ever had with a woman. His affairs were usually short, ending before any hint of commitment came into them. He didn't know anything about Jenny's sex life before she met him, and he didn't want to. If ever he started to wonder where their relationship was going, he quickly shut the thought out of his mind. One important bond they had was that they both worked long, erratic hours and understood when the other had to call off a date at five minutes' notice. But this was not one of those days.

Jenny had taken no chances. She had insisted on driving them out for lunch in her own car to a Thameside restaurant well outside the Metropolitan Police area. She used her asthmatic Metro because she knew Harry was quite capable of 'accidentally' knocking on the switch of his police radio and deciding there was an emergency that only he could deal with.

As it was a weekday the restaurant, despite its reputation, wasn't overcrowded, so they could get a window table overlooking the river. While they were eating their hors d'oeuvres Jenny suddenly asked Harry, 'What made you join the police?'

'Nothing *made* me join. It was a free choice. Instinctive.'

'Did your careers adviser at school suggest it?'

'We didn't have one. It wasn't that sort of school. The headmaster wanted me to try for university.' Almost before he had finished speaking, Harry Timberlake regretted saying it. Jenny looked up sharply, surprised. 'Why didn't you?'

He tried to put an end to this line of conversation with a dismissive shrug.

At school he was by far the best pupil in his class. At first this made him thoroughly disliked by his classmates: they reckoned that Harry was being a show-off who was trying to make them look stupid. Harry never thought of himself as 'brilliant' or even 'clever'. He just said he had a knack for learning. He would have swapped it for being good at football. As he was never cocky they gradually accepted his oddness with the same indifference as they would show to someone with short sight or a bad leg. Most of the time.

So, Harry tried to keep his head down and be one of the crowd, but it didn't always work. In any group activity he instinctively started to take the lead and try to run things, which reignited old resentments.

Jenny Long persisted. 'What did your headmaster think about your not trying for university?'

Harry remembered the interview clearly. His headmaster bounced about with pleasure at the thought of one of the pupils from his 'special area' school going on to university. He explained eloquently and at length all the reasons why Harry *should* go to university. But Harry said he didn't want to, thank you very much.

14

'Why not?' asked the headmaster, going rather pink.

'What's the point?' Harry asked. 'There're university graduates sweeping streets, driving lorries and stacking supermarket shelves.' Before the headmaster could interrupt Harry added, 'And I don't fancy myself as a teacher.'

'What *do* you fancy yourself as, may I ask?' the head asked acidly.

'Dunno.'

Threats, promises, cajolery and plain lies had no effect. Harry simply would not try for university. Finally the headmaster could only splutter in speechless frustration.

'But why the police?' Jenny asked.

'I told you. It was an instinctive decision. And the right one,' he added firmly. In fact he couldn't imagine himself as anything other than a policeman, and nor could anyone else who knew him. He worked long and hard because he enjoyed it, was ambitious and had an unquenchable enthusiasm. It was only surpassed by his hatred for criminals as enemies of an ordered society. Privately he sometimes admitted that he didn't think all that much of society, either. Timberlake didn't realise it, but he was a puritan.

The waiter arrived with their main course. Harry was having steak and kidney pie, boiled potatoes and cauliflower. 'My God,' said Jenny Long, looking at his crowded plate. 'It's a wonder you don't look like Cyril Smith if that's one of your usual meals.'

'It's not. Most of the time I seem to eat on the run.'

'I'm surprised they do typically English meals like that here.'

'It's for the foreign tourists.'

Jenny's own meal was some exotic concoction made from lamb cutlets. They were presented looking like three small round islands in a creamy-brown sea of what was undoubtedly a delicious sauce. A few tiny French beans were carefully lined up like boats drawn up on the shore.

'You know why they give you so much sauce?' Harry asked.

Jenny shook her head.

'So you won't realise how empty the plate is.'

'You're a cynic.'

'I prefer realist.'

'What did your parents think about your joining the police?'

'I thought I was supposed to be the interrogator,' Harry said, not altogether amused.

'Doctors have to do it, too. Much the same sort of situation, really. We question people who are scared, and don't want to tell the truth.'

Harry thought for a moment, then nodded.

'Well?' Jenny said. 'How did your parents take it?'

'They were acutely embarrassed. By then I was living with them in a high-rise flat on a rough estate, and the news that their son was a copper, one of the Old Bill, spread more quickly than crabs in a Bombay brothel and was about as popular.'

'You have a charming turn of phrase.'

'I thought doctors weren't shockable. Anyway, I moved out, much to everyone's relief, including my own. Now, can we leave it? My steak and kidney pie's getting cold.'

The man stopped breathing while he painted the thinnest of lines along the length of the car's coachwork in a single stroke. He put down the fine, camel-hair brush and slowly let out his breath. He took off his glasses with the clip-on magnifiers, polished them, put them on again and leant forward to study his work. Perfect.

It was one of his finest pieces: a 1/24th scale model of a Mark II Jaguar with steering that actually worked. The wire wheels, made with piano wire, were minor masterpieces on their own. In addition to other refinements, the bonnet catch operated from the driver's position. It lifted to reveal a perfectly shaped model engine. The miniature oil-filter cap could be unscrewed and there was even a scale-size dipstick that could be removed. The man had painted the bottom of the dipstick with brown lacquer to give the impression that there was oil in the sump.

He switched off the strong fluorescent lamp on the bench and covered the model with a glass dome so that no dust would stick to the painted coachline, then set to tidying his workbench so that everything was lined up in its proper place like a troop of guardsmen. By the time he had finished, the attic workroom would have made an operating theatre look scruffy.

The last thing he did was to go to a large cork wallboard covered with newspaper cuttings and photographs. There was also a typewritten list. He studied one photograph for a long moment before turning out the lights. Finally he carefully locked the door behind him – he did *everything* carefully – and went downstairs to the living room.

The woman was putting a meal on the table as he entered the dining room.

'Finished it?' she asked.

'Yes.'

'That's good.' She paused, and then asked diffidently, 'Are you going out this evening?'

'Yes.'

She asked for no explanation, and he offered none.

He never did.

WPC Sarah Lewis, known to her colleagues at Terrace Vale police station as the Welsh Rarebit, was normally a fairly cheerful young woman, but she also suffered from Celtic gloom on occasion. Right now she was pissed off. Anyone within earshot of her would have realised this at once, because she said, right out loud, 'I'm pissed off. Thoroughly pissed off,' she added, to chase any lingering doubts.

It was the morning after Harry Timberlake's day off. Sarah was on patrol in Elm Park Square, in one of Terrace Vale's better areas. The houses were large and occupied by single families to whom bank managers were always pleasant: people like international actors, private bankers, pop stars, television personalities, very superior call-girls and one MP member of the loony far Left. There were no bedsitter tenants here. Parking space was hard to come by at kerbs lined with expensive cars with new registrations.

The reason for Sarah's ill humour was that she was forced to live in one room of a house where the landlady was a sharp-tongued, narrow-minded, screwed-up old bitch. No, not screwed-up, Sarah thought.. That's probably her trouble. It was Sarah's own trouble, as a matter of fact. Her boyfriend was a constable at Terrace Vale – although none of their colleagues had guessed at the relationship yet. If any of their superiors even suspected, one or both of them would be posted away. The boyfriend, PC Greg Davidson, lived in police accommodation for single men. It meant that he and Sarah had about as much sex life as an inmate of an open prison. If only she or Greg could find a small flat . . . Her knees felt weak at the thought of long afternoons or long nights in bed with Greg. Or even long afternoons *and* nights . . .

17

These pleasant thoughts were cut short by a scream. It was no squawk of pleasure, surprise or skylarking. That sort of squeal wasn't unusual in this Sloane Ranger outpost. This was a retching, throat-rasping scream of terror. A scream like that in broad daylight in Elm Park Square brought up goose-pimples on Sarah's back. She hurried towards the sound without breaking into a run. A police officer running when not actually in pursuit of a criminal caused public alarm, Sarah remembered, but that scream, followed by another, wasn't doing much for public calm.

This second scream made it easier for Sarah to locate the source of the trouble. She quickened her pace up the pathway to the front door of a large double-fronted house.

A middle-aged, inexpensively dressed woman leant against the doorframe. She was clutching a cloth shopping bag to her chest with one hand and holding a bunch of keys in the other. She took a deep, shuddering breath ready to scream again when Sarah said crisply, 'It's all right. Now, what's the trouble, madam?'

The woman made no reply and continued to stare fixedly into the hallway. Sarah followed her eyeline. The door to the first room on the right was open.

Sarah peered in, then fought back the vomit that started to rise in her throat.

Ted Greening took the bottle from the bottom drawer of his desk and poured himself a large Scotch in a paper cup. He had got half of it down when Sergeant Rumsden stuck his head through the door. 'Hi!' he shouted cheerfully. Greening coughed and spluttered as some of the cheap spirit went down the wrong way.

'For Chrissake don't make me jump like that,' Greening complained. He finished his drink then took a handful of cashews and threw them into his mouth.

'What's up, Ted? Was the Chief Super rough on you?'

'Him? Rough? You ever had your balls nibbled by a rabbit?'

Rumsden thought about it. 'Can't say I have,' he said at last.

'As if I haven't got enough troubles,' Greening moaned.

'You've got more now.'

'Bloody hell. What?'

'WPC Lewis just called in.'

'Oh, the Welsh Rarebit. What's she on about?'

18

'There's been a murder.'

'That's all I need. How does she know it's murder?'

'The body has a chopper stuck in the top of its head. It seems a fair guess.'

Green swore nastily as if it was all Sarah's fault. He asked, 'Where is it?' Rumsden handed over a piece of paper with a name and address written on it.

'Oh, fuck!'

'I thought you might say that.'

'Howard Foulds, Q bloody C. It would have to be someone like him. SOCOs and doctor been warned?' Rumsden nodded.

Greening thought about having another drink and reluctantly decided against it. For the moment, anyway. He had a half-bottle in the car. 'Give Harry Timberlake a shout for me on your way out, will you, Tony?'

'He's already left.'

'What?'

'The call came in half an hour ago, while you were getting your balls nibbled. Harry said he'd take care of things.'

'I bet he bloody did,' Greening said.

By the time Ted Greening arrived at Elm Park Square there were more flashing blue lights than at a disco. Half a dozen jam butties – police cars so nicknamed because of the yellow-red-yellow lines along their sides – were parked with maximum inconvenience to traffic. A milkman was complaining that he couldn't get his float out of the square. Nobody was taking much notice. At last he bumped the vehicle up on to the pavement with a great jingling of bottles and escaped that way, waving goodbye with two fingers at a police driver.

Greening noticed the police surgeon's car and the SOCOs' – scene of crime officers' – vehicle as he walked across the pavement to the house. The uniformed men had already put up tapes on either side of the house, winding them round the plane trees – there were no elms in Elm Park Square – and were keeping people well away.

Harry Timberlake, Sarah Lewis and the woman who had screamed were all in the hall, just beyond the open door of the room where the body still lay. The local police doctor was straightening up from over the body. In a case of sudden death the very first thing that must be done, even before the SOCOs get to work, is for a doctor to pronounce the victim dead. It doesn't matter if the head is a couple of feet from the body: the doctor has to confirm that the corpse is definitely dead.

'Hello, guv,' Timberlake said. Greening nodded.

The doctor made his way to the door, keeping to the narrow track marked out for him by the SOCOs so that he would make minimal disturbance of any physical evidence like dust, or a hair, left by the killer. The SOCOs, wearing their clean white overalls and overshoes, moved into the room.

'He's dead all right,' the doctor announced unnecessarily. He scratched the side of his nose and, indicating the axe in the victim's skull, said, 'I've had hangovers that felt like that.' He thought himself something of a wag. It was a minority opinion.

'Who found him?' Greening asked grumpily.

Sarah Lewis answered. 'Mrs Sanders here. She's the cleaner. She let herself in with her key and saw the— Mr Foulds on the floor there inside the sitting room.'

Mrs Sanders gave a small sound like a computer bleep and nodded in confirmation.

'I was passing, heard her scream and came in.'

'Anyone else in the house?'

'No,' Harry Timberlake answered. 'Mrs Foulds is on holiday in Italy.'

Greening addressed Sarah again. 'Did you search the place?'

Harry Timberlake looked at him in surprise.

Sarah was unruffled. 'No, sir.'

'So whoever did it could still have been here.'

'I didn't think that likely, sir. It was obvious that he'd been dead for some time, and the light was on. I reckoned that he'd been killed last night. In any case, the back door's bolted – you can see it from here, down at the bottom of the hall, and no one has come past us.' Put that in your pipe and stick it somewhere, Sarah thought savagely. She was rather proud of the way she'd coped with everything and Ted Greening was spoiling it all for her.

'You did very well, WPC,' Harry Timberlake said.

When Ted Greening had done everything he could at the scene of the crime, which wasn't much before the scientific squad and doctor had finished, he turned to Harry Timberlake.

'You take charge at this end, Harry,' he said with as encouraging a smile as he could manage. 'I'll get back to the nick and start organising things – incident room and all the rest, ready for when the AMIP mob turn up.'

In other words, leave me to do all the real work and carry all the cans, Timberlake thought bitterly. Then he brightened up. It might be a chance to shine in front of the hot-shot superintendent leading the AMIP team. These days it's no longer a question of 'calling in the Yard' to help with the investigation of a serious crime like murder. London is divided into eight areas and each has an Area Major Investigation Pool or AMIP commanded by a detective superintendent. As soon as the major crime is reported, an AMIP team is despatched from Scotland Yard.

While the SOCOs were examining the room where Foulds's body was found, vacuuming the carpet around the body, taking photographs and all the rest, and the fingerprint officer was gently dusting promising surfaces with aluminium powder using a feather-soft brush, Timberlake organised a search of the house. All that the detectives learned was that the late Howard Foulds QC wasn't short of a bob or two.

There was no sign of a break-in, and robbery didn't seem to be the motive. There were all sorts of expensive portable items in plain view, including a small cashbox containing about £200 on the desk top.

By some strange mental telepathy or intuition, Professor Peter Mortimer timed his arrival for five minutes after the scientific men had packed up their gear, leaving the scene of the crime clear for the pathologist. Mortimer, almost invariably referred to in popular newspapers as 'the eminent Professor Mortimer', would have been about six feet three inches tall if he'd ever stood up straight, but a lifetime of bending over dead bodies on slabs had made him stoop-shouldered. The top of his head was only six feet above the floor when he was wearing shoes. He had a rather long, scraggy neck with a prominent Adam's apple that made him look as if a walnut had stuck halfway down his throat. He was rather like a decayed Gary Cooper. On his sixtieth birthday Mortimer tried to calculate just how many cadavers he had cut up in a lifetime of forensic pathology. He gave up counting as an impossible task, which depressed him deeply. He should have retired years before, but he had no home life. His wife died, his colleagues said, in self-defence against increasing boredom and in a last desperate attempt to get her husband to take a close look at her at least once.

21

Despite the low rate of pay for forensic pathologists he was comfortably off, thanks to income from books and lectures. His problem was that he didn't know what he would do if he retired. He had absolutely no outside interests. And Peter Mortimer was very good at his job.

If anyone asked him why he became a pathologist, he said it was predestined with his initials. It was the nearest he had ever come to a deliberate witticism in his entire life.

Although the cause of death of a man with a hatchet buried deeply in his skull would seem fairly obvious to most people, Mortimer took nothing for granted and carried out a detailed examination *in situ*.

'Post mortem at midday tomorrow,' he informed Timberlake.

Harry Timberlake took Mrs Sanders into the kitchen and got her to make them both a cup of tea while he questioned her.

'I don't suppose you know anyone who'd want to kill Mr Foulds?' he asked genially.

Mrs Sanders considered the question gravely before declaring that she didn't.

'Did he get any unusual phone calls while you were here?'

She shook her head.

'What about strange people knocking about the place?'

'I haven't noticed anybody.'

'How has Mr Foulds been acting recently?'

She shrugged. 'Same as usual.'

'This is a big house for you to manage on your own. Aren't there any other servants?'

'There's a married couple. Spanish, I think they are, or Portuguese. Foreign, anyway. And a Dutch au pair.'

'Where are they?'

'They went on holiday at the same time as Mrs Foulds.'

'When was that?' Harry Timberlake asked.

'Last week. Italy.'

The address and telephone number were on a memo pad on Foulds's desk. When Harry rang her to give her the news it took a long while to get her to the phone. There was a lot of laughing and talking in the background, with noises like glasses clinking. Lucia Foulds didn't lose her presence of mind. 'I hope you aren't tramping all over my house, making a mess,' she said, sounding like a mature Sloane Ranger who wanted to bring back capital punishment for sheep stealing.

'When will you be coming back?' Harry asked her as politely as he could manage.

'Perhaps some time next week. Or the week after,' she added reluctantly. 'Our solicitor can take care of the . . . arrangements for my husband. I'll have him get in touch with you.'

'I see.' Harry Timberlake was a little thrown by her self-possession.

'There's no point in my coming before. I can't help you with your enquiries, Inspector. I know nothing of my husband's professional affairs, and I certainly don't know of anyone who would want to kill him. Coming, darling,' she added to someone at her end. She sounded only slightly put out by her husband's murder, as if the garage had told her that the car wouldn't be ready tonight after all and she'd have to pick it up in the morning. At last it must have got through to her that she wasn't making a very good impression. 'I'd come back tonight, but my nerves . . . the shock . . .' Harry thought that she was as easily shocked as a rhinoceros. 'I don't think I could stand the journey. I need a few days to get over this.'

Her voice throbbed with all the sincerity of a politician on polling day.

Harry Timberlake hung up.

It had been a hell of a day for everyone, and longer for Sarah Lewis than most. She was the first one to be involved in the case. She'd hardly been off her feet all day, and they throbbed like a blacksmith's bellows – which was probably a good thing, because it took her mind off her other problems. After a rotten day doing house-to-house and typing up her report, she had gone for a meal with Greg Davidson. It had been great to sit down for a while, but agony keeping their hands off each other. She didn't know whether it made things easier or harder to bear that they were going away together for the weekend, to a hotel in Westcliff-on-Sea.

'At least we've got that to look forward to,' she told Greg.

'Thinking above it only makes it harder,' he said unthinkingly. Sarah snorted with laughter all over her lasagne.

Almost immediately afterwards her own frustration increased, and as she thought of all the weekend promised, she felt almost dizzy. For a moment the young couple remained silent, and when they did speak they snapped at each other until they realised why.

That was a couple of hours ago. As she got to her front door, she turned and waved at Greg in his car. He waved back, blew her a kiss and drove off. Sarah put her key into the Yale lock and went inside the house. She found the button of the automatic-shut-off light, pressed it and started upstairs. The door of the front room opened and the landlady peered out.

Mrs Ena Culliford was dressed in a dusty-pink dressing gown of quilted nylon, buttoned from ankle to neck. Her streaky hair was pulled back so hard that her eyebrows were set in permanent surprise. She had a thin, downturned mouth with a noticeable moustache above it. It was rumoured that a Mr Culliford existed somewhere in the back of that room.

Mrs Culliford was about to make some unpleasant remark when she caught the full force of Sarah Lewis's angry stare, which would have stopped a runaway horse. The older woman bolted back into her room. Sarah went upstairs and unlocked her own room. She had made it neat, tidy and homely, and she hated it. She wanted a place where Greg could come and visit her if they felt like it, and they felt like it almost all the time. She shut the door behind her and said a couple of words that nice young women weren't supposed to know.

Before Ted Greening left the Incident Room that had been set up in Terrace Vale police station he made a phone call.

'Ted Greening. You busy?' The answer satisfied him. 'See you in about a quarter of an hour, then.'

A little more than fifteen minutes later he pressed one of a battery of doorbells in a rundown early Edwardian house. The bell had no nameplate next to it. The entryphone crackled. 'Ted,' he said. There was a buzz and the doorlock clicked. He pushed the door open. The room he had rung was on the first floor. Its door was slightly ajar.

The two-roomed apartment was as pink as the late Jayne Mansfield's bedroom. Even the kitchen corner had a pink glow, reflecting the pink lamps and pink wallpaper. The open bedroom door revealed a pink bed with pink rugs on each side. There was a large pink velvet elephant perched on a pink-painted dressing table.

'Hello, Rita,' Greening said. He flopped into a pink easy

chair. As he glanced round the room he wondered if Rita took the *Financial Times*.

Rita shut the door behind him and turned the key in the lock. Without speaking she poured them both large Scotches. The amber whisky clashed with the colour scheme.

Rita was tall, with long legs and high breasts. She was wearing high-heeled slippers, a see-through *peignoir* which she left open, and nothing else. The pink lights traced interesting patterns on her black skin.

'You on this murder case?' she asked, sitting on the floor near him, her legs curled up beneath her.

He nodded.

Prostitutes are among the most valuable of police informants. Villains tell all sorts of secrets to whores, even when they are sober. Maybe the ultimate intimacy they share with the women gives a sense of professional secrecy to their relationship. Whatever it is, men boast of their crimes to them. It could be that a man who has to go to a prostitute has some inadequacy and he tries to compensate for it by boasting how tough he was when he blasted a security guard with a sawn-off shotgun, and how clever he is at fooling the pigs, the Bill or the Filth. Ted Greening had never bothered himself too much why villains opened their mouths as soon as they took off their trousers. He just took advantage of the fact.

'Heard anything?' he asked.

'It's a bit soon,' Rita said. 'If there's anything I'll call you.' She stirred her drink with her finger and looked up at him. 'You want to fuck?' she asked.

Greening stood up and took off his jacket. He was the only man with whom she went to bed here. This was where Rita lived: her working address was a few streets away.

When Greening got home his wife Marjorie was in bed. Even asleep – if she was asleep – her mouth was like a drawstring purse. She was wearing a grey flannelette nightdress that would have killed the lust of a Japanese sailor just back from a two-year whaling trip. Majorie was forty-eight, and looked as if she had been for the past ten years. She dutifully gave Ted Greening two children early in their marriage, then developed a permanent bedtime headache that had lasted for a good twenty-six years.

For twenty-four of them Greening hadn't cared. Soon after the marriage Ted Greening began to ask himself why he'd married Marjorie Spinks. As a nineteen-year-old Boots shop assistant she was attractive, with a seductive figure and an inviting manner. It was only after some months that it dawned on him that her air of sexual provocation was assumed and had been learned from films in the belief that it would make her appear adult and sophisticated. He soon learned that her reluctant approach to sex wasn't timidity: she genuinely had an eyes-closed, teeth-clenched, tight-fisted reaction to It.

As her husband got into bed beside her, Marjorie wrinkled her nose in disgust. He stank of whisky, cigarettes, cheap scent and another woman. She silently vowed to pray for him when she went to arrange the flowers at the church in the morning.

Harry Timberlake drove his Citroën BX GTI into his garage at the block of flats where he lived in Clapham. Since he first owned a car he had always driven Citroëns because of what he called their matchless suspension and the fact that they were always years ahead of their time. Harry Timberlake firmly believed that André Citroën was one of the major geniuses of the twentieth century, but then Harry was also a Fulham supporter. As he came out of the garage he noticed a light shining through the blinds of his window. It gave him the first feeling of warmth he'd had all day. Jenny was asleep in his bed when he entered, but she woke at his slight touch on her shoulder. She was fully awake in seconds as usual. Her ability to do that never failed to surprise him. In her job she was always being woken up in the middle of the night.

'Hello, darling,' she said. He looked at her with a sense of wonderment that had not diminished despite the time he had known her. In his bed she was an entirely different woman from the one who had been to lunch with him a couple of days earlier. In fact, he admitted to himself, she was half a dozen different women at different times. No matter how often he saw her there was always the same tiny shock of pleasure as if it were for the first time. It was a new experience for him, and the unaccustomed emotion it aroused in him made him a little uneasy. Jenny gave him a soft kiss, warm from the bed, that immediately stirred him.

'Hi, doc,' he greeted her.

'What time is it?'

'Just gone two. I didn't know whether I ought to wake you.'

'Don't be silly. I heard on the radio about the murder. I guessed you'd had a long day and needed cheering up.'

'You're a bloody marvel, d'you know that?'

'Yes.' They both chuckled.

Jenny always slept naked when she wasn't on duty at the hospital. She sat up in bed, looking spectacular. 'Can I get you something?'

'You've got it right there. I'll just have a Scotch and a quick shower.'

She got out of bed with a flash of slender limbs. 'You get into the shower. I'll bring us both a drink and scrub your back for you.'

'Thank God for the National Health Service.'

'Don't kid yourself. This is strictly private treatment, Inspector.'

Chapter 2

As soon as the murder of Howard Foulds was reported to Scotland Yard, the wheels were set in motion to send an investigation team to Terrace Vale. At 8 a.m. the following morning, Detective Superintendent Charles Harkness of the AMIP arrived to take charge of the Foulds murder enquiry. He began by making a courtesy call on Chief Superintendent Liversedge. The Chief Superintendent had rank and ten years' seniority over Harkness, but the younger man left him feeling uneasy and inferior. It made Liversedge talk rather too loudly, with a forced heartiness.

'Yes, I'll be leaving here fairly soon,' Liversedge said. 'I'm going to the Yard. Traffic Planning.' Liversedge's tone was defiant, although both of them knew that was a sort of 'In Charge of Paper Clips' posting.

'Ah,' Harkness replied.

'I don't mind admitting that I'll be glad to get out of Terrace Vale. Reported crime has been going up more than the rate of inflation. Tinpot "diplomats" breaking the law and claiming immunity, armed robbery, West Indian drinking clubs, muggings, drugs, prostitution, squats . . .' Liversedge knew he was talking too much, but couldn't help himself. 'You're not going to find it easy here, Mr Harkness. Relations with the public are bad, and the place is swarming with God knows how many local committees, all of them unofficial, and all of them pains in the arse.'

'Really,' Harkness said, wishing he could get the hell out of it.

'Committees for racial equality, sexual equality and the civil rights of pimps and muggers when they're arrested. Nobody worries about victims, though. They haven't got any committees.'

'Perhaps it might be an idea if you started one,' Harkness said without expression. Liversedge looked at him, wondering if he was trying to be sarcastic or something. Harkness gave him a

28

smile that made him seem even colder. 'Isn't there a local Victims' Support Group? A number of areas have them.'

Liversedge didn't answer, and regarded Harkness more closely. The man sitting across the desk from him was neatly dressed in a suit that looked as if it was made from something as creaseproof as armour plate. He wasn't very tall, probably just made the minimum height for the Met, when they had that qualification; slender but wiry, clean-shaven, thin-lipped. His eyes were the most noticeable feature; they were dark for his medium colouring and deep set. Before most of the sand had run out of Liversedge he'd stared down some pretty brazen criminals and sharp solicitors in his time, but Harkness's gaze made him wriggle uncomfortably and wonder how much the other man knew about him. 'Well, any help you need from me . . .' he said at last.

'Thank you, Chief Superintendent,' Harkness said with his usual icy politeness. 'I may ask you to let me have a few of your CID men. I'm afraid we're rather under strength at the moment.'

Liversedge nodded. 'Now, I suppose you'll want to start your conference with my people who began the investigation.'

'Good idea,' Harkness said, as if Liversedge had just invented the wheel.

Liversedge couldn't make out Harkness at all. He hoped to God that he'd find Foulds's killer quickly and leave him alone.

At the first conference with Harkness were a detective inspector who looked like a defrocked bank manager, Detective Sergeant Braddock, who was Harkness's driver and bag-carrier, some other AMIP men, Ted Greening, Harry Timberlake and Sarah Lewis, who had been the first officer on the scene.

'What has the house-to-house turned up?' Harkness asked, after introductions and all the preliminaries had been gone through.

'Nothing, sir,' Ted Greening said, trying to sound efficient. 'So far,' he added quickly at Harkness's look. 'No suspicious characters, no strange cars parked.'

'Scientific evidence?' Harkness was always precise with his language. He knew, if most policemen didn't, that forensic does not mean scientific.

'Nothing there yet, either, sir,' Harry Timberlake broke in. 'Of course, it's been less than twenty-four hours. They did manage to say that the axe was a standard Woolworth's model of about five years ago. They must have sold tens of thousands of them.'

'No fingerprints, of course?'

Timberlake shook his head. 'No, but there was one hair, mid-brown, long, and very probably from a man. The daily said she vacuumed the study the previous day, so it might be helpful.'

'What were your impressions of the scene, WPC? You were the first there,' Harkness said, but Greening wasn't going to be upstaged: 'I had a pretty good look at the place. No traces of a struggle. All the signs that it was somebody Foulds knew.'

'Or somebody who didn't seem dangerous,' Sarah Lewis said.

'Yeah,' said Greening, annoyed that he hadn't thought of that himself.

Harkness thought for a moment. 'We'll have a couple of local people go down to Mr Foulds's chambers to see if they can help. Perhaps someone he prosecuted held a grudge. Once we get a list we can check it against people who've been released from prison recently.'

'Or somebody he sentenced,' Harry said unexpectedly. Harkness looked at him sharply. 'He was a recorder, as well as a counsel. He occasionally sat as a judge in the crown court.'

'How do you know?'

'I looked him up: *Who's Who* and the *Law List*.'

Greening knifed him with his eyes.

'I see. Anything else I should know?' Harkness said, expressionless as ever.

'I put a call into the Italian police asking them to check that Mrs Foulds was in Italy on the night of the murder. They'll phone the Incident Room when they've got an answer.' Harry avoided Greening's eye.

'Thank you, Inspector.' Harkness turned to Ted Greening. 'Did you question the daily help, Mrs . . . er . . . Sanders about her keys? Whether anyone could have got hold of them?'

'I was going to do that this morning,' Greening said smoothly, with all the conviction of the practised bullshitter.

'She was pretty badly shaken up yesterday,' Harry said.

Greening glared. He didn't want his help.

'Can you spare me a couple of men to interview her, Chief Inspector? Your chief superintendent said it would be all right.'

'Certainly, sir. Detective Sergeant Brolly and . . .' He thought, then: 'Detective Constable Webb. They often work together.'

Harkness rose. 'Good.' He glanced at his watch. 'Time for us to go to the post mortem.' He hesitated, then addressed Harry. 'How's your workload at the moment, Timberlake?'

If Harry was surprised at Harkness using his name, he didn't show it. It meant that Harkness had moved on two stages away from the complete formality of 'Inspector', through 'Mr Timberlake' to plain 'Timberlake'.

'About normal, sir. I've only got one big case on at the moment – series of robberies. And I'm up against a brick wall.'

'I'd like to borrow Inspector Timberlake as well, if I may,' Harkness said to Greening. 'Just for the moment, anyway.'

'Oh, yes, I can spare him,' Greening said, trying to make it sound that he'd be no great loss.

When Harkness, Greening, Timberlake and Harkness's bag-carrier arrived at the Pathology Department of St Lawrence's Hospital for Foulds's autopsy – Professor Mortimer was important enough to have bodies brought to him for post-mortem examination instead of having to go to the chilly morgue – the Professor was in the middle of the post mortem on Titus Lloyd, the hit-and-run victim at Wallsend. A bored-looking detective sergeant named Tommy Perch was in attendance. In a few minutes his expression was going to change drastically.

'Come in, Harkness,' Professor Mortimer called out. 'I'm afraid I won't be ready for your client for another half an hour or so. I was called out to Heathrow this morning and I'm running late.'

'That's all right, Professor,' Harkness replied. He wasn't over-awed by the great man. 'What would you like us to do?'

'You can stay and watch this one or have a coffee and come back at about a quarter to.'

Greening licked his lips. 'I think I'll just nip out and have a coffee, it that's all right with you, sir,' he said to Harkness. The Superintendent didn't answer directly.

'Timberlake?'

'I'd like to stay.'

'Yes, you might learn something,' Mortimer said. He didn't mean to be arrogant, patronising or rude, but sounded all three.

'Perhaps I'll stay after all,' Greening said grudgingly, cursing

31

Harkness, Harry Timberlake and Mortimer under his breath. Especially Timberlake.

After fifteen minutes' work on the body lying on the stainless steel table with its deep channels and drain holes, Mortimer said, 'This isn't a hit-and-run case. It's murder. The man was run over by a car, which then came back and ran him over again. Certain injuries are ante mortem, others are post mortem.' He launched into a technical explanation about 'infiltrated blood in some of the wounds and only a slight degree of blood extravasation in the rest.' Although it wasn't Timberlake's case he couldn't help saying, 'Couldn't another car have run over him while he was lying dead in the road, and the driver was too scared to report it?'

'It was the same car. The driver knocked him down, reversed back over him and then drove over him once more. The tyre marks on the body are quite conclusive.' He turned to Tommy Perch. 'Your Mr Titus Lloyd is a murder case, Sergeant.' The pronouncement was as unarguable as stone tablets.

Sergeant Perch left the path lab looking surprised and dejected.

Timberlake had seen Howard Foulds QC in court a few times, including on a couple of cases in which Timberlake had been involved, although he had never been subjected to a Foulds cross-examination. He had been a large, impressive man with a carefully cultivated port-wine voice that boomed. His face was round and red, his lips full and sensual. The untidy pile of flabby, greyish flesh lying on the dissecting table had no resemblance to the living, domineering man.

The body was on its stomach, the face turned towards Timberlake and the others so that the wound in the back of the head wasn't visible. The false teeth had been taken out of the mouth and the face, with shrunken cheeks and thin, sucked-in lips, was quite unrecognisable.

Mortimer glanced up and caught Timberlake's expression. He seemed to read the detective's thoughts, for he said sardonically, 'Don't worry, Inspector. We'll make him look quite presentable again when we've finished with him.'

Before Mortimer opened up the body and took out the organs, he carefully examined the exterior of the body for any wounds or unusual marks. This was standard practice, and the reason why he began with the back, which he studied closely for some time. Once he had done that, he had the body turned over. After an examination of that side, Mortimer made the standard big incision from under the chin to the base of the abdomen, and out came the organs for separate examination and analysis. Next, Mortimer sliced the scalp with a T-shaped incision, peeled back the skin, sawed open the top of the skull with an electric saw, and then removed the brain. Timberlake had known better moments – and worse, too.

While Mortimer was examining the dead man's brain, Harkness asked him, 'Was death instantaneous, Professor?'

'Almost certainly. That is evident from the amount of blood lost and the fact that the brain stem was severely damaged. Head injuries can sometimes be quite unpredictable in their effects, of course.' Mortimer launched into one of his famous boring anecdotes. 'I recall one reported case of a man who sustained a wound of some five centimetres in length from a blow with an axe. He had a depressed fracture of the skull, which involved the inner table of the parietal bone which was broken into four pieces over an area of some eight to ten centimetres. Naturally there was extensive extradural haemorrhage and the brain tissue was bruised. The victim walked from his house to the local police station to have his wound dressed, but he refused to await the arrival of a doctor, went home and spent the afternoon and evening in drinking. He died late that same night.' Then he added, 'Of course, nothing like that happened here.' Ted Greening was becoming thoroughly fed up with Mortimer's manner, and badly needed a drink. He was wondering how he could get away from the post-mortem room when Mortimer lit the fuse of a small bombshell he had been keeping to himself since early in his examination. Mortimer had no sense of humour, but a strong sense of the dramatic.

'There is one thing that may affect your enquiries, Superintendent. It's quite clear that Foulds was a passive homosexual and had been for many years. There are also indications that he indulged in sado-masochistic practices – bondage, flagellation, perhaps more – again, as the passive partner.'

There was a heavy silence for a moment. Then Greening said nastily, 'In other words he was a screaming poofter who got his kicks from being whacked.' He had the brief satisfaction of seeing Mortimer wince.

'Was Foulds suffering from AIDS?' Harkness asked quietly. Greening involuntarily took a step back from the table.

33

'Revenge? Yes, that would be a motive,' Mortimer observed. 'I'll let you know. I'll also let you know how long after his last meal he was killed, which may help you with the time of death.'

Lester Bradford QC, next in seniority to Howard Foulds, the late head of chambers, was the complete opposite of his predecessor. He was as thin as a goalpost, and if Foulds's voice had been like port wine, his was like battery acid. Harry Timberlake could well believe that people gave in to his arguments just to shut him up. With Timberlake was Darren Webb, a bright young detective who might do well if he could rid himself of a diffidence uncharacteristic of CID men.

Lester Bradford declared himself shocked by the murder, and totally unable to suggest who could have committed such a dastardly crime. He agreed to put his staff on to preparing a list of all the cases Foulds had prosecuted over the past five years where the defendant had been given a prison sentence of six months or more, together with the names of defendants he had sentenced to the same period while sitting as a recorder.

'When you want to know something about an officer, don't ask the other officers. Ask the sergeant-major,' Harry advised Webb. So, when they had finished talking to Bradford, they had a quiet chat with Percy Hoskin, the clerk to the chambers. Clerks in barristers' chambers are men of great influence and knowledge.

They had their talk in a local pub, which is always a good place for encouraging confidences. 'D'you know anyone who might have a grudge against him? Anyone who might want to kill him?' Timberlake asked.

'Half the bloody Bar,' Hoskin said, whose loyalty to his chief died with him. 'Bloody big-headed, tight-fisted and never did anybody a favour. Except yesterday.'

Webb looked at him enquiringly. Timberlake provided the answer. 'Getting himself knocked off.'

Hoskin winked at him. 'If you ever catch the bloke who did it, they'll have a whip-round in the Temple to brief the best counsel there is to defend him.'

Timberlake suspected that Hoskin might be exaggerating but, even so, it was clear that Howard Foulds QC had been a high-grade stinker.

Percy Hoskin introduced them to a clerk from another set of

chambers, Tony Bain, who had come in for a stiffener before undertaking the rugged journey home to Upminster. He confirmed Hoskin's assessment of Foulds.

'What about women?' Timberlake asked. 'Could some husband have had it in for him?' He had heard what Professor Mortimer had said about Foulds's sexual habits; he was simply avoiding approaching the subject head on.

The other two men looked at each other blankly. 'He'd know more about that than me,' Bain said, nodding towards Hoskin. 'I've never heard any of my people say anything.'

'Me neither,' Hoskin admitted. 'He didn't seem to be all that interested in women.'

'Too busy counting his money, I expect,' Webb said. His expression was innocent and his voice unemphatic.

Hoskin wasn't fooled. 'Nah,' he said. 'Foulds wasn't ginger.'

'Well, you'd know,' Harry said. 'My shout.'

The smell of the dissecting room was strong in Professor Mortimer's office, but he hadn't noticed it for thirty years. Whenever he went away for a rare holiday he thought the countryside smelt odd.

Mortimer picked up the phone and dialled the number of the Incident Room at Terrace Vale.

'Incident Room, Inspector Timberlake,' came the answer.

'Professor Mortimer. Is Superintendent Harkness there?'

'No Professor.'

'Never mind, you'll do.' Mortimer was being his usual charming self.

Timberlake took a deep breath. 'What can I do for you, Professor?'

'Nothing. It's what I can do for you.'

Timberlake put his hand over the phone and swore hard.

'Foulds: I'll send you a full report tomorrow. I thought you'd like to know that he was not suffering from the Acquired Immune Deficiency Syndrome.' Anyone else would simply have said AIDS. Mortimer paused, waiting for Timberlake to ask him what all that meant, but Harry didn't give him the satisfaction. 'Secondly,' Mortimer went on, 'death occurred about two hours after his last meal. Roast lamb, mint sauce, peas, boiled potatoes and something that looks like apple charlotte. With about half a bottle of red wine,' Mortimer said like a waiter confirming an order. 'Good evening.'

Mrs Sanders had told them that when he ate on his own Foulds always had the evening meal she prepared for him between half past eight and nine o'clock. So this second piece of information meant that the time of death could be fixed on something around 10.30 and 11.00 p.m.

For all the good it did anyone.

The man didn't speak while he was eating his meal; he clearly had something on his mind. The woman sitting opposite him wasn't eating, but she made no attempt at conversation. The man was silent because he was considering for the sixth or seventh time whether it was safer to use his own mini-van rather than a stolen vehicle for what he had to do that evening. For the sixth or seventh time he decided on the mini-van.

He finished the jam tart the woman had baked for him. 'Very nice,' he said of the meal.

The woman smiled mechanically. She paused before asking, 'Are you going to stay in this evening? There's a good programme on television.'

'I shan't be out long – an hour or two, that's all. Just something to deliver.' He stood up, ready to leave the room.

'Do you have enough money?' the woman asked.

'Yes, thank you.'

'You sure?' She moved towards the sideboard.

'It's all right,' the man said as firmly as his quiet voice could manage.

'If you want any, you only have to say. After all, it'll all be yours when I'm gone.'

The man clenched his fists in his pockets as he went to his workroom.

Trawling Terrace Vale's gay clubs and bars was largely an undertaking for the area's local detectives. Timberlake for one was lumbered with the job, which he hated. His natural puritanism made him prejudiced against homosexuals, an attitude he acknowledged and had to fight to overcome. Timberlake wasn't hopeful of finding much locally. 'Foulds was too intelligent to shit on his own doorstep,' he said, but pressed on nevertheless.

36

Routine, covering all the possibilities; dreary routine, that was how crimes were solved. If they were solved.

The Sad Mac Club was situated in a short cul-de-sac just off a shopping street, which was just as well for the club, for it meant that there were no residents to complain about what went on inside and outside the place during its night-time-only opening hours. The appearance of most of the members was enough to cause a lot of lively comment. Those of its members who spoke French would find it amusing that the club was situated in a cul-de-sac.

Harry Timberlake wasn't looking forward to continuing his enquiries there, but he had no choice. The fact that he was accompanied by the young Detective Constable Darren Webb didn't make him feel any better.

'Clever name, that,' Timberlake said. 'The Sad Mac.'

'How's that, guv?' Webb asked interestedly.

Timberlake wished that he hadn't tried to show off. He explained that it had nothing to do with an unhappy Scotsman, but came from the names Sade and von Sacher-Masoch respectively.

'Bit classier than a bent spieler we had in my last area,' Webb observed. 'The Bum's Rush.'

The Sad Mac was in a semi-basement beneath some dubious offices. The entrance area was littered with disgusting-looking rubbish which hinted at some very nasty practices. There were four crumbling, greasy steps down to the doorway.

'You stay just inside the door. If anyone tries to slide out, collar 'em,' Timberlake told Webb. The younger man looked nervous, but Timberlake guessed that it would be fairly dark in the club and no one would notice his uncertainty. Beyond the front door the atmosphere was like the inside of the exhaust of a Porsche. The noise level wasn't much better. The dark walls were covered with swastikas, SS insignia and photographs of some rather brutal-looking Nazis. There were other pictures of very muscular men wearing bizarre leather clothing with studs and spikes. There were a lot of spikes and studs and chains being worn by the customers in the place.

Behind the bar was a large, sweaty man. He was wearing an open leather waistcoat, no shirt and a spiked dog collar that must have been made for a healthy St Bernard. A big beer-belly hung over the top of his leather trousers, but his arms were heavily muscled. On his head was a peaked cap with the SS Death's Head insignia.

'Are you the owner?' Timberlake asked him politely . . . to start with.

'Who wants to know?' The voice was almost girlish.

Timberlake flashed his warrant card and said, 'Inspector Timberlake.'

'Oh, the Filth.' He giggled.

Timberlake ignored it. He produced a photograph of Howard Foulds. 'You ever see him in here?'

The fat man looked him straight in the eye and said 'No.'

'Look at it.'

'Sod off.'

'Don't piss me about. I'm on a murder enquiry and I'm not in a very good mood.'

'Ooh, hark at her.' He gave another giggle, but there was a menacing undertone to it. Some of the drinkers near the bar moved a step closer.

Timberlake let his cockney accent broaden and he fixed the fat man with his penetrating look. 'If I get the least bit of aggro from you or your members, there'll be a mobile outside this club every night, with an officer taking photographs of everyone who goes in or out. Anybody with a car, motorbike or tricycle will be breathalysed as soon as he's gone ten yards. Anyone who even farts on the pavement'll get done for creating a disturbance and half a dozen other charges. This'll be the deadest place this side of the morgue. Now, Fatso, look at this photograph and tell me if he ever came in here.'

The man behind the bar glared hate at Timberlake, but eventually looked at the picture.

'Before you say anything, if you tell me 'No' and I find out he used to come in here, I don't fancy your chances of staying open for another forty-eight hours.'

'He's not a regular. I don't think he's ever been in here.'

Timberlake showed the photograph to some of the heavies near him. They all shook their heads. Timberlake nodded. He didn't really think that Foulds would have frequented a cesspit like this so close to his own home. He turned away and went out, ignoring the looks he knew were aimed at his back. Webb nipped out behind him very smartly.

'Not exactly the Athenaeum,' Timberlake said. Webb didn't know what he meant, but he could guess.

They stood on the pavement beside their car for a moment to get some fresher air. Just as they were about to get in the car, a soft voice from behind them said, 'Inspector.'

Timberlake whirled round. A mild-looking city-gent type complete with umbrella, bowler hat and £500 Harrods suit was standing there.

'May I see the photograph, please? The light wasn't very good inside.' It took Timberlake a moment to recover.

'You were in there?'

'Yes.'

Timberlake didn't say anything. There didn't seem much to say. He produced the photograph again. The man took it to the nearest lamppost and studied it. 'I'm sure it's the same man. I've seen him before.'

'In there – The Sad Mac?'

'Oh, no. A place in the West End. The Double-V Club. We call it the Vice Versa.' He smiled wryly. 'It has much the same interests, but with rather more style and a much better class of member. No pun intended.' The man looked at Harry Timberlake and guessed what he was thinking. 'We are what we are, Inspector. But that's no excuse for killing us.' He nodded sadly, raised his hat and turned away. Webb wanted to stop him, but Timberlake checked him.

'He can't tell us any more. Give the poor sod credit for coming forward like that. Good for him.'

The man picked up a foot-long mild-steel rod as thick as a man's finger and looked along its length, turning it slowly, like a billiards player examining a cue; then he tested the sharpness of the machined point with his finger. After that he checked the balance of the rod. The man nodded, satisfied. The whole procedure was unnecessary. Although the rod would be used only once, he had made it with all the meticulous care he gave to his superb models, but he was an obsessively thorough man who left nothing to chance. As he frequently said, with no sense of conceit, he never made mistakes.

When he put the rod in a large, plastic bag it clinked against something metal.

Before leaving, the man went over to the wallboard and studied one of the photographs. Finally, as he always did, he locked the door behind him.

Reg Barclay was a creature of habit. Maybe it was working for an airline with its books of rules and work schedules and timetables that helped make him that way. Before every flight he always drove his Volkswagen into the multi-storey car park behind his local supermarket and picked up the food he couldn't get abroad: Mars bars, Ovaltine, Danish bacon in packets, Shredded Wheat, bitter marmalade, tea bags – things like that. His job as steward on a jumbo meant that he could count on all sorts of perks, such as liquor, cigarettes, perfumes and boxfuls of toiletry goodies from the First Class lavatories. Nevertheless, he needed his stock of good old English grub to make life tolerable in an eastern Mediterranean glass-and-concrete sleeping factory that was called an international hotel.

He parked his car on the second floor with its direct lifts to the store. He glanced at his watch: just gone seven. Nearly an hour to do his shopping; more than enough. Then another hour to get to Heathrow. As he walked towards the lift, a mini-van pulled into the space next to his car on the right. Less than half an hour later he was back at the car, carrying a plastic shopping bag. He opened the door of his car and put in the bag. At that moment the door of the van opened and a man got out. Barclay didn't get a good look at him, but it wouldn't have mattered if he had. All he noticed was that the man was holding a large plastic bag in front of him.

'Excuse me,' the man said politely.

Barclay turned back towards him. 'Yes?' he replied, and waited for the other man to speak, but he said nothing. After a few seconds Barclay added, 'Just a moment. Don't I know you? Aren't you—?'

'That's right,' the man said with satisfaction. He dropped his bag, and brought up a wicked-looking crossbow in his other hand. Barclay blinked. The crossbow was armed, and had a foot-long bolt with a deadly sharp point in the groove. He was just about to say 'Hey, be careful with that thing!' when the bolt pierced his chest and ripped his aorta before going on to damage his spinal cord. The awful wound and the massive shock it caused killed Barclay in a matter of seconds.

While Barclay was still upright the killer pushed him into his Volkswagen. Barclay fell back across the front seats. The killer bundled his legs into the vehicle and shut the door. The body was out of sight of anybody who wasn't standing right next to the car and deliberately looking inside.

Quite unhurriedly now, the man picked up the plastic bag he had been carrying, put the crossbow and car keys in it, threw it into the van and drove away, out of the car park.

Luck was with him. The car park closed half an hour later, and no one had noticed the body in the Volkswagen.

At Heathrow the man in charge of the crewing roster rang Barclay's home to see if he'd left, but there was no answer. Reg's wife Tina was already on her back, levelling the score with her husband in the cheating game so enthusiastically that she ignored the ringing phone. She would have done better to miss this particular bonking session. When she eventually found out that Reg was lying dead in his car while she was being laid by a betting-shop manager, even though she was hardly on good terms with her husband a sense of guilt gave her an enormous psychological block to lovemaking for a couple of years that earned her a reputation for being frigid.

Later that night the man stopped his van in the middle of Waterloo Bridge among all the parked cars belonging to theatre-goers. No one noticed when he slipped the crossbow and keys from under his coat and dropped them into the river. They were never seen again.

The Incident Room for the Foulds murder was on the second floor of Terrace Vale police station, up thirty-six wooden stairs with lino that had holes worn in it from civilian typists' shoes. The lino dated back to the first days of stiletto heels. The room itself was large and tastefully furnished with battered wooden desks, rickety folding chairs, typewriters, telephones and half a dozen computer terminals. The air was thick with cigarette smoke.

There were some twenty or more detectives already there when Harry Timberlake walked in for Superintendent Harkness's regular morning conference. Ted Greening spotted him across the room, signalled and moved over.

'You want the good news or the bad news?'

'Oh, shit. The bad news.'

'Phantom Flannelfoot has been at it again. Did a place in Paddock Grove last night. The posh end.'

Timberlake sighed. 'That's all I need.'

'Hang on, there's more.'

'Bloody hell. What?'

'There was a burglar alarm. When the owner and his wife got back it was switched on. The wife was with her husband, saw him take out his key and switch the sodding thing off. There's no mistake about it. Chummy Phantom Flannelfoot got past a burglar alarm as well this time.'

Timberlake looked gloomy and remained silent for a moment. Then he said, 'Ted, don't mention it to the guvnor yet. I don't want to get taken off this murder enquiry.'

'That's all very well, but who am I going to put on this one? We're short-handed enough as it is with the AMIP borrowing our bodies.'

'You can find somebody.'

'Okay. But you owe me one.' Greening never missed an opportunity to put people in his debt, even when it cost him nothing to do the favour.

'What's the good news?'

'The good news is that that's the only bad news.'

Timberlake felt like secretly pissing into the half-bottle of Scotch Greening kept in his desk. The trouble was, Greening drank such awful whisky that he probably wouldn't notice anything wrong.

The morning conference wasn't the high spot of the day. It began very grittily for some of the detectives. Harkness walked into the smoke-filled room and managed to make disconcerting eye contact with everyone there before he spoke. He said, 'Good morning, gentlemen. I'd rather you didn't smoke in here unless you really can't help it.' No one was bold or thick-skinned enough to keep puffing away with Harkness looking at them. There was a moment's chaos as everyone reached for the nearest ashtray. No one felt like stubbing out his cigarette on the floor under Harkness's gaze.

The conference was short and there wasn't much to report or to discuss. No one had any bright ideas to offer, until right at the end. The AMIP men who were working through the list of criminals Foulds had either prosecuted or sentenced hadn't found a credible suspect. House-to-house enquiries by local detectives had turned up nothing. Ted Greening reported that Mrs Sanders, the housekeeper, was absolutely positive that no one had got their hands on her keys.

The only lead that offered any real hope was Harry Timberlake's discovery about Foulds's membership of the Double-V or Vice Versa Club, and that was thin enough. As soon as he reported it, Timberlake had the sick feeling that enquiries at the club would be handed over to another detective, probably one of the AMIP team, leaving him out in the cold. Harkness looked at him without expression, and said, 'You'd better follow that up yourself, Inspector.'

'Yes, sir,' Timberlake said, trying to keep his voice level. Greening was looking at him with a strange expression. Then Harry Timberlake had his brainwave.

'Sir,' he said, 'there's another set of possible suspects.' The room went silent except for the scraping of chairs as detectives turned to look at him. His self-confidence burst like a pricked bubble. Harkness looked at him politely. Harry cleared his throat and went on.

'We've been concentrating on the cases where Foulds prosecuted and forgetting the ones where he defended.' One or two detectives turned away from him again, embarrassed or pitying expressions on their faces. Ted Greening gave a just audible snicker of derision. Harkness remained expressionless. Harry Timberlake ploughed on.

'If we're reckoning that this was some sort of revenge murder . . .' – a flash of comprehension went across Harkness's face, but he didn't interrupt – 'maybe clever-dick Foulds got some villain off and the victim felt aggrieved and decided to take it out on the brief. Or it could be a civil case where a lot of money was involved.'

'Thank you, Timberlake,' Harkness said thoughtfully. 'That's very perceptive. You might well be right.' Greening looked like a badly carved totem pole. 'That means another visit to Foulds's chambers.'

Harry Timberlake felt glum. Despite the helpful attitude of Lester Bradford, the new head of chambers, on his first visit, he had the gut feeling that the reception would be a lot frostier the next time round.

Five minutes after the meeting broke up, Timberlake had

made an appointment to see the Secretary of the Double-V Club. He sounded like a Very Superior Person.

Just as Timberlake put the phone down, news came in of the discovery of the murder of Reg Barclay. A youth looking into the car had seen the body. He called the police and eventually a tow-away unit with a box of keys arrived and opened up the Volkswagen. A second murder so soon after the other one hit the Terrace Vale nick with a shock that was worth a good few points on the Richter Scale.

When the dust had settled, Chief Superintendent Liversedge and Superintendent Harkness agreed that for the time being Ted Greening, Harry Timberlake and other Terrace Vale officers as necessary would be allowed to continue working with the AMIP team on the Foulds murder. When the second AMIP team arrived from Scotland Yard, the whole personnel situation would be reviewed. In the meantime, Greening and Timberlake could make the preliminary investigation at the car park.

Even with headlights on, blue lamp flashing and siren whoop-whooping away, their police car covered the last half-mile of the journey at little better than walking pace. The main road was jammed with other police vehicles, cars whose drivers had slowed to a crawl to try to see what all the excitement was about, buses that were threading their way through the traffic like camels through eyes of needles, and passers-by who spilled into the roadway in the hope of seeing something.

'It must be a bomb,' said one loud-mouth know-all. An uneasy ripple ran through the crowd until a uniformed PC declared firmly, 'It's not a bomb, but move along please. There's nothing to see. Move along, please.' Canute had more luck with the ocean.

Inside the car park it was even more chaotic, as people with supermarket trolleys full of food tried to get to their cars on the second floor and above. The whole building echoed with angry demands for explanations, staccato metallic voices hissing from personal radios and loud wails from children. Police photographers' flashguns added lightning flashes to the scene.

Before anyone was allowed to his car, registration numbers were noted down and names and addresses taken, although the policemen realised the almost-certain pointlessness of it all. It was clear that the murder had taken place the previous evening: the parking ticket inside the car underlined that. Later, the police surgeon gave a rough time of death as between four o'clock and midnight the previous day. Still, somebody might have been there the previous evening, somebody might have seen something.

The actual murder weapon was a puzzler. After the SOCOs had tested it for fingerprints and found none, the police surgeon removed it from the body with the help of a muscular policeman. 'Bloody hell,' the doctor said, 'Whoever bunged this in him must have been built like a cement karsie.' No one responded to his predictably bad attempt at humour.

'What the hell is it?' Bill Bailey asked.

'Looks home-made,' one of the scene of crime officers said. 'We'll know better when we've had it in the lab.'

All the noise and confusion and general commotion did something unexpected to Ted Greening. Suddenly he felt the old heady thrill of power. He forgot his jealousy of Harry Timberlake for his performance at the conference. Here, he was in command. He was the guvnor. Whatever his shortcomings, Greening could still be a great man-manager when he had to be. For the first time in years he felt a sudden surge of enthusiasm. Instead of handing over to Timberlake and returning to the nick, he called up reinforcements and deployed a small army of policemen.

Under his direction uniformed PCs carefully searched every square foot of the floor. They noted down where everything was found before putting it into plastic bags.

He sent a team of detectives and uniformed men to the supermarket with the receipt for the groceries the victim had purchased the previous evening. First they'd find the cashier at the checkout to see if she could remember anything about Barclay: whether he was on his own, whether she'd noticed anyone out of the ordinary. Then everyone else who'd been on duty in the supermarket would be interviewed on the off chance that they'd seen something. Greening didn't hold out much hope. Cashiers at checkouts had to concentrate on goods, not people.

Identifying the victim had been no problem. He was in uniform, and his wallet contained his airline ID card, as well as credit cards and driving licence. His wallet also had more than £200 in it. The facts that robbery was obviously not the motive for his murder and that he was an airline steward immediately raised all sorts of suspicions. Was Barclay a courier of some sort? If he was, there could be any number of reasons for killing him:

because he was double-crossing the other members of a gang, for example, or skimming the top off profits, or doing deals on his own account, or because he was going to blow the whistle on someone and had to be shut up, permanently. Oh, there were possibilities, all right.

So, Greening detailed three detectives to go to Heathrow to dig around, beginning with a good look in Barclay's locker.

Timberlake was beginning to feel as useless as a second boot to Long John Silver. 'D'you want me for anything?' he asked Greening.

It was the sort of question Greening himself would have asked if he were pulling one of his strokes, and it made him immediately wary. 'Why?'

'I've got a call to make for the Foulds case. I might as well do that if there's nothing more for me here.'

Greening considered this from all angles, but failed to find anything suspicious. 'All right,' he said finally.

The last act of the untidy drama in the car park began with the SOCOs driving off in their van. Their principal – their only – exhibit was the murder weapon, which they'd already found was free of fingerprints. The would-be whimsical police surgeon cadged a lift from a panda driver; and a black, anonymous, undertakers' van removed the body. Another policeman, wearing gloves, clamped a steering wheel over the Volkswagen's steering wheel, covered the driver's seat with plastic sheeting and carefully drove the car to the police garage where it would be vacuumed and every speck of dust and grit examined. It would all be for nothing.

Chapter 3

The exterior of the Double-V or Vice Versa Club was expensive, discreet and thoroughly in keeping with the neighbourhood. The place was studded with shops that sold hand-made hats, shotguns and leatherbound books for noting down the details of the carnage of inoffensive birds and fish, luggage that would be a certain come-on to thieving baggage-handlers, and hand-made shoes at a few hundred pounds a pair.

Harry Timberlake was shown into the Secretary's office. Major Gavin Broadbent looked as if he kitted himself out at the local shops. His hair was cut short, and was plastered to his skull with a brilliantine that had sold well to officers in Lord Raglan's forces. He sported a moustache that seemed to have been modelled on the camel thorn bushes used to keep out the Fuzzie-Wuzzies. His eyes and a network of tiny ruptured veins on his cheeks betrayed that he was a heavy drinker.

The walls of the Major's office were covered with prints of soldiers, most of them sword-brandishing cavalry officers with rolling eyes, looking as if they were trying to scare the enemy to death. The room had the unmistakable odour of money and influence.

'Detective Inspector Timberlake? How do you do,' said Major Broadbent, not offering to shake hands. 'How can I help you?'

'Interesting name, Double-V,' Timberlake said with a completely straight face. 'What does it stand for?'

'Vincent Villiers. He founded the club in 1766,' the Major replied, even straighter-faced. 'But I'm sure you aren't here to discuss our club's history.'

'No, sir,' Timberlake replied. He paused. 'Howard Foulds.'

'Ah. A very sad business. I was discussing the matter here only last night with one of your Commanders.' The message was delivered in a quiet Guards officer voice, but was as noticeable as a kick in the crutch.

47

'He was a member here,' Timberlake said, trying to sound unruffled. 'Howard Foulds, I mean.'

'I wonder who told you that?' Major Broadbent mused.

'As you know, we don't reveal our sources.'

'Very wise.'

'Discretion. And that's the keynote of my enquiry.' With a flash of inspiration he added, 'That's why I've come here on my own.'

'To what end?' Broadbent asked, unaware of any *double entendre*.

'I shan't beat about the bush, Major. What I'm trying to find out is whether Mr Foulds had any special friends here. A particular, close friend.'

'What makes you think that I would know that?' Broadbent answered questions with another question with the automatic reflex of a dodgy politician or a psychoanalyst.

'I have the impression, Major, that there's nothing that goes on in this club that you don't know about.'

Major Broadbent considered this statement, and decided that it was meant as a compliment. 'Perhaps.' He went to a small cupboard, took out a bottle with an unfamiliar label and a couple of glasses. 'Have a malt.' It sounded like an order to come to attention.

Timberlake sipped the clear, golden liquid. It was like nothing he'd ever drunk before.

'How do you find it?' Broadbent asked.

'Quite superb,' Timberlake responded, repeating a line he'd heard on TV or somewhere. Then, with a flash of inspiration, 'but discreet.'

The Major's liver must have been ninety per cent scar tissue. By the time he'd got halfway through his second glass he was already half drunk.

'Just between you and me,' he said thickly, 'just between you and me, Foulds did have a special friend. God knows what he saw in the man . . . Not really our sort of chap. Didn't know how to behave. Had two shocking rows with Foulds, right here in the club. They carried on like two—' He was going to say 'women', but managed to change it to 'fishwives'. 'Right here in the club,' he repeated. 'I had to tell them, you know. Any more exhibitions like that and they'd be out. Cashiered,' the Major said, confusingly.

'Who is this friend?' Timberlake asked mildly.

'Bloody awful man. Don't know how he ever became a member. Total outsider. Even his name . . . Terry – not Terence, mark you – Terry Luckwell. Lives in Earls Court, for God's sake.'

Two drinks later Timberlake managed to get out of the club. He made straight for Earls Court.

Ted Greening decided to go and break the news to the unsuspecting widow himself – not because he considered himself particularly diplomatic or sensitive, but because he wanted to see if Barclay's home showed any signs of an unusually high standard of living. After all, this might open up into a big smuggling case, maybe a drugs operation – a chance for him to get a good result. But by this time Ted Greening's earlier zeal was fading fast. The first indication was the old familiar need for a couple of drinks. He had been on the point of telling Harry Timberlake to go in his place when the remains of an old pride pricked him.

'I suppose I'd better go and tell his wife,' Greening said. 'I want to have a look round his place. I'll take a WPC with me. I've seen the Welsh Rarebit knocking about here somewhere. She'll do. See if you can raise her for me, will you.'

If Reg Barclay was involved in anything dodgy, there was no outward sign of it in his house: a modest three-bed semi in a working-class road not far from Hammersmith. Still, you can't always tell from the outside, Greening thought. Same as with people. Before he got out of the car he took a deep breath.

'You ever done this before? Had to break the news about someone being killed?' he asked Sarah Lewis, who was trying to look composed as she sat next to him. Not trusting her voice, she just shook her head.

'There's no easy way. Best thing you can do for them is make a cup of tea and get somebody to come and stay with them if they're on their own.' He sighed. 'Come on.'

Tina Barclay opened the door. She was an attractive, slightly lush young woman. As soon as she saw Sarah Lewis's uniform, her eyes widened with shock.

'Mrs Barclay?' Greening asked. Tina nodded. 'I'm Detective Chief Inspector Greening, and this is WPC Lewis. May we come in for a moment?' Without a word she turned and walked inside.

Greening and Sarah followed her into a comfortably furnished front room. When she turned round all colour had gone from her face, making her make-up look badly overdone.

Before Greening could go through the formula of saying that she had to prepare herself for some bad news, Tina said 'It's Reg, isn't it? Something's happened?' Greening nodded and was about to speak when she hurried on. 'Where was it? I haven't heard anything on the news about a crash. Is he . . . is he . . . ?'

'It's not a crash, but I'm afraid it's bad news, Mrs Barclay . . . very bad,' Greening told her, but she'd already guessed. His immediate reaction was one of disappointment. If Barclay had been into something crooked, his wife didn't know anything about it.

'I'll make a cup of tea, if that's all right,' Sarah said with a surprisingly firm yet kind voice.

'I'll have a drink first.' Tina Barclay went to a sideboard and poured herself a large whisky, which she downed in one go, then gagged a little. The sight and smell of the Scotch made Greening ache for a drink himself. If Sarah Lewis hadn't been there, he'd have asked for one.

Somehow they all struggled through the next long minutes. Sarah made some tea, then called Tina's sister, who lived in Wimbledon and said she'd be right over.

Tina soon had herself under control: perhaps a little too soon and a little too much control, Greening thought, but you could never be too sure about people's reactions at a time like this. 'Do you feel up to answering some questions?' he asked her, as Sarah poured out another cup of tea.

Tina nodded. 'If it'll help.' So, he went through the usual list about whether her husband had any enemies, whether he'd shown any signs of being under strain recently, whether there had been any odd phone calls or letters: all the routine enquiries. Greening asked if her husband always went to the supermarket on the way to his work at Heathrow. 'Only on the longer flights,' she told him.

Greening nodded. 'From the car-park ticket and the bill from the checkout it's pretty certain that your husband was killed some time between seven o'clock and midnight last night when the car-park closed.' He carefully avoided using the word murdered, which was much more upsetting. 'I have to ask you this, Mrs Barclay. Where were you during those times?'

50

'I stayed home. Watched television.'

'Were you alone? Did anyone call?'

She hesitated. 'No.'

'Can you remember which programmes you watched?'

'I . . . must have dozed off.'

'I see,' Greening said with heavy neutrality. 'And no one phoned?'

'No.' The voice was barely audible.

Sarah hated herself for it, but she had to ask. 'Didn't anyone from the airline ring to ask why your husband hadn't reported for duty?'

Ted Greening looked at her with a mixture of reluctant admiration and annoyance for beating him to the thought. That's the second bloody time, he told himself. Once again the colour drained from Tina's face. Her mouth opened once or twice, but no words came out. Greening waited.

At last she said, with a nonchalance that sounded horribly cracked, 'Actually, a friend called. He spent the night . . . the evening, with me.'

So that's it, Greening thought. He and Sarah were careful not to look at each other.

'I see,' he said without expression. 'Would you mind letting me have your friend's name and address? It's only routine, Mrs Barclay.' He smiled reassuringly. 'And if it all checks out the enquiry will be in the strictest confidence, I promise you.' Though it doesn't really matter much now, Sarah thought.

After a long pause, Tina said in a low voice, 'His name is Wayne Dysart. Seventeen, Vicar's Walk, Putney.' She paused awkwardly. 'He lives with his mother. If she knew . . . Me, a married woman . . .'

'Of course. Do you know where he works? It might be easier for him if we saw him there.'

Tina brightened. 'He's manager of a betting shop in Stratford.' She gave the address. Sarah noted it down.

Tina's eyes suddenly widened. 'Why are you asking me all this? You don't think I . . .'

'Like I said, it's routine.' Greening tried a reassuring smile but it came out like a bad confidence trickster's smirk. 'Standard practice,' he added. 'We always eliminate relatives and close friends first. One last thing. Did your husband have a study, or a desk where he kept his papers? I'd like to have a look, if you don't mind. It might give us a lead to whoever . . .' He left it dangling.

'He's got . . . he had a desk. It's in the other room,' she said, but didn't move until Greening stood up, then she led him to it. There wasn't a great deal in the desk: receipts and bills, none of them out of the ordinary; house and car insurance policies; a few personal letters and postcards.

In a drawer all on their own were two insurance policies. One was an endowment policy to cover the mortgage of £85,000 on the house, the other straightforward life insurance. When Greening saw the amount, he whistled silently.

'What did you think of her?' Greening asked Sarah as they drove back to Terrace Vale police station.

'I'm not sure. At first she seemed pretty shaken. Then she recovered and was almost . . . unfeeling. I don't think she was all that fond of her husband. But when you asked her where she was when he was killed I thought she was going to break up.'

'Guilty conscience.'

Sarah stared at him. 'You're not suggesting that she . . . ?'

'Of course not. It was because she realised that while her husband was being murdered she was being screwed by her boyfriend. That sort of thing can be very upsetting to some people.'

By the time Greening had typed out his report, the three detectives were back from Heathrow. 'Bloody place smells like a paraffin shop,' one of them grumbled.

'Bugger the environmental bulletin,' Greening said. 'What did you find out?'

'If Barclay was up to anything dodgy he managed to keep it hidden. Nothing in his locker, and none of his mates reckoned he was into any villainy. And he was never flash with money.'

'So who could have wanted to knock him off?' Greening asked, not really expecting an answer.

'Husband or boyfriend. Our Mr Barclay was a right one for the birds. Jumped on everything that stood still for a second.'

'Or might be some bird he'd elbowed,' said the second detective. 'Hell hath no fury, and all that.'

'Then all we've got to do is find a female gold-medal javelin thrower,' Greening said acidly. 'That spear thing was bunged into him as if Rambo had done it for a bet.' He thought for a moment and said, 'I wonder if his wife knew he was playing around?'

The first detective answered him. 'She knew all right. She gave him a couple of right bollockings in front of some of his mates.'

'That's interesting,' Greening said. 'So, she had a double motive. Jealousy . . . and money. Apart from an endowment policy for the mortgage, he had another life policy.' He paused. 'For a hundred grand.'

It has often been said if you sit long enough at a pavement table at the *Café de la Paix* in Paris, everybody you know will eventually pass by. Much the same is probably true about the Good Pull-up for Carmen in Wapping, or the steps of the Albert Memorial, if you're prepared to wait long enough. By the same token, everybody in, or on the fringes of, show business lives in Rancliffe Square, SW10, at some time in their careers. Why, nobody knows. Theories for this phenomenon include one that it has the same irresistible attraction for failed actors and writers as clifftops have for lemmings. Another is that there is an atavistic race memory in show people which draws them there like salmon being drawn back to their original spawning grounds. It could also be that the whole area is a rabbit-warren of not-too-expensive bedsitters within easy reach of the West End.

Terry Luckwell occupied one of the garden flats on the less fashionable side of the square, a two-roomed dump offering a permanent bird's-eye view of the front room to all the passers-by, and a back room opening on to a patio just big enough for a potted geranium and a bird bath for small birds. Harry Timberlake went down the steps leading to a blistered and peeling front door and rang the bell. After a moment the door was opened with the security chain left on.

'Mr Luckwell?'

The man who opened the door was in shadow and Harry Timberlake couldn't make out his features. 'Who wants him?' the shadowy figure asked in a slightly cockney voice. Harry could hear, even if he couldn't see, why Terry got up the red-veined nose of Major Broadbent of the Double-V Club.

'I'm Inspector Timberlake, Terrace Vale police station. I wonder if I could ask you a few questions?'

Luckwell looked shifty. 'It's not very convenient at the moment. I was just going out and—'

'It won't take very long.'

Luckwell made no move to open the door any wider. 'What's it about?'

Timberlake raised his voice. 'It's a police enquiry, Mr Luckwell. I can ask you the questions here, if you like, but I think it'd be better if—'

The door closed briefly, there was the rattle of the doorchain, and then the door opened wide. 'All right,' Luckwell said. 'You'd better come in.'

The door gave directly on to the main living room, if you could call it living. Harry Timberlake guessed that the place was let furnished. It looked as if it had been kitted out from the furniture equivalent of Oxfam by a dozen different people, some of them colour-blind. There were a few photographs of Luckwell of the sort that actors and models send out when they're looking for jobs.

Terry – 'not even Terence' – Luckwell was tall and cheaply handsome with collar-length wavy blond hair. At first sight he looked about thirty-five, but when he was careless enough to stand in a good light he looked at least five years older, and probably more. His mouth was full, with lips that seemed unnaturally red, but Timberlake was sure he wasn't wearing lipstick. His suit must have cost somebody three hundred quid at the very least.

'So what's this about, then?' Luckwell said. He looked Harry Timberlake straight in the eye and tried to sound belligerent, but there was a hollow ring to his tone.

'I'm enquiring into the murder of Mr Howard Foulds.'

Timberlake felt a sudden thrill of excitement at Luckwell's reaction. Just for a moment his bold, almost challenging gaze went out like a broken light bulb and his eyes flicked away from Harry Timberlake's regard. He pulled himself together almost at once, but it was too late.

'Why ask me?'

'You are a member of his club and according to my information you were a close personal friend. Very close.' Luckwell didn't deny it. He licked his red lips, making them glisten even more.

54

Maybe he was wearing lipstick after all, Timberlake thought. 'I also understand that you had a serious quarrel the day before he was killed.'

'I never!' he cried in pure Eliza Doolittle English. After a moment of silence Luckwell qualified his answer and got his accent under control once more. 'It wasn't serious. It didn't mean anything. The sort of barney that all friends have.'

Barney. No wonder the gallant Major at the Vice Versa Club couldn't stand Luckwell. Timberlake suddenly found himself becoming irritated, with himself as much as with Luckwell, for being intolerant. This made him even more short-tempered.

'And lovers?' he snapped.

'What you mean?' It was as unconvincing as it was ungrammatical.

'Oh, come on. That club is a poofs' paradise. You were Foulds's special chum, weren't you?'

'I didn't kill him. Why would I want to?'

'Jealousy. Where were you on Thursday night, the fourteenth, between nine o'clock and midnight?'

The door to the bedroom smashed open. 'The bastard was with me! He is every Thursday! But not any more!'

A small, well-dressed woman of about forty-five, bristling with energy and indignation, came bursting out of the bedroom. She ignored Harry completely and raced over to Luckwell.

'You were that disgusting old queer's boyfriend, were you? Laura said you were a . . . And I didn't believe her! God, you're disgusting! Revolting!' She paused while she searched for a better adjective, failed and repeated 'Disgusting!' a couple of notes higher. 'To think that you . . . with him . . . then did that with me! God, I feel dirty! Dirty!'

She wound up like a baseball pitcher and gave Terry Luckwell a slap across his perfumed chops that made Harry Timberlake's head ring just to see it. 'You filthy shit! I'm going home to have a bath and try to scrub myself clean again.'

Terry Luckwell was opening and closing his mouth like a goldfish at feeding time. Before he could string two words together, the woman had run out of the room and up the concrete steps.

'I didn't realise anyone was listening,' Timberlake said. 'You should have told me. I'm sorry.' He wasn't sorry in the slightest.

As a matter of form he asked for the woman's name and

address, but he instinctively knew that she was kosher and telling the truth. Luckwell wrote it down for him, and added viciously, 'Do me a favour, and give her some of the same. Try to see her when her husband's there. I was getting tired of the supercilious bitch anyway. She was getting to be a right pain in the arse.'

Harry stifled the urge to make a clever remark.

It was a long time since it had been used, but it was still in perfect condition: the man was very careful with all his possessions, particularly mechanical ones. Before it had been put away the shotgun had been carefully oiled and covered with grease, then wrapped in plastic sheeting together with a large sachet of silica gel to absorb any moisture.

After he had cleaned off the grease, leaving the gun looking shiny and new, with some regret the man separated the barrels from the breech and stock and put them into a vice. He had respect for well-made objects, and he was unhappy about what he had to do next. It would be a long and laborious task, but he had plenty of time, and there were other preparations to be completed as well. He began cutting the barrels to half their length, turning a handsome sporting gun into a gangster's murderous weapon.

After another day trawling more of the Terrace Vale bars and other hangouts frequented by the so-called gay community Harry Timberlake was thoroughly sick of the whole exercise. Not only did he find some of the gay bars among the saddest places he'd seen, but his conviction was growing that he was on the wrong track to find Foulds's murderer. At first he thought his gut instinct that Foulds's homosexuality had nothing to do with the crime was due to his own aversion to working in that community. Immediately he had the thought he became angry with himself for mentally reacting to the word 'homosexual', even though it was unspoken. Trying to be as objective as he could and to dismiss all prejudice from his mind (the fact that he was doing it proved that he *was* prejudiced), Timberlake decided that he genuinely believed he was on the wrong line of enquiry.

Jenny Long was due to come to his flat that night, but with his luck he was sure there'd be an emergency with a bad case of piles or severe dandruff or something to keep her at the hospital. But maybe the stars slipped a cog: his luck changed. Jenny turned up looking as cute as a bathing beauty on a travel brochure. Her arrival made him feel a lot less jagged.

Harry Timberlake was very limited as a cook so he concentrated on simple meals with the emphasis on quality. They had smoked salmon with French toast, fillet steak with broccoli, and out-of-season strawberries. The wine was a superior but reasonably priced Rhône which he'd found in a supermarket and kept secret from everyone in case the store ran out of it.

Timberlake and Jenny ate slowly, enjoying their food the more because of what they knew was to follow. Harry was a pure-jazz fan, and he had taped all his precious jazz records, some of them rare 78s. He put on one of his favourite tapes that he played only when he was feeling rather special. The room was filled with a brilliant cascade of piano notes. Jenny looked up in surprise. Her own musical tastes were an odd combination of Mozart and Wagner, for which Harry Timberlake generously forgave her.

'Good heavens,' she said. 'He could play the "Minute Waltz" in forty seconds. Who is it?'

'Art Tatum. But he's not just a speed merchant. Listen to the harmonies he puts in between the line of melody.'

Jenny stopped eating and gave Art Tatum the attention he deserved. After a moment she said, 'That's not jazz. That's *music*.'

'What the hell do you think all jazz is, you perverse woman!' Harry said with an exasperation that wasn't totally pretended.

'Sorry,' Jenny said. 'I'm not prone to argue.' Harry grinned.

Later they made love unhurriedly and successfully on three different pieces of furniture. As they lay quietly in bed, gently touching each other lovingly but without passion, she ran her finger down his nose. She asked him, 'How did you break it? Playing football or something?'

'No.'

'A jealous husband?' As Harry remained silent she insisted, 'Well?'

Reluctantly he said, 'In a punch-up when I was a woodentop . . . uniformed PC. It was just after the pubs had closed. Three tearaways trying to mug an old man. Half a dozen people were watching. Doing absolutely fuck all,' he added bitterly. 'I went in to break it up. One of the thugs nutted me while the others were punching me. So I got out my stick and whacked them. I handcuffed two of them together and kept the other one quiet while I radioed for transport to pick them up.'

'What about the people watching? Didn't they help?'

'Did they buggery. When it was all over they started talking about police brutality. Typical. It makes you ask yourself why you bother, sometimes. What the point of it is.'

'Service to others.'

'No,' he said firmly. 'I don't have a lot of time for the majority of the great British public.'

Jenny was shocked. 'That's rather a sweeping generalisation, isn't it? I can't really believe that you mean it, otherwise you wouldn't be doing your job.'

'I'm a copper to stop criminals, that's all.'

'That's service to others.'

'Only as a by-product. The primary object is to punish the wrongdoers.'

'That's a bit Old Testament, isn't it?'

'So?'

Jenny decided to leave it. After a moment she said, 'I know a good surgeon who could fix it for you.'

'No, thanks.'

'Actually, it's an improvement. You must have been unbearably good-looking beforehand. I bet you devastated all the girls at school.'

'Not really.' There was an odd note in his voice.

'No?' Jenny prompted him.

'I didn't have the sort of small talk most of them expected and wanted.'

Suddenly Jenny understood something about Harry Timberlake. His avoidance of any commitment to women was because he was basically uneasy with most of them.

The last thing a detective – particularly an off-duty one – expects is for someone to shadow *him*. So, when the detective left the nick to go home, he had no idea that the man had spotted him and slipped out of a hamburger bar to follow him. As the man set off he glanced at his watch and nodded to himself.

The man was lucky. In this part of the main road there were a couple of hamburger joints, a greasy spoon caff, and a Fried Chicken Eatery and Takeaway, for God's sake, all of which commanded a view of the corner of the street leading to the Terrace Vale police station. It meant that he could keep a lookout on the corner from different places each time and so avoid making himself conspicuous.

The street was quite busy at this hour with people on their way home from the pubs and two local cinemas, so the man following the detective found it easy to remain unobtrusive.

The policeman went into the Underground entrance on the main road. The man carried on past it, took the first turning past the station and went in by the side entrance. The detective bought a 70 pence ticket, which would have been a useful tip if the man had needed it, but he already had his own Travelcard in his pocket. He let his quarry go into the lift before him and stayed at the back, keeping other passengers between the two of them.

When the train came in, the man got into the next carriage where he could keep an eye on the detective through the communicating doors, just in case he deviated from his usual pattern. The detective, absorbed in doing a newspaper crossword, seemed totally unaware of his shadower. Suddenly, without warning, he turned his head and stared hard at the man.

The man froze.

If the detective had recognised him after all he was in great danger.

He slowly let out a deep breath. He realised that the detective was looking at him with the blank, unseeing eye of a man searching for a word. He looked down at his paper again and wrote something on the crossword.

It was the last train of the night, so a lot of passengers crowded out, most of them noisy and boisterous, which made it simple to follow anyone unnoticed up the stairs and into Southington Court Road, formerly nicknamed Kangaroo Valley and now known as Camel Alley, reflecting the change in immigrant population.

The man continued tracking the detective quite closely for about one or two hundred yards along the still-busy street with no danger of being noticed, but abruptly the character of the area changed. The traffic and pedestrians melted away: there were no more shops and restaurants; this part was all residential. The tall, dark houses presented closed eyes to the virtually deserted streets. Now he had to be careful.

He let his quarry get a hundred yards or more ahead of him; he knew where he was going now. As the detective reached a certain point in his regular journey the man glanced at his watch once more, and nodded with satisfaction. There hadn't been a variation of more than three minutes in five occasions. As he turned for home he began to hum cheerfully.

After making love with Jenny, Harry usually slept as soundly as if Mike Tyson had hit him twice. This time, instead of being as unwound as a broken watch, he lay awake while Jenny slept fitfully beside him. He studied her with the wide eyes of discovery, as if it were the first time they had slept together. Her breasts were uncovered, and as he looked at her he was surprised to see her nipples become erect and harden. He wondered what she was dreaming.

Two thoughts elbowed their way through a crowd of others to the front of his consciousness. The first was that this was the longest relationship he'd ever had with a woman, and it gave no hint of becoming boring. Following on from that: everything between them was so easy, natural and unspoken. He didn't want to go through all the process of learning and adjusting with another woman.

The logical implication of this last thought struck him almost like a physical blow. He was actually contemplating a permanent arrangement . . . being faithful to one person. Oddly enough, for a man who was in a profession that was near the bottom of the league for marital fidelity, that didn't bother him a great deal. After all, he hadn't slept with any other woman almost since the first days of his relationship with Jenny. Although he knew that beginning a new affair could sometimes be as fresh and stimulating as other occasions were wearisome, he had no real yearning for the excitement of novelty.

Harry felt a great surge of tenderness for her. He was astonished to hear himself say, 'Jenny. Look, supposing we got married?'

Quite clearly Jenny replied, 'The television isn't working. It needs new shock-absorbers.' She snuggled down deeper in the bed and gave a little ladylike fart.

Timberlake didn't know whether to be sorry or glad that she hadn't heard him.

* * *

Breakfast with Jenny was one of Harry Timberlake's major pleasures in life. They sat facing each other, freshly showered bodies under loose dressing gowns. The fact that they'd almost invariably made early-morning love was only part of the pleasure. There was an intimacy about breakfast that no other meal could offer. Real coffee, high-fibre cereal – she wouldn't let him eat cholesterol-packed bacon and eggs – wholemeal toast and marmalade, all combined to make the world a very agreeable place.

'You going to get new shock-absorbers for your telly?' he asked her suddenly.

'What are you talking about? Tellies don't have shock-absorbers, although God knows they could do with them with some of the stuff they have on them.'

'In your sleep last night you said your telly needed new shock-absorbers.'

'Good heavens.' She gave a wildly exaggerated leer. 'Shock absorbers . . . very phallic. Big tubes with a spring in them . . . Maybe I was feeling unsatisfied.'

'Good morning, Messalina,' said Harry, who'd read a few books. He hesitated, wondering what to say next. He couldn't quite bring himself to mention marriage directly so he temporised. 'I'd just asked you a question.'

'Oh? What?'

The phone rang, shattering Timberlake's fragile sense of purpose again. He picked up the receiver.

'Yes?' he said grumpily.

'Harry?' It was the unmistakable voice of Ted Greening.

'Hello, Ted,' he answered with a bitterness that would have scorched anyone without a skin as thick as Greening's.

'What're you doing?'

'Having breakfast.'

'Well, finish it off and come straight in. I want a couple of words.'

How about, 'Piss off'? Harry thought, but settled for 'I'm not due in to see Superintendent Harkness till twelve. I was working late last night.'

'Hard luck. Get a move on.'

'But—' Timberlake said, too late. Greening had hung up. 'Oh, shit!' he exploded.

Jenny guessed the situation. This wasn't the first time for

61

either of them. She shrugged resignedly and then said 'What was the question? The question you asked me last night?'

'Oh, nothing important.'

Terrace Vale nick on a cold, wet day of early spring was not – although many of its police officers frequently insisted otherwise – the arsehole of the world, but it definitely came low on London's list of tourist attractions. Harry Timberlake entered the building in a stinking mood. He was still as mad as a wet cat at being dragged away from Jenny. At the same time he was feeling angry and confused by being twice frustrated in his attempt to propose marriage to her. To make matters worse, although he'd tried to propose he wasn't sure he really wanted to be married anyway. The final element in the complex compound of Harry Timberlake's suppressed anger was the realisation, provoked by the sight of the Terrace Vale nick, that he had another day of dragging round gay haunts. He was looking forward to that as eagerly as if he were volunteering for mumps.

Despite the fact that Terrace Vale police station was a rambling building with a lot of large rooms, Harry Timberlake's office was little better than a large cupboard with an inadequate window. Because the ceiling was high, the room had the awkward proportions of a shoebox standing on end. He went there first to hang up his coat before going to Greening's office, but Greening was sitting in Harry's own chair. This succeeded in winding up Harry's resentment another couple of notches.

Briefly Timberlake wondered if the reason Greening was up so early – for him – was that he hadn't been to bed yet. At first sight he looked sober, but it was always difficult to tell with him. A second look revealed that Greening had changed his clothes since the previous day. He also had a piece of cotton wool stuck to his cheek like a certificate that he'd shaved, more or less.

Seeing Greening in the nick this early was as unexpected as hearing the first cuckoo in January. More than that, he seemed excited about something. At the same time he was unusually affable, which threw Harry Timberlake off balance and made it difficult to keep his anger simmering.

'What's up Ted?'

Like Timberlake, Greening had spent a night with unexpected thoughts ricochetting around inside his head. To his surprise the buzz he'd got from being the guvnor at the car park had come back and set his adrenalin surging.

'The car-park murder. There's something I want you to do.'

'You got me in here for that? But I'm on the Foulds job,' Timberlake interrupted. 'I'm working for Harkness.'

'You're Terrace Vale. You're working for me,' Greening said with unexpected authority.

'The Chief Super said he'd lent me to Harkness. Besides, the second AMIP team'll be here today to take over the Barclay murder.'

'They won't be here till tomorrow. There's been some cock-up at the Yard. Their super's giving evidence to some poxy Royal Commission or other. If we dodge about a bit smartish we might get a quick result before they get here.'

Greening sounded wildly optimistic to Timberlake. Alcoholic euphoria, he thought at first, but there was something slyly cocky about Greening's manner. Harry decided to go along with him for the moment and try to talk him out of it later when he ran out of steam.

'Okay, Ted. What's the form?'

Greening leaned forward. 'A randy wife getting bonked by a boyfriend.'

'What? Christ! If every wife who was having it away with somebody else got her husband murdered, half the male population would disappear.'

'Sexual jealousy's the number one motive for murder, you know that as well as I do. Besides, there's more to it than that.'

'But Barclay was an airline steward. He was away from home more than he was in it. The wife and the boyfriend could screw each other all they wanted to with no problems. What would they want to kill him for?'

Greening grinned nastily. 'A hundred grand's worth of insurance, plus the mortgage insurance.'

Timberlake blinked. That, he had to admit to himself, was a pretty solid motive.

'I told you there was more to it,' Greening said smugly. 'And there's something else. The killer had to know that Barclay would go to the supermarket before going to work on this particular occasion and at what time. That narrows it down for a start, right?' Timberlake nodded.

Greening went on, 'It's a racing certainty that Barclay was murdered between seven and eight. The car-park ticket fixes the first time, and the fact that he was due at Heathrow by about eight fixes the second.'

'So?' But Timberlake knew what was coming.

'Go and see the wife and the boyfriend. The wife said she didn't go out, and spent the evening with the boyfriend. Apparently it was a regular arrangement. But something doesn't smell right. The more I think about it, the more I'm sure. When I spoke to her there was a moment when she was dead shifty. It was only a moment, but it was there.'

'Maybe she was just embarrassed at having to admit to having a boyfriend.' Timberlake kept a neutral expression. 'Or there's the faint possibility that she was upset at learning her husband had been killed.'

'Don't be sarky with me,' Greening snapped in his normal unlovable manner. He quickly became confidential and matey again, reinforcing Harry Timberlake's certainty that Greening wanted something from him. 'Come off it, Harry,' he said with an ingratiating smile. 'You're a copper and a bloody good one. I don't have to tell you about having an instinct for something that's not kosher.'

Timberlake didn't reply for a moment. 'What d'you want me to do?'

'Check the timings. It's always iffy when suspects give each other alibis. Go through them with a microscope. Statistically it's odds-on that one or both of them knocked him off.'

'If you think you might get a result, why aren't you doing it yourself?'

'Don't think I wouldn't like to, but I'm in court at eleven till God knows what time. I can trust you. I know you won't try to hog all the credit.'

Harry Timberlake recognised a snow job when he heard one. Nevertheless, he felt a change of attitude coming over him. He decided to accept the inevitable and relax. He might even enjoy it.

Greening slipped a piece of paper from underneath a folded newspaper on the desk in front of him. 'Here are the two names and addresses.'

The boyfriend's name was Wayne Dysart. Harry Timberlake disliked him before he had even met him: he couldn't stand men named Wayne Something. Wayne went with very few surnames: he once knew a villain named Wayne Bullwinkle. Timberlake was sure that the man had become a criminal out of sheer resentment of his name. Harry stood up and was about to go out when he checked.

'Hold on, though, Ted. What about Superintendent Harkness?'

'He's away. Another one of those sodding useless seventh-floor conferences. His chief inspector's in charge while he's gone, and he won't know Harkness didn't give his okay for you to scc Mrs Barclay and what's-is-name.'

'But Harkness will find out as soon as he sees my reports.'

'Don't you worry about Superintendent Toffee Nose. Leave it to me. I'll square it with him. I'll just tell him I sent you.'

But Greening, being Greening, forgot. Or didn't bother.

The place was a dump. *Sunny studio flat; lrge livg/bedrm; k & b* sounded reasonable enough, even without the *sthn aspect* to make it sound better. But the aspect turned out to be over a car-breaker's yard and a refuse lorry depot. Sarah Lewis grumpily told herself she should have guessed it was a dump from the price of £45,000. This was the first flat for ages that she'd found that was within her price range.

The price was the first clue to what the place would be like. The estate agent's attitude was the second clue. It began with his greeting: 'Oh, I didn't know you were a . . .'

'Police officer?' Sarah finished for him.

'That's right,' the agent said, quickly putting back his plastic smile. 'You didn't say on the phone.'

'Can we get round to see the place?' Sarah asked shortly. 'I'm due at the station soon. We're very busy at the moment.'

The estate agent said that life was tough all over and he was busy too, so would she mind going round to see the flat on her own so he could have a sandwich lunch in the office?

That was clue number three.

He gave Sarah the address and handed her a Yale key for the front door. It was then that she should have smelled a rat, Sarah told herself afterwards. In fact she didn't smell a rat until she got into the sunny studio flat. And if it wasn't a rat, it was something even more unpleasant, like a long-dead skunk. The peeling wallpaper had a series of stains on it that looked as if they'd been

65

painted by Picasso with a hangover. When she went over to the window to see the southern aspect, a section of the floorboards felt spongy and soggy underfoot. She wouldn't mind betting that the place had a combination of rising damp and dry rot.

Sarah stamped back to the estate agent, dug the key from her shoulder bag and slapped it down on to his desk.

'I'm sure I could get the owner to consider a reasonable offer,' the man said with no real conviction.

'Try "Drop dead",' Sarah said, slamming the door behind her. Sarah's Black Thursday, or whatever it was, had begun.

Tina Barclay's home was nearest to the station so Timberlake decided to start there. When he identified himself to the widow there was a flash of something almost like panic in her expression. Maybe Ted Greening's instinct was good after all, Timberlake thought. She recovered almost immediately, and although she looked drawn and as if she'd been crying a lot, she seemed composed enough.

There was a man in the living room, about the same age as Tina, tall, powerfully built and good-looking in a sort of silent-film hero way. Timberlake disliked him on sight and decided he wouldn't take his word for tomorrow being Friday even with a certificate from the Astronomer Royal.

'This is a friend, Wayne Dysart,' Tina said, not hesitating a second over the choice of the word 'friend'. Timberlake decided that his first instinct was right.

'Oh, yes, Mr Dysart,' Timberlake said. 'I was going to come to see you at work today.'

'It's my day off. Thursday's a slack day – day before payday,' Wayne replied, with a smile that had all the sincerity of a bomb-site car salesman.

'Mrs Barclay, you told my colleague that on the night your husband was killed you stayed in with Mr Dysart.' His tone was as expressionless as a talking weighing machine.

'That's right,' Dysart answered for her smoothly. 'I arrived at about quarter past seven and I stayed until about midnight.'

'Did you come here from Putney?'

'No, from work, as usual. I left there about six. It takes me a good hour or more with the evening traffic.'

Timberlake nodded. He wondered what excuse Dysart gave

his mother for coming home so late, but decided that the question wouldn't be relevant. In any case, there was no certainty that his mother was home herself at that time. She could be working in an all-night hamburger joint or out with a sailor.

'What time did your husband leave home?' he asked Tina Barclay, although he already knew the answer.

'Between half past six and a quarter to seven.'

'Cutting it a bit fine, weren't you?' Timberlake turned to Dysart. 'Supposing he was delayed and you turned up while he was still here?'

'I always ring from the phone box on the corner,' he replied, with no hint of embarrassment.

Timberlake felt that there was something passing between Tina and Dysart that he wasn't getting.

He summarised in his mind: Barclay was killed between 7.00 and 8.00 p.m., almost certainly much nearer 7.00 than 8.00 p.m. Allowing for it to take fifteen minutes from the supermarket to the Barclay home, it would have been cutting things very fine for Dysart or Tina Barclay to have killed Reg Barclay and got back to the house by 7.15. Too fine to be believable. So, Tina and Wayne Dysart were probably in the clear. If, of course, they were telling the truth.

'Thank you both,' Timberlake said formally. He turned and looked directly at Tina Barclay. 'I'm sorry I had to worry you at a time like this.'

'That's all right,' Dysart said with a smile.

It all sounded very plausible, but there was a nasty nagging feeling in Timberlake's gut that had nothing to do with anything he'd eaten. He decided to call on Dysart's mother and see if she had anything to say that might help him, but she was out.

'You looking for Mrs Dysart?' asked a nosy woman neighbour in an overall and old-fashioned curlers under a turquoise chiffon head square. 'She's gone to her sister in Kingston. She won't be back till this afternoon. Shall I give her a message?' she volunteered eagerly. 'Can I tell her who called?' she raised her voice. Harry Timberlake continued to his car, pretending he hadn't heard.

Whether it was a happy coincidence or cynical design it was impossible to say, but Eldorado Bookmakers Ltd was situated only three doors from the local social security office. Its name had a curious relevance. El Dorado was the South American city of gold sought by the first Spanish invaders. They never found it because it existed only in their imaginations.

The architectural style of the betting shop was Early Dilapidated, and it had been untouched by the recent revolution in the interior decoration of betting shops. Eldorado's customers needed no fitted carpets, Muzak and satellite TV sets to encourage them to press their money on the proprietors. Harry Timberlake wasn't a gambler, in the financial sense, that is. An occasional pools entry and a couple of pounds on the Derby and Grand National were the extent of his involvement in gambling. He could never understand why men with frayed collars and holes in their shoes queued up to give money to other men with camel-hair coats and big houses in Wembley.

Behind the glass-fronted counter was a stonefaced young woman whose knobbly blouse suggested she was wearing a bra made of Lego. When Harry announced himself as 'Detective Inspector' he heard the shuffle of uneasy feet behind him. The door opened as some punters suddenly remembered important appointments elsewhere.

'I'd like to see whoever's in charge.'

'Jocko!' Miss Stoneface screeched. It was as unexpected as if a gravestone angel had suddenly taken flight.

Jocko appeared from the back office. He was a Glaswegian with an accent as thick as cold porridge. He wore a moustache of a style very familiar to Harry Timberlake from his recent visit to gay bars. He invited Harry into the office, which was dominated by a large safe and a woman with a figure like a telephone directory. She was clacking away at a computer with fierce concentration.

Jocko started to explain that he was the assistant manager. 'Mr Wayne Dysart, the manager, is—'

'I know,' said Timberlake. 'I'm making enquiries about a hit-and-run accident,' he explained. 'We've only got part of the registration number and we're checking on all the possibilites.'

Jocko nodded.

'I understand Mr Dysart leaves the shop at six.'

'Aye.'

'I'd like you to cast your mind back to Tuesday. Do you remember it?'

'Do I remember it?! Too friggin' right I do. Bastard!'

'Oh?'

'Practically every favourite on the card came up. Cost us a friggin' fortune.' He said it with as much venom as if he'd had to pay out the winners from his own pocket.

'That's not quite what I meant,' Harry Timberlake said politely. 'Did Mr Dysart leave at his usual time?'

'Oh, aye, I think so.'

'No he didn't,' said the woman at the computer without taking her eyes from the screen. 'He left about twenty to five. It was just after the result of the four-thirty at Yarmouth. Sparafucile.' She pronounced it Sparafoosyle.

'Och, aye,' Jocko said. 'Five to four on. Favourite,' he added bitterly. 'Bastard!'

Timberlake looked at him in astonishment. He didn't think that the Scots actually said 'Och, aye!' any more than the French said '*Oo-la-la*!' – which they did, of course.

Jocko went on: 'I mind it well now. He said he had to get off early and left me in charge.'

The woman at the computer made a noise suspiciously like a suppressed snort of laughter.

On the way back to west London, Harry Timberlake did a lot of thinking. Why had Wayne Dysart lied about what time he left work on the day Barclay was murdered? It didn't affect the crucial time. Unless . . .

The police had been working on the assumption that Barclay was killed between 7.00 and 8.00 p.m. Supposing it was much earlier? Tina Barclay or Wayne Dysart could have driven into the car park at 6.45 p.m. and swapped their parking ticket for Reg Barclay's. The bag of groceries could be a plant, as well. He wondered it anyone had checked the supermarket receipts to see whether there was a cheque or a credit card slip that matched the total on the bill.

'Ted Greening, you lucky sod, maybe you'll get your result before the AMIP team turn up after all,' Harry Timberlake said out loud as he drove his car through the city traffic.

69

Chapter 4

Wayne Dysart's home in Putney was one of thousands of identical houses designed for maximum economy in materials and labour. They were built between the wars and could be bought for a deposit of £5 and practically a lifetime of mortgage payments for the remaining £500. The exterior had been repainted twice since the war, both times badly. The mean little house depressed the hell out of Timberlake. As he got out of his car he briefly thought of Jenny Long, then dismissed as absurd any similarity between a life with her and the sort of existence this house symbolised: a succession of dreary days of cramped existence, tied to a dreary wife as disillusioned as her dreary husband. Timberlake shuddered. If Wayne Dysart had to live here with his mother he felt sorry for him, and could understand Dysart's affair with the lively Tina Barclay.

When Timberlake rang the doorbell Dysart answered. He seemed unsurprised to see the detective, but not very pleased. If Timberlake had to describe Dysart's attitude, he would call it furtive.

'May I come in?' he asked sharply. 'I have some questions to put to you.' Dysart hesitated but could see no way out of it. He opened the door a little wider for Timberlake to squeeze through and led him into a back room. It had French windows on to a dusty, ill-kept garden where weeds were winning the war. The furniture was surprisingly cheap-looking, even for this house. Much of it was the type that is 'delivered in kit form, easily assembled with just a screwdriver, and can be either painted or polished'. It was turning into a thoroughly depressing day.

Harry Timberlake waited for Dysart to offer him a drink so that he could refuse it, underlining that this was an official call, but Dysart didn't offer him one.

70

'Mr Dysart, you told me that on Tuesday you left work at six thirty and went directly to Mrs Barclay's home, where you arrived at about seven fifteen. Two witnesses say that you left work much earlier, at about a quarter to five. That leaves some two hours unaccounted for.'

Dysart walked about the small, crowded room as much as the crammed-in, tatty furniture would allow, making up his mind what to say. Finally he replied, 'As a matter of fact I think I did.' He gave a mirthless grin. There were small beads of sweat on his upper lip. 'I was going to tell you about it eventually, but I didn't think it was all that important as I was with Tina at the important time.'

'Tina who?' came a voice from the door. Standing there was a woman of about thirty-five. She had improbably blonde hair, thick, darkish eyebrows and a sharp, pointed nose. It was the only thing sharp or pointed about her because she was a good twenty pounds overweight and refused to admit it, even in the way she dressed, which made her appear even dumpier. Her mouth was set in a thin, straight line like a cut-throat razor. She had all the charm of a ratcatcher. And yet . . . There was something about her that suggested that she had been an attractive and perhaps warm young woman not too long ago. She had obviously just come in, unheard, for she was wearing a topcoat and she was carrying a bag of groceries.

'Tina who?' she repeated, in case Wayne and the neighbours hadn't heard her first bellow. She looked at Timberlake. 'And who are you?'

Dysart did the introductions. The woman was unimpressed by Harry Timberlake's rank. On the other hand, he was a little taken aback when he was told that the woman was 'my wife, Julie'. So Dysart wasn't an unmarried man living with his mother, but a definitely married man living with his spouse.

Harry Timberlake gave Mrs Dysart the same story that he'd used at the betting shop: he was checking on a hit-and-run case. She hardly listened to him. She wasn't the sort of woman who did a lot of listening. Timberlake could see the storm signals and the fast-approaching thunder clouds. In his time as a uniformed copper he had attended many 'domestics' or family rows, but this one turned into an all-star, wide-screen epic with stereophonic sound, very loud. He tried to make himself inconspicuous as Julie

71

and Wayne Dysart went at each other hammer, tongs and poker, but he needn't have bothered. They were so involved in each other that they wouldn't have noticed him if he'd waved a flag. He let the row rage between them because more home truths escape in rage than in drunkenness.

When they stopped for breath, Harry Timberlake managed to slip in a couple of questions. To his surprise he learned that on the night of Barclay's murder Dysart had arrived home at about 7.15 p.m. and gone out again at 8.30 p.m. Mrs Dysart, who clearly didn't want to do her husband any favours, nevertheless confirmed his times of arrival and leaving home.

This opened two more cans of worms. Mrs Dysart's story seemed to put Dysart in the clear, if the murder had been between 7.30 and 8.00 p.m. But it meant that Tina Barclay's alibi had been exploded.

Secondly, there was an unexplained gap in Dysart's timetable: he left the betting shop in Stratford at about 4.45 p.m. and didn't arrive home, a journey of about an hour and a quarter, until 7.15 p.m., which left a gap of an hour or more. If the time of the murder had been disguised and the actual killing had taken place earlier, then Dysart could be guilty.

That missing hour suddenly became important, and Timberlake prepared to press Dysart on the point. Mrs Dysart did it for him, and with much more vigour than he could have allowed himself. She bellowed an accusation that he had gone 'straight from work to fuck that scraggy bitch Sandra again!'

'Well, at least she doesn't look like a bleeding beached whale!' Dysart retorted unwisely.

As Harry Timberlake let himself out, Julie Dysart was looking for something heavy to throw.

Harry drove on to Putney Heath and a car park, where he made an entry in his diary and then wrote up his notebook, which is referred to officially as a pocketbook. Harry Timberlake always took the time to do his notes before returning to the station. This stratagem occasionally led to an interesting exchange in court. When Harry asked permission to consult his notebook, the defending lawyer would sometimes ask in a deprecating tone, 'And when exactly did you make this note?', expecting an answer that would give him an opening. Harry would pause and say clearly, 'Ten minutes after the interview.' It impressed the hell out of the jury and discomfited the supercilious counsel.

He put away his notebook but made no attempt to start his car. He thought at first of the Barclays and Tina's obviously frequent rows with her husband, because, in Sergeant Bailey's elegant phrase, 'He jumped on anything that stood still for a second.' Tina Barclay herself was being banged by a married betting-shop manager who was apparently triple-crossing his wife and Tina with some scraggy bitch named Sandra.

Harry supposed that Reg and Tina Barclay had loved each other once; that they had actually believed in a long, happy life together. The odds were that Julie and Wayne Dysart did as well, at the beginning. Julie Dysart had probably been a slim, cheerful girl in love with the superficially – in Harry's opinion, anyway – handsome Wayne. Maybe when he was younger he was less of a turd, Harry conceded.

He sighed. In other words, he told himself, both couples then were like he and Jenny were now. He switched on the engine and looked through the windscreen. The sky was dark and overcast. He couldn't remember what it felt like to be in the sun.

Sarah's angry disappointment over the flat persisted through her late duty at the Terrace Vale nick. It was her turn for the mind-numbing job of transferring to computer disc the statements – such as they were – taken on door-to-door interviews. They included the usual trivia, mild paranoia and vicious gossip-mongering; but hidden in all the chaff might be a couple of grains of valuable information that would be shown up by the computer's cross-indexing.

About a quarter of an hour before Sarah was due to go off duty came the second black spot of her day. PC Paul Todd, inevitably called PC Plod by his colleagues who should have known better, brushed by her chair and knocked her shoulder bag off the back. He trod on it with a size nine shoe that had more than thirteen stones bearing down on it, breaking a ballpoint pen and squashing a criminally expensive lipstick, among other things. Oddly enough, a mirror was unbroken.

Todd's apologies and offers to pay for the damage, repeated like a stuck gramophone record, only made Sarah more furiously exasperated. He was abject, and refrained from saying that it was a stupid place to put a bag anyway. So Sarah didn't have even the satisfaction of a shouting match that would have lanced the abscess of her filthy mood. She set to cleaning the squishy red goo from the inside of her bag and its contents.

Harry Timberlake suddenly realised that he was hungry. He always had an enormous appetite after a night and morning with Jenny. Greening's early call had interrupted his breakfast and he'd had nothing since. Hunger overcame judgement and he settled for a burger with a powerful seasoning that could disguise the taste of anything from horse to kangaroo, and a plastic cup of coffee-coloured tea. They didn't do a great deal to sustain him, but they positively ruined his appetite. When he returned to the Barclay home he felt and looked sour.

Tina Barclay didn't seem in the least alarmed to see Timberlake again, although he was pretty sure she'd been crying.

'When I spoke to you before, you told me that Mr Dysart arrived here at about a quarter past seven.'

'No. *He* told you.'

'That's right. So he did. But in fact he didn't get here until after half past eight, did he?'

Tina didn't hesitate. 'No, he didn't.'

Timberlake said nothing, waiting for her to go on. After a moment she added, 'I suppose I should have said something, but I was sort of surprised. After you left I asked him about it, and I said I was going to tell you, but he begged me not to.'

'Why?'

'Actually, he was home with his mother, but he didn't want you going round questioning her. She's not very strong, and he didn't want her upset. Besides, she might find out about us. Me and Wayne, I mean. Anyway, I knew he couldn't possibly have done it.' She avoided the obvious word, and settled for, 'You know . . . What happened to Reg. Wayne, he couldn't. So, I agreed to keep quiet.'

'Until now.'

'Well, you know, don't you?' A thought struck her. 'You've seen his mother, then?'

'I've seen Mrs Dysart, yes,' Timberlake said carefully. 'She says Mr Dysart was with her until half past eight.' He didn't point out to her that now she had no alibi for the time of the

74

murder, but he was absolutely certain that she wasn't involved in it in any way. Nevertheless, it wasn't in Harry Timberlake's character to cut corners.

'Mrs Barclay, do you have a car? Besides your husband's, that is?'

She shook her head. Her eyes filled with tears at the mention of her husband. Timberlake was sure they were genuine. But again, he was thorough: she had to be told.

'Mrs Barclay, I must warn you that lying to the police can get you into very serious trouble. If you're not involved in anything, it's always best to tell the truth. We usually find out anyway.'

Tina was going to apologise when the doorbell rang. She hurried to it. Wayne Dysart stalked in.

He glared at Timberlake with a sulky expression that was ludicrous in a man of his age. 'You *would* be here. I suppose you've told her,' he said petulantly. Timberlake managed to keep his temper, but his dislike of Dysart was growing rapidly.

'Yes, I know all about it,' Tina Barclay interrupted.

'Look, darling, I can explain,' Dysart said, turning on all the charm he could manage. He hurried on. 'Everything's been over between us for years.'

Tina Barclay was still in a state of shock. All she could manage was, 'What?'

'Darling, you've got to believe me. She means nothing to me. It's just a marriage in name.'

Harry Timberlake winced heavily. He didn't think anyone outside paperback romances ever used that cliché. And because Dysart could think only the worst of people, he had given himself away. Spectacularly. One thing's for sure, Timberlake told himself. Maybe Dysart's good at arithmetic and knows horses, but apart from that he's stupid – much too stupid to be mixed up in anything as heavy as murder without betraying himself.

Tina just stared at Dysart, and then pitched into him. Her grief made her anger even sharper. Wayne Dysart, the very poor man's Lothario, must have wondered what hit him. For the second time in a couple of hours he found himself being sliced up by an angry woman's sharp tongue. At last he managed to pull himself together enough to answer back.

'You're a fine one to talk! All right, so I'm married,' he

75

yelled at her. 'But so were you! That didn't stop you screwing me! What's the difference?'

'You *knew* I was married, while you told me a lot of bull-shit about living with your poor old mum! That's the difference!'

Timberlake didn't think about God a lot, but now he wondered if God was trying to tell him something. Twice in one day, just after he'd asked Jenny Long to marry him, he'd been given an insight into what marriage could become. In fact, it dawned on him that he didn't know of any really happy marriages more than a couple of years old.

He was shaken out of his introspection by Dysart turning on him. Dysart was furious: he could see himself losing a trouble-free bit on the side.

'It's all your fault,' he told Timberlake, viciously. 'I bet you bloody told her I was bloody married. It was none of your bloody business! I got a bloody good mind to report you!' His vocabulary was as limited as his imagination.

Harry Timberlake moved towards the door. 'As it happens, I didn't tell Mrs Barclay that you're married. But if you want to make a complaint about me, that's your privilege.' He stopped at the door and turned. He couldn't resist saying cheerfully, 'Anyway, you've still got Sandra.'

'Who's Sandra?' Tina demanded shrilly.

What Harry Timberlake had done was unprofessional, but very satisfying, and he whistled briefly as he let himself out. It was about the only good thing that had happened to him since he left home that morning.

The gremlin who was running Sarah's Black Thursday, or whatever it was, had one more stroke to pull, a sort of step-in-a-dog-dirt surprise for her. When she arrived home that night, her head buzzing from having stared at a computer screen all evening, she dug into her handbag for her key and jabbed her finger into a blodge of lipstick that had escaped her earlier.

Cursing, she found her key. It went into the lock half an inch, then stuck. Sarah joggled and pushed at it but the key stubbornly refused to go all the way in. She took it out again and looked at it carefully. The damned thing was bent, the victim of PC Todd's heavy foot. She vainly tried to straighten the key with her fingers, and briefly her Celtic temper almost pushed her into trying her teeth on it.

Sarah rang the doorbell.

And again.

Mrs Culliford opened the door against the security chain and peered out. She was wearing her dusty-pink dressing gown. She had evidently dressed in a hurry, because the top button was undone.

'Oh, it's you,' she said, as if she were welcoming the Angel of Death. She stood motionless.

'Well, are you going to let me in?' Sarah said. Only her lips moved; her teeth remained tightly clenched.

'Haven't you got your key?'

Sarah breathed out noisily through her nose. 'Do you think I'd've rung if I had?'

'I hope you haven't lost it. I don't want burglars getting in here with your key,' Mrs Culliford said with alarm.

'It's not lost. It's bent.' She held it up.

'What did you do that for?'

The asininity of the question defeated Sarah. She moved forward. She must have looked menacing, for Mrs Culliford jumped back, startled. She recovered, pushed the door almost shut and released the safety chain with a rattle that sounded like Traitor's Gate being opened.

'You'll have to pay for a new key,' Mrs Culliford said accusingly. She muttered something about 'waking respectable people in the middle of the night . . . no consideration . . . the sort of thing you'd expect . . .'

Sarah started up the stairs, stopped halfway. She said with the sweetness of cyanide-laced ice-cream, 'Oh, I'm sorry if I interrupted you and Mr Culliford . . .' and then, with a nudge-nudge wink and a lascivious leer, 'in the middle of something.'

Mrs Culliford looked as if a stake had just been driven through her heart. Sarah continued on upstairs, a satisfied smile on her face. There was as much likelihood of the Cullifords indulging in sexual activity as of Ian Paisley sending the Pope a birthday card.

So ended Sarah's Black Thursday, or whatever it was.

Although she didn't know it yet, she had just had the biggest stroke of luck in her entire police career.

The name Westcliff-on-Sea was established before the Trade Descriptions Act, otherwise the municipal council might find itself in trouble. Westcliff-on-Sea, like its neighbours Leigh-on-Sea and Southend-on-Sea, is on the Thames Estuary. It is affected by the tide, but so is Hammersmith, which doesn't claim to be Hammersmith-on-Sea.

Westcliff's claim to be a seaside town couldn't have been further from the minds of the Welsh Rarebit, WPC Sarah Lewis, and PC Greg Davidson. They couldn't care whether Westcliff was on-sea or halfway up a mountain. Although it was midday, they were still in bed at one of Westcliff's better hotels. To give them due credit, at least they were sitting up. They felt no urge to visit the town, or to watch the cold rain falling on the expanse of grey mud exposed by the ebbing tide. They didn't have the strength, either. They had been making the most of their weekend together, and had had a very strenuous time of it.

'You know,' Greg said, 'we're earning enough between the two of us. We should be able to find a place to rent, for a start.'

'As soon as you say you want to move out of the section house, people'll begin to get nosy. And when someone notices your home address and mine are the same . . .' She mimed an exaggerated nudge-nudge, wink-wink.

'So what?' he said unconvincingly.

'Oh, come off it, Greg. If they knew at the nick that we were seeing each other, one of us'd get posted away. It's standard practice. And even if living together wasn't against regulations, think of all the mickey-taking – and worse – we'd get from some of the foul-mouthed sods we've got at the Vale.'

'Not if we were married.'

'Don't kid yourself. Besides, we agreed: we don't get married until we've both got our promotion.'

'*You* agreed.'

Sarah snuggled down under the bedclothes. She slipped a practised exploratory hand along Greg's thigh.

'Oh, no,' he groaned. 'Not again. Aren't you ever satisfied?'

'Almost invariably. That's why.'

'Only almost?'

'I don't want to give you a swollen head,' she said, emphasising the last word.

'Give it a rest,' Greg pleaded. 'I'm not Superman. I've had it.'
'Come on,' she said. 'It's our last day.'

Greg managed to stop himself saying 'Thank God'. Sarah continued to work on him with firm expertise. After a few moments he said reflectively, 'I don't know, though . . .'

Later, after they had rested, got up, eaten three Shredded Wheat each and gone back to bed again, Sarah suddenly said, 'I know why I couldn't get it in that time!'

Greg was startled into full awakeness. 'Wha'?'

'I know why it wouldn't go in.' She looked at him. 'Oh, not *that*.' She started to explain.

Ted Greening took a deep breath, and knocked on the door. 'Come in,' Harkness called out. Greening adjusted his expression to what he hoped was one of amiable respectfulness. He sat on the chair next to the desk for a second or so before Harkness said quietly, 'Sit down, Chief Inspector.'

Ted Greening shot sideways glances at Harkness while trying not to show it. As usual, the senior man looked as if he'd stepped straight out of Harrod's window. His face gave nothing away, but Greening began to feel uneasy. He took a cigarette from a battered packet and put it to his mouth. He had got as far as fumbling for a match when Harkness said without emphasis, 'Don't smoke in here, please.' The timing was beautiful. It left Ted Greening as off balance as a slalom racer who has just lost a ski. He cursed himself for falling into the trap of behaving with Harkness as he always had with Chief Superintendent Liversedge. He began to sweat.

'Mr Greening,' Harkness began with icy politeness, 'did you instruct Inspector Timberlake to leave his enquiries on the Foulds case and go to interview witnesses in the car-park murder while I was away?'

Oh, Christ, Greening thought. He managed a nod.

When he came out of the office a quarter of an hour later his shirt was soaked with sweat. He shut the door behind him and leant against the wall of the corridor for a moment before taking out the badly needed cigarette he had been denied earlier. He gulped down a great cloud of smoke, sucking it down to the bottom of his lungs. He let it out slowly, luxuriously, spoiling the effect with an explosive cough.

Ted Greening had no fancy way to describe his feelings; not even something simple, like being skinned alive or sandpapered all over. It was outside his powers of creative imagination to think of something like that. He just felt totally sliced up and wrung out. He cringed at the memory of how Harkness had humiliated him, without raising his voice or using the vulgarities that Greening himself would have used and felt more comfortable with. It wasn't only the matter of diverting Harry Timberlake from his work without mentioning it to Harkness, let alone asking permission. There was Greening's failure to produce his own reports of the investigations into the Foulds murder that he had made before the AMIP team turned up. On top of that, Greening had failed to follow instructions to chase up and collate the reports of the other Terrace Vale officers involved in the enquiries. Guiltily Ted Greening remembered that the reports were all on his desk, somewhere.

It was the worst quarter of an hour Greening could recall since a blistering cross-examination at the Old Bailey when he was a young police constable and he had unwisely tried to embroider his evidence a little.

There was a moment when Greening tried to answer back to Harkness and point out that he and Harry Timberlake were Terrace Vale officers, not members of the AMIP squad. Harkness wasn't their guvnor.

Harkness took his scalpel to that. He 'reminded' Greening that his own chief superintendent had instructed him to co-operate with the head of the AMIP squad, and had specifically seconded Harry Timberlake to the team.

Yet this was not the worst of it. What griped at Greening's guts and made him feel so shamefaced was the pitiless mirror that Harkness had held up to him. Instead of seeing a reflection of friendly, hail-fellow-well-met, jokey, good old Ted Greening who was as good a copper as you'd find anywhere, Greening was acutely aware that the real image was a disaster. He was a mess: overweight, unfit, badly shaved, yellow-eyed and dressed in a wrinkled suit that badly needed cleaning to get the smell of stale sweat and tobacco out of it. He felt so depressed that he couldn't even console himself with the memory of his commendations and the knowledge that he was a first-class thief-taker. Or at least, he had been, a long time ago. A very long time ago.

He straightened up and returned to his own office. On his way along the corridor he met Harry Timberlake.

Timberlake looked at him hard. 'You all right, Ted?'

'Oh, yeah. I'm bloody great. Fine friend you turned out to be.'

Timberlake didn't pretend not to understand. 'I'll always cover for you, Ted, but not with my own neck.' He continued, less sharply, 'The Super asked if my report was right, and I said it was. It didn't occur to me that you hadn't told him you'd sent me on enquiries. I'm sorry, Ted, but it was bound to come out anyway.' Greening thought hard, trying to find some excuse for blaming Harry Timberlake, but there was no way.

He pushed past Harry and went into his office and banged the door shut, too hard, and it bounced back to remain ajar. Automatically he reached in the bottom drawer of his desk for the whisky bottle, but there were only a couple of spoonfuls in it. He swore, silently and viciously. Dimly he realised that he'd been drinking even more than usual lately, but he stifled the thought. He started to get up to go to his car with its emergency bottle in the glove compartment, then checked and reached for the phone instead. He dialled a number and while he waited for an answer he drank the one finger of whisky.

'It's me,' he said sharply. 'I'm coming round. Now.' The person at the other end apparently protested. 'Shut your mouth,' Greening said. 'If you know what's good for you, you'll be there.' He slammed down the phone.

He picked up the bottle again and tilted it back to get the very last drop. As he threw the bottle into the wastepaper basket Greening noticed Sarah Lewis standing in the doorway. From the look they exchanged he knew that she had seen him draining the whisky bottle.

'What the hell do you want?' he said, rising. He looked so angry that for a moment Sarah actually thought he was going to attack her.

'Have you got a moment, sir?'

'What for?'

The enormity of her presumption suddenly overwhelmed Sarah and her face went beetroot. But she had guts. She swallowed hard and said, 'I think I know how Phantom Flannelfoot is getting into those houses.' As she said it she was acutely aware of how pretentious she sounded.

81

'Oh, piss off, WPC. Go and see some old ladies across the road, and leave CID work to the men.' Greening brushed past her.

In for a pound, Sarah thought. Her anger rose at Greening's boorishness. 'At least it's an idea—' she began.

'Go and waste Inspector Timberlake's time,' he said over his shoulder.

There were five prostitutes that Ted Greening took turns to visit. His favourite was the black girl, Rita, who was not only the best-looking and the best technician at her trade, but also the best snout. Ted Greening owed some of his successes to her tips. Before calling on four of the girls he always phoned in advance to ask them if they were busy. This wasn't courtesy on his part. It was simply that he didn't want to waste his time by calling on a whore who was already on her back with a paying customer. He always had other girls he could turn to.

He went to the fifth girl, Greta, when he was in the wound-up state that he was now. He didn't ask her if it was convenient; he just said he was on his way and that was that. She didn't seem to have much going for her; she wasn't pretty and her figure was average at best. But she was special: she was submissive. Greening didn't get his kicks, or as the Americans would say, get his rocks off, by whacking Greta or being whacked by her. He simply acted brutal; he played the super-macho stud. As best he could, that was.

As he banged into Greta, breathlessly insulting her through clenched teeth, she wailed and moaned, swearing that he was screwing her to death and she couldn't take much more, which only encouraged him. While she was acting the suffering victim she was thinking, *One of these days the bastard's going to have a heart attack on me*. Then, with enormous surprise, she discovered that she was almost enjoying it for a moment.

When he had finished, unlike most men in this situation, Greening suffered no self-disgust or lack of satisfaction. In fact, he felt much better. The tension had gone out of him, and most of his strength as well. Yes, he felt great.

Greening walked out into the street. His luck was holding: there was a black cab approaching with its For Hire sign alight. He was about to raise his arm to hail it when he saw another would-be passenger was already signalling. The cab pulled up ten yards beyond the other man, which gave Greening his chance.

As the man opened the door of the taxi, Greening lumbered up and roughly elbowed him aside. Curiously, he made no protest. Greening flourished his warrant card and said, 'Police business.'

'That means no fucking tip,' the taxi-driver muttered to himself. 'Where to, guv?' he said out loud. He meant to give the other man an apologetic shrug, but he had already moved away.

The man gave a rare, secret smile as the cab drove off. He had recognised Greening from the long nights of keeping watch on the Terrace Vale nick. He bet Greening would have liked to recognise him.

Chapter 5

Sarah Lewis was a darkly attractive young woman who looked a little like a young Liza Minelli whose face had been put together with greater care. She had a full figure and a countrywoman's clear complexion, which all earned for her the nickname of the Welsh Rarebit. She lived her first eighteen years in mid-Wales with her parents who ran the general store and sub-post office in a small village. Life wasn't too bad during her school years, for she had to travel on a bus some ten miles to the nearest small town. It meant she got away from the stifling existence of a village where everyone knew everyone else, and everything about them. There were no secrets; and the central exchange for all gossip was the village shop. When she read *Clochemerle* on her trips to and from school – it was the sort of book she had to hide from her parents – there was a passage which reminded her irresistibly of her own village. It was to the effect that, if someone coughed at one end of the village, at the other end the chemist was already wrapping up the cough mixture before the patient got there.

Once Sarah left school she was expected to stay at home and help run the shop. There was an ambivalence about Sarah's attitude towards the village. Although she found it unbearably constricting, she enjoyed being at the centre of all the gossip. On the other hand, there were no opportunities to be alone for five minutes with any of the young men of the village, even if she had wanted to. Robert Redfords they weren't. Not even Tom Joneses.

Her father was strict chapel and strict everything else. His sense of honesty made him pay her for working in the shop and post office, but it wasn't quite strong enough for him to pay her a fair wage. On her eighteenth birthday Sarah withdrew all her money from her post-office savings account and took the train to London.

She managed to avoid the pimps and prostitution-recruiters at the terminus and found a cheap room. A strong native wit and a natural suspicion enabled her to settle in London quite quickly, but her money melted away much faster than she had expected. She had no shorthand or typing, so jobs – other than as a counter clerk in a post office, which she simply refused to consider – were hard to come by. As a last resort she applied to join the police. She passed the entrance exam and did very well during her probationary period.

At the time of the Foulds murder Sarah was a mature, yet still young, woman of many moods. There were times when it was easy to visualise her in traditional Welsh dress with a riverboat-funnel hat, plunking a harp; other times with a truncheon thumping a large disturber of Her Majesty's peace; yet others looking sexy enough to make the bed smoulder. However, at no time could anyone imagine her as lacking confidence or courage.

Her rejection by Ted Greening had given her a severe jolt, but by the time she came off duty that same evening she had almost completely recovered. Even so, while she waited for Harry Timberlake to return to his office, some of her resolution leaked away. Her knock on his office door was a trifle hesitant. When there was no answer she was on the point of turning away. She heard Timberlake moving around inside, which provoked a surge of bloody-mindedness in her. She knocked again, more positively this time.

The irritated 'Yes?' from inside almost scared her away, but she persisted and went in. Timberlake was at his desk, looking as knackered as someone who has failed to complete the London Marathon. When he saw who it was, his expression lightened a little. 'Come in, Sarah. Sit down,' he said.

Sarah went to the least uncomfortable-looking of the chairs, took a deep breath and said without preamble, 'Phantom Flannel-foot: I think I know how he might be getting into those places.'

She waited to see how Harry Timberlake would react, but he remained impassive. At least that was a lot better than Greening's insulting dismissal of her, she thought.

'What about the burglar alarm?'

'That, too.'

'I see.' There was a long pause as she looked at him nervously.

Timberlake said, 'Well, are you going to tell me, or is it all a big secret?'

She told him, beginning with the night she couldn't get her key into the front door of her digs. It wasn't because it was bent, as she had thought, but because it was the key to the ghastly flat she had been to see earlier that day. She had given the estate agent her own key and kept the wrong one.

Harry paid her the compliment of listening carefully to her. Occasionally he unconsciously rubbed the bump on his nose as if he were trying to smooth it out, a sure sign that he was thinking hard.

'And that's it,' Sarah finished. The fact that Timberlake hadn't interrupted her once with a comment or a question unnerved Sarah. She looked hard at him, hoping to see some hint of a reaction, but he remained impassive, still rubbing his nose.

After a long pause he asked her, 'Have you mentioned any of this to Mr Greening?'

'I tried to, but he told me to go and— He told me to go away.'

'Uhuh. Wait there for a couple of minutes,' Harry said, and went out.

When Harry Timberlake arrived downstairs, Sergeant Anthony C. Rumsden was at the desk with a civilian whose flat had recently been burgled. Rumsden was showing him a sealed and labelled plastic bag containing a collection of cufflinks and medals that had been found in a public park. 'No, they're not mine,' the man said without regret. He nodded and left.

'I bet he's pleased,' Rumsden observed to Harry. 'He's already put in his insurance claim and he wouldn't want to alter it – particularly if he bumped up the value of the stuff on his claim. Now, what can I do for you?'

'I'd like you to lend WPC Lewis to CID.'

'What for?'

'The Phantom Flannelfoot business. She's come up with a good idea, and I'd like her to follow it through. I could do with the help, with all these other flaps going on. Besides, I think she'd make good CID material.'

Rumsden sighed. 'Oh, don't do that to her, Harry.'

Timberlake looked at him in astonishment. 'What are you talking about?'

'I used to be CID. Didn't you know?' Timberlake shook his

head. 'It nearly ruined me. Out all hours the devil sends . . . Not always able to ring the wife to say I wouldn't be home till late . . . Falling in the front door smelling like a fire in a brewery because I'd had to meet informants or villains in a pub . . .'

'Come off it, Tony,' Harry Timberlake said. 'It's not that bad.'

Anthony Chamberlain Rumsden continued as if Timberlake hadn't spoken. 'With the best will in the world, any wife is bound to get suspicious and jealous eventually. Another month in CID and my wife would have walked out on me. So I chucked it. It's all right for you; you haven't got a wife.'

'Nor has Lewis.'

'Ha, sodding, ha. But she might want to get married one day, and CID's no life for a married woman.'

'There's quite a few successful ones about. Anyway,' Harry said with increasing irritation, 'don't you think that's something for her to decide? Maybe she has career ambitions.'

Rumsden sighed again. 'You're not a bad sod, Harry, but you do have tunnel vision about police work. There's another world outside, you know.'

'So they say. Well, can I borrow Sarah Lewis?'

'If she wants to.'

WPC Sarah Lewis most certainly did want to.

'I thought you would,' Harry said. 'Mind, it's only a temporary attachment. But if you put up a good performance . . .' Sarah looked as if she'd be ready to run through the wall if Harry asked her. 'I'll fix up for you to have a desk. Get hold of the files and start making your calls tomorrow. Report back to me.'

'Yes, sir. We should know quite quickly whether or not we're on the right track.'

'One more thing.'

'Sir?'

'From now on it's "guv". Right?'

'Right, guv.'

Sarah left Timberlake's office calmly, but once she had closed the door behind her she punched the air as if she had just scored the winning goal in the Cup Final.

The man's stillness was almost inhuman. No hunter waiting for the most dangerous prey in the night jungle could have remained more motionless: he hardly seemed to breathe. Despite

87

the bright street lights only yards from where he stood hidden, he was virtually invisible in the cover of a tree and bushes, the shadows of their gently moving leaves breaking up the outline of his black-clad form.

He hardly moved his head to glance down at his wristwatch. If the policeman didn't come within the next six minutes, he wouldn't be coming at all. In all the times the man had stalked him, the policeman had not varied his times by more than five minutes.

Someone was approaching from the right direction. Although the policeman was still a good fifty yards away with the light behind him, the man in the shadows recognised him at once from his walk. The several nights of quiet surveillance had been worth the time and effort. The policeman was forty yards away now . . . thirty . . .

Very slowly, so that there would be no sudden movement which might give away his position, the man brought up the shotgun. There was no need for the man to check that it was loaded; he had done that before taking up his position and he felt no compulsion to check again. He didn't make mistakes. Although he was about to kill someone, the man's hand was as steady as a surgeon's.

The policeman was ten paces from being dead in line with the shotgun's sights . . . eight . . . five . . .

There was a sudden screech of tyres and the sound of breaking glass. A battered Ford Cortina, hard down on its springs with six passengers crowded inside, swayed drunkenly into the street. Another empty wine bottle came looping out of a window to smash on the roadway. The revellers in the car cheered.

The man with the shotgun said to himself, *Madmen! They might kill someone!*, not seeing the massive incongruity of his thought. Yet he didn't waver: he still steadily aimed the gun at where the target would appear next; but the policeman had swung round and run into the roadway to try to take the number of the car. He shook his head and continued across the road to walk on.

The man with the shotgun allowed him to get out of sight before preparing to move off. He felt no sense of anticlimax or frustration. There would be another occasion.

* * *

88

By midday the following day Sarah Lewis was ninety-five per cent certain that her theory about Phantom Flannelfoot was right; two hours later she was totally convinced. She went into Harry Timberlake's office. There was no need for her to speak: she glowed like a Roman candle about to burst into brightly coloured sparks. Her enthusiasm was infectious; Harry felt a sudden wave of excitement himself.

'So you're right?' he said.

Sarah nodded. 'Every one of the houses done by Phantom Flannelfoot in this manor and the two neighbouring ones were sold through estate agents within the previous two years.'

'All of them?'

'All except one,' she conceded, 'but the file on that one has a big query against it. The collator doesn't reckon it was a Phantom Flannelfoot job. The owner probably went out and left the front door unlocked and didn't want to admit it. It all fits,' she went on, her words spilling out eagerly. 'I'm sure that at each house Flannelfoot managed to get hold of the front-door key from the estate agent just long enough to take an impression and make a duplicate, then went back a couple of years later and walked straight in. I mean, how many people change the door locks when they move into a new house?'

'Yes, all right,' Harry said, not unkindly. 'I got the message last night. Now calm down and get your breath back.'

'Sorry, sir . . . guv.'

'Now, we've got a pretty good lead on how he gets in, but that's less than half the problem. The question is, how do we find him?'

Sarah stared at him. She could kick herself; she'd been so full of herself at guessing how Phantom Flannelfoot had been getting into the houses that she hadn't stopped to think about tracking him down.

Harry let her down lightly. 'Of course, you've realised that by now it's no good asking the estate agents for a list of people who visited the houses. Chummy wouldn't have given his right name and address anyway.'

'Right.'

'So this is what you do. You mark up on a map all Chummy's jobs, with dates, and see if there's any pattern in the way he moves. Find out how much the houses cost. Then you call on all the local estate agents and get from them a list of houses in the right price bracket they've had on their books in the last couple of years.'

'And try to forecast his probable next targets.' Her Welsh accent became more pronounced as her enthusiasm mounted again.

'Two things,' Harry said. 'First of all, don't think CID work is all glamour and excitement. A hell of a lot of it is deadly dull and boring – like this job you'll be doing for a start. Second, keep what you're doing on this case to yourself. And that reminds me. Go and write a report of everything you've told me, right now, and time and date it. You don't want anyone nicking credit for your idea.' Harry Timberlake was, after all, an exceptional copper.

Sarah met Greg late that evening in a small restaurant well away from Terrace Vale. She was tired, but happy after a long day of getting from collators lists of houses that Phantom Flannelfoot had robbed and marking them up on a map; then going through local papers and Yellow Pages for names of estate agents and making phone calls to them. She was, she admitted to Greg, thoroughly knackered.

So when he asked her, 'What have you been doing all day?' she told him in detail. He was rather surprised, like someone who asks casually 'How are you?' and gets a full medical report. Sarah rattled on so enthusiastically about her theory and how Harry Timberlake had set her to work as a CID aide that Greg had finished his soup before she had taken a couple of spoonfuls of her own.

'All this is going to keep you pretty busy, isn't it?' Greg asked. Sarah cheerfully admitted that it was.

'What did you want to get involved in all that for? God knows we don't see much of each other as it is. If you're going to work CID hours we'll be practically strangers. You might as well be in a monastery.'

'Convent.'

'You know what I mean.'

There was a note in Greg's voice that made Sarah look at him sharply. 'But, darling, if I'm right, and we actually collar Phantom Flannelfoot, think what it'll do for my career.'

'What good's a career if you haven't got a private life?'

'It could mean quicker promotion, and then we could afford to get married.'

Greg seemed unimpressed. 'And in the meantime . . .' He paused, and added incautiously, 'Fat chance we'll have of getting together. You know.'

Sarah studied him as he avoided her eye and looked down at his empty soup plate. She supposed that she should have guessed that Greg might be slightly jealous of her success as well as pleased for her. But there seemed to be something else in his attitude. She began to wonder.

Detective Constable Geoff Robson always went to the Terrace Vale nick by public transport. He had a car, but it was a toss-up whether he owned the car or it owned him. Robson would no more think of using it for work and risk getting it dirty or scratched than he would of sending his mother out on the streets to sell bootlaces. His colleagues pointed out that he was losing money by not using it on enquiries and claiming mileage, particularly as everyone knew that there were about 880 yards to every expense-sheet mile. DC Robson was a civilised man who had his priorities well established. Money was no substitute for peace of mind, he said.

So Geoff Robson travelled home by Underground – two stops – or night bus if the Underground had stopped running, to his four-year-old Rover which didn't look its age. He lived in a tiny mews house in Southington, the adjacent Metropolitan Police area to the south of Terrace Vale. The house was worth its weight in gold bricks to Geoff Robson, for it had a garage. The final part of his journey was on foot into a large square with a miniature park in the middle.

Like almost all of the Terrace Vale policemen involved in the Foulds case, he was thoroughly fed up with the routine door-to-door enquiries. As he walked into Whitecliffe Square he wished for the thousandth time that he could get a transfer to the Royal Protection Group. No more nasty streets with menacing shadows in doorways, no more gulped-down hamburgers and horse-piss tea, no more aggro from hooligans and muggers, no more abuse from the people he was trying to protect. Instead, better than first-class travel everywhere, eating and sleeping in castles and palaces.

The trouble was, Geoff Robson had no idea how to get a transfer to the Royal Protection Group. He was sure you had to know someone who could pull a string . . . but he didn't know anyone.

As he walked through the square, with cars parked nose to tail along the kerbside, vulnerable to thieves and addicts of malicious damage, Geoff Robson thought of his own Rover, snug in its locked and heated garage. If the weather was good tomorrow, and the rain kept off, and the traffic wasn't too bad, he might take it for a drive.

He heard an odd noise from the other side of the railings and hedge forming the border of the small garden square. Probably a couple of dropouts humping in the bushes among the discarded French letters and empty beer cans, he thought. He turned his head towards the sound. For a millisecond he was conscious of a great flash of yellowish light, and for another millisecond he felt a sharp pain. Then he saw and felt nothing as most of his head was splattered against the parked cars in a mixture of bone fragments and brain matter by the simultaneous blasts of both barrels of a sawn-off shotgun.

The gunman ran across the deserted garden to the other side of the square. He looked weirdly top-heavy, with a massive, swaying, featureless head. When he ran through the light of a streetlamp it highlighted his shiny black crash helmet and dark visor. He broke the shotgun into its two parts and dropped them into a large pannier bag on a motorcycle. The engine roared into life at the first kick of the starter.

A lot of people heard the shot and the sound of the motorcycle starting up, but no one was quick enough to see the killer or the motorcycle.

The murder took place at 43 minutes past midnight, or 00.43 a.m. The anonymous 999 call was logged at 00.54 a.m. after a resident looked out of his window and thought he saw somebody or something lying on the pavement, and debated with his wife for nearly ten minutes before winning the argument about whether or not to call the police.

When Sarah Lewis turned up for work next morning, she wondered what on earth had happened. The Terrace Vale nick was like Gatwick Airport on August Bank Holiday. All it lacked were some screaming kids and belligerent drunks. In addition to the normal full complement of uniformed and plain-clothes officers, there was the AMIP team of detectives dealing with the Foulds case, looking sour and hungover as they waited for their morning conference to start, together with their civilian workers who were helping with the increasing mass of paper and computer work. Unusually, almost all of the Vale's CID officers were in the station. On top of all that there were a lot of bodies, obviously policemen, whom Sarah had never seen before. The air was thick with cigarette smoke and the buzz of a score of conversations. She caught the eye of Harry Timberlake, who was talking to one of the strangers.

'Good morning, guv,' she said, the word coming awkwardly off her tongue. 'What's up?'

'DC Robson, Geoff Robson, was shot last night. All these people are from Southington nick. It happened in their area.'

'Christ. Killed?'

Harry nodded. 'Shotgun.'

'Do we have any idea who . . ?'

'Not yet.'

Detectives from Southington were already at work, questioning their Terrace Vale colleagues about Robson. It was an unusual situation, but the Terrace Vale men weren't appreciating the novelty.

There was one of those unexpected silences that sometimes occur in a room noisy with chatter. At that moment Ted Greening said in a loud, peevish voice, 'As if we haven't got enough on our plates already.' Every head turned towards him, but he either didn't realise that everyone was hating him or, more likely, he didn't care. He was more concerned with the taste of old pennies in his mouth and a nasty-looking pimple he'd noticed that morning when he was pulling on his Y-fronts.

Greening, who had apparently shot himself in the foot with his remark, then kneecapped himself with another observation.

'As if two sodding murders weren't enough.'

It was the act of someone who knows he has behaved badly and perversely aggravates the situation. Greening, never fully functional or agreeable before the pubs opened, was feeling especially shitty this morning. He had been dragged out of bed by the murder before he'd had time to sleep off the whisky he'd drunk. And there was that damned pimple.

'You rotten bastard,' came an anonymous voice. There was

a murmur of agreement. It is traditional, and firmly ingrained in policemen, that they take attacks on their own kind very badly. In their eyes, the murder of a policeman is equalled only by the sadistic murder of a child. So Greening's remarks managed simultaneously to get up their noses and get their backs up. What made his blunder even worse was that many of the Terrace Vale men half agreed with him, and they tried to minimise their own guilt by resenting Greening.

The trouble was that, although nobody actually disliked Geoff Robson, nobody positively liked him much, either. He was amiable, but unremarkable; he was friendly to everyone but had no close friends. No one knew anything about his private life – or even if he had one – apart from his devotion to his car. In fact when Terrace Vale was informed that he'd been murdered, no one could say offhand who his next of kin was. The duty sergeant had to look up his records to find that his closest relative was an aunt, Mrs Lily Eckersley, who lived in Totnes. She turned out to be an elderly woman who had been a widow for forty years. When she was eventually informed of Geoff Robson's death she looked vague and said, 'Who?' Sergeant Bill Brolly summed it up perfectly. 'I don't get it,' he said, scratching his chin. 'It's like somebody killed Mary Poppins.'

There were the Southington detectives, questioning DC Robson's Terrace Vale colleagues and going through his reports. They would soon be joined by detectives from the AMIP group investigating the murder. They would be hanging around Terrace Vale for a long time. Although they did not know it yet, the Southington CID men and the AMIP team would spend weeks on thorough house-to-house enquiries, on studying all Geoff Robson's recent, and then less recent, cases. Between them they would come up with one solid piece of information. Just one. The murderer probably – although not positively – used a motorcycle which was stolen from Richmond-upon-Thames and was subsequently found abandoned in Woolwich.

The intensive investigations in Southington and surrounding areas would produce the side effects of two minor drug busts and the uncovering of a stolen-car ring, but nothing of value in the murder case was turned up. The murder made an interesting item for *Crimewatch* and *Crimestoppers* on television but nothing came out of these programmes either.

So, after some thousands of man-hours of investigation compressed into a relatively short period, the AMIP and Southington detectives would still be at square one. A murder enquiry is never closed, the murder of a police officer never forgotten; but with sinking hearts everyone could see that the whole operation would wither away.

Unless, of course, they had a totally unexpected stroke of luck. That would come from Terrace Vale, and from Ted Greening, of all people.

In the meantime, policemen milled around Terrace Vale nick like ants in an ant-hill. The traffic had been increased by the arrival a few days earlier of the AMIP team sent to investigate Reg Barclay's murder in the car park.

The officer in charge was Superintendent Frank Ward. He was a walking deception, a human piece of camouflage, the complete antithesis of Charles Harkness. Ward was very large and seemed to lumber rather than walk, but elephants can manage 25 m.p.h., which is faster than Carl Lewis or Ben Johnson can do with or without the aid of stimulants, and elephants can run a lot further. He appeared balder than he was because his remaining hair was blond and fine, the same as his eyebrows and eyelashes. The total effect was to make his countryman's face look totally guileless. This went well with his voice, which sounded like someone's bad imitation of John Arlott.

His tweed suit was clean, but wrinkled. At the Yard it was generally agreed that Ward slept in it, probably standing up like a horse, and that it had never been pressed. This last part was not true; Ward had pressed it himself before going on plain-clothes duty for the first time at the Coronation.

The final element in Frank Ward's marvellously deceptive persona was his lugubrious air of a bloodhound that has lost its sense of smell. Criminals and cocky young coppers often made the mistake of thinking that Ward's mental processes plodded along like a plough horse in a muddy field. There was a naturally avuncular, friendly air about him that was priceless when he chose the right moment to put his arm round the shoulders of a criminal and say, 'Why don't you tell me all about it? It'll make you feel a lot better once you've got it all off your chest.' Before Chummy fully realised what he'd done, he was looking at his own signature at the bottom of a full statement, given in strict accordance with the Police and Criminal Evidence Act 1984.

The only trouble was, Frank Ward didn't have anyone he could be a friendly uncle to. So far, all the team had learned was that the murder weapon was very probably a crossbow. The scientific experts were ninety-nine per cent sure that the bolt that had killed Reg Barclay was home-made: it wasn't mass-produced or a standard size. Half a dozen detectives were given the boring routine task of checking with crossbow dealers on sales made across the counter and by post. What made the job even more mind-numbing was the stone-bonker certainty that it was all for nothing. Anyone who buys a crossbow to murder someone isn't going to visit his local shop and give his right name, or pay with a credit card. And as one detective pointed out, if the murderer had made the bolt, there was a fair chance that he had made the crossbow as well.

The general air of barely controlled chaos was aggravated by the appearance of a team of British Telecom engineers who had come to put in new lines for the second AMIP team. The telephone gang were the last straw for Ted Greening. 'The place is a bleeding madhouse,' he observed loudly to anyone within earshot. No one gave him an argument. He slipped his half-bottle of Scotch into his pocket from his desk drawer and set off for the loo. He hoped that a hair of the dog that had bitten him the previous evening would chase away some of the old-pennies taste in his mouth and stop his head throbbing. It wasn't a very earnest hope.

The two AMIP teams broke up into their separate groups to hold their conferences. Although Terrace Vale station was large, the arrival of all the extra detectives put a serious strain on the building's resources, and Superintendent Ward's team were given a large top-floor room which was normally used for storage of all sorts of junk that no one quite knew what to do with or would take responsibility for throwing away. The different layers of dust would have fascinated an archaeologist. Meanwhile, the detectives from Southington continued to interview Geoff Robson's colleagues, who were surprised to realise how very little they knew about someone they worked with every day.

Superintendent Harkness's conference with his AMIP team and the Terrace Vale detectives followed the depressing pattern of most of their recent conferences: no one had much to offer towards finding Howard Foulds's murderer. Detailed, patient house-to-house interviews had turned up nothing more than gossip, rumours and flights of fancy, all of which had to be carefully checked even though the detectives knew that it would all be for nothing. But they had to go through the motions. There was always that one chance in a thousand or ten thousand that there just might be a faint clue hidden among all the rubbish.

When it was Harry Timberlake's turn to report, he told Harkness he was now convinced that there was no homosexual element in the motive for Foulds's murder. 'He was too careful and too discreet to get mixed up with any rough trade,' Harry said. 'None of his closest colleagues who'd known him for years had any suspicion he was homosexual and apart from one minor row with a boyfriend named Terry Luckwell, who Foulds dropped immediately and who's in the clear anyway, there's no hint of his being involved in any serious lovers' quarrels.'

'But Foulds was into bondage and flagellation,' observed the AMIP detective who had been at Foulds's post mortem. 'He must have had some pretty dodgy chums.'

'Yes, but . . .' Timberlake said. He hesitated for a moment. 'Most – maybe all – murders provoked by homosexual jealousy involve multiple wounds, repeated blows or stabbings, almost frenzied in the number and random nature of the injuries. Foulds was killed by one single blow to the head with an axe.'

'So what line do you suggest we follow instead?' Harkness asked.

'Well, about all we have left is looking into some of the cases where Foulds defended. Like I said the other day: a victim could feel aggrieved because Foulds got a villain off.' With a sudden access of boldness Harry volunteered, 'I could go down to his chambers and have a word.' Harry tried not to notice that some of the AMIP team were giving him dark looks for his pushiness.

'Very well,' Harkness said without expression. 'By the way, do we know when Mrs Foulds is due back?'

'In a couple of days,' Harry said. 'The housekeeper gave me a ring.'

'You might as well see her as well.'

Some of the dark looks aimed at Harry for this favouritism were practically audible, but the older members of the AMIP

97

group knew from their own experience what Harkness was up to. He was sizing up Timberlake with a view to getting him into the team. And Harry realised it himself.

As he left the conference room he noticed Sarah Lewis busy on the phone. He went over to her.

'How's it going?'

'Slowly. I never realised how many estate agents there are. Some of them have been quite helpful. They've got everything on computer and they've given me lists of possible houses they've had on their books during the past couple of years.'

'And the others?'

Sarah grimaced. 'About as organised as a dogfight. I've had to go through old circulars and advertisements myself.'

Harry Timberlake grinned sympathetically. 'Nobody said it was going to be easy. Good luck.'

'Thanks, guv.' She still felt awkward using the nickname.

Harry Timberlake guessed right. When he went to see Lester Bradford QC for the second time, Howard Foulds's successor as head of chambers made him feel as welcome as an attack of gout, as he had expected. As soon as Timberlake explained what he was after, Bradford put on the courtroom act for his benefit. The total effect, with the addition of Bradford's grating voice, made Harry want to hit him.

'Let me see if I understand you,' Bradford said in the patronising manner he would use in court to belittle a witness and suggest he was weak in the head. 'You think that the victim of an alleged crime' – even in private conversation Bradford automatically said 'alleged' – 'might have sufficient grievance . . .' Bradford paused to wipe his lips with a handkerchief taken from his breast pocket as if to get rid of an unpleasant taste. His tone made Harry's idea sound preposterous even to Harry himself.

'The alleged victim', Bradford amended, 'might have sufficient grievance to murder Mr Foulds, simply because Mr Foulds had successfully defended the person charged with whatever it was.'

'Had got off a guilty person,' Harry gritted. 'Yes, something like that.'

'Interesting theory. Most imaginative,' Bradford said with undisguised contempt. 'I should have thought that the er, alleged victim would have been more inclined to take his revenge on the alleged perpetrator, rather than on the perpetrator's counsel.'

You're slipping, Harry thought. You missed out an 'alleged'. 'He could have done both,' he said out loud.

'Yes,' said Bradford dismissively, 'be that as it may,' which was his way of diminishing a good point made against him. 'What it amounts to is this. You want me to give you a list of clients Mr Foulds defended in the past eighteen months where he persuaded the jury to give the defendants the benefit of the doubt to which they were entitled.'

'I wouldn't put it quite like that, but yes.' Harry Timberlake replied. His version would have been more like 'a list of the villains that Foulds managed to get off'.

'You must realise it's quite out of the question. You are asking me, by implication, to suggest that certain clients were in fact guilty although the juries found otherwise.'

Harry took a deep breath. 'Mr Bradford, we are trying to find the person who murdered your former head of chambers, and we're running up against brick walls. We need all the help we can get, official or unofficial.'

'I wish you luck,' Bradford said with a voice like a door closing. 'As for your request . . . I'm sorry.' He sounded as sorry as a challenger who had just knocked out the champion. As Harry got up, Bradford seemed to relent slightly. 'All the cases where Mr Foulds appeared are a matter of public record, you know.'

'I realise that. I was simply hoping there might be a short cut. Thank you for your time.' As Harry left the room he muttered, 'Shakespeare had the right idea.'

'I beg your pardon?' Bradford asked.

'Nothing.' Harry Timberlake was thinking of Dick's speech in Act IV, scene ii of *Henry VI, Part II:* 'First thing we do, let's kill all the lawyers.'

Perhaps he'd have better luck with Mrs Foulds. Perhaps they'd have a White Christmas in Bermuda.

But then he had a brainwave. He was too impatient to wait till he got back to the station and he asked Percy Hoskin, the clerk of the chambers, whether he could make a phone call from the clerks' general office.

'Feel free,' Hoskin said. 'D'you want the STD code for Australia?'

'No, thanks,' Harry smiled.

'D'you know anyone in Hong Kong, then?' Hoskin asked.

'Just a local call.'

'Pity,' said Hoskin.

Harry called a national newspaper, and he was in luck. The man he wanted to speak to, Claud Salter, the paper's crime correspondent, was in.

'Harry Timberlake.'

'Hello, Harry. What's up?'

'I need a favour.'

'I'm broke.'

Harry chuckled. 'No, it's not that. Tell me, are all your cuttings on computer now?' Major newspapers have always maintained enormous libraries of press cuttings. Large staffs spend all their working days going through the major British newspapers, cutting out the stories, indexing and cross-indexing them, and filing them in special stiff envelopes. In recent years most papers have stored the 'cuttings' on computer.

'Yes, they've all been transferred.'

'Claud, could you get me a printout of all the cases in the past two years where Howard Foulds defended?'

'Why? Are you working on that case?'

'Sort of. I'm co-operating with the AMIP team down at our nick.'

'What's in it for me?'

'I'll owe you one.' He paused. 'I'll tell the guvnor of the AMIP team you did me a big favour and ask him to give you an edge with the story if – when – we get the killer. No guarantees, but I'll do my best,'

'You're on.'

'Thanks.' Harry hung up the phone. He felt like blowing a raspberry in the direction of Lester Bradford's room.

When he got back to the station Sarah Lewis had a message for him.

'Hello, guv. The collator was asking for you.'

'What did he want?'

'He didn't say.'

The collator was PC Brian Pegg, who managed to look like a dubious second-hand car salesman even in uniform shirt and trousers. He also had the ready chat of a market trader of cheap crockery. He was basically quite a decent chap. As a beat constable, however, he was about as useful as a lead lifebelt. Pegg's trouble was that he knew *Moriaty's Police Law* from cover to cover, and he often browsed through *Stone's Justices Manual* – all three volumes – for pleasure. As a result he knew a great deal about the law, but little about justice, and as it happened, less about common sense. Somebody once said of Brian Pegg that if he arrested anyone fleeing from an armed robbery, the first thing he'd charge them with would be having insufficient tread on the tyres of the getaway car.

All this knowledge meant that he couldn't walk half a mile along a peaceful street without seeing a dozen offences being committed. On early morning turn of a typical day he saw a paperboy who rang doorbells when he delivered the papers, which, Pegg knew, was 'wilfully and wantonly disturbing any inhabitant by pulling or ringing any doorbell, or knocking on any door', contrary to the Town Police Clauses Act 1847, as amended by several subsequent Acts.

In the market PC Pegg noticed that a fishmonger was 'exposing for sale a crab with spawn attached to the tail', which was an offence against the Sea Fisheries (Shellfish) Act of 1967. Not far from that scene of a crime, two lads were leaning against a pillar box and kicking it with their heels as they talked, which is expressly forbidden by the Post Office Act 1953, as amended by the Criminal Justice Act 1967, the Criminal Law Act 1977 and the British Telecommunications Act 1981 (although what telecommunications had to do with pillar boxes was unclear to Pegg: still, that was what the book said). The Post Office Act states that 'no one shall do or attempt to do anything likely to injure a post office box . . .'

Walking through Terrace Vale Park, PC Pegg noticed a youth flying a large kite which must have weighed more than two kilogrammes which, Pegg considered, was an offence against the Air Navigation Act 1980. But his *pièce de résistance* was when he saw old Mrs Joseph noisily trying to stop Mr Potter, the local greengrocer, from serving another customer with potatoes because she, Mrs Joseph, was there before her. Most coppers would have given the old lady a friendly talking to, but PC Pegg saw Mrs Joseph's action against Mr Potter as 'an intent to deter him from buying, selling . . . grain, flour, meal, malt, or potatoes . . .', contrary to the Offences Against the Person Act 1861.

His prodigious memory for detail, however, made him an ideal collator, concerned with every form of intelligence about criminals and shady characters.

PC Pegg was working on cross-indexing some of his filing cards when Harry Timberlake entered his office.

'Hello, Peggy. You got something for me?'

Pegg had long since given up trying to get people not to call him Peggy and did not even wince.

'Ah, yes. Remember the Wilson brothers?' This was rather like asking Churchill if he remembered Hitler. The Wilson brothers, Lennie and Billie, were leaders of one of London's most vicious and dangerous gangs of the Seventies, notorious for their murder and torture of rival gangsters. As a sergeant, Harry had arrested them for the murder of Bertie 'Bootsie' McCann, so nicknamed because he took size thirteen shoes although he was only five feet ten inches tall. Somebody once observed that he would have been quite tall if he hadn't had so much leg turned up for feet. There were subsidiary charges, including causing grievous bodily harm, alternatively actual bodily harm, to both McCann and Andy 'Tin Ear' Robinson, a former boxer. Harry Timberlake knew the Wilsons had killed McCann – they boasted of it to him, but not in front of witnesses – and tortured Robinson in the cellar of their east London home on the same night; but knowing they were guilty of murder and proving it were two different matters.

'I thought you'd like to know they're out,' said Pegg.

'Of prison? They can't be.'

'They got twelve years. Four years off that for good behaviour . . .'

'Christ. Is it eight years already?' Despite the passage of eight incident-packed years, Harry remembered parts of the Old Bailey proceedings with great clarity, particularly the turning point of the trial. The Wilsons never appreciated how close their counsel had come to getting them off all the charges, but Billie Wilson, the younger brother, insisted on giving evidence on his own behalf against the urgent advice of his brother Lennie and their lawyer. Billie, unstable at the best of times, disintegrated under the hammering of the prosecution's merciless cross-examination. All self-control gone, he ended by screaming curses at the prosecuting counsel; worse, he made threats. His performance would have been enough to make the jury find the brothers guilty of murdering Bootsie McCann, but in his summing-up the judge strongly emphasised that the evidence on that charge was strictly circumstantial. Tin Ear Robinson gave evidence against the Wilsons but he couldn't say definitely that he'd seen McCann dead and no trace of McCann's body had ever been found. The judge also reminded the jury that, as far as McCann's disappearance was concerned, the defence counsel had pointed out that McCann had had his own very good reasons for dropping out of sight.

At the time Harry Timberlake feared that the jury might find the brothers not guilty of the murder, but he was confident of a guilty verdict on the grievous bodily harm charge, for which the maximum sentence could be life imprisonment. The judge, a well-known booby, gave the brothers twelve years.

Harry Timberlake looked at Pegg. 'I don't get this. Why are the Wilsons on your list? They're not local.'

'They are now. They're living in Terrace Gardens Square. A snout told DC Webb, and he told me. They're a right choice couple, by all accounts. They were lucky to get away with twelve years.'

'How did you know abut my connection with them? It was all before your time, and in a different area.'

'The Wilsons were famous and—'

'Notorious.'

'Okay, notorious. Everybody's heard about them. As soon as I was told they'd moved in, I checked with Records and saw you were the original arresting officer.' Brian Pegg gave his unfortunate salesman's smooth, insincere smile which made it difficult for people to like him. 'And when I saw that Howard Foulds was the prosecuting counsel . . .'

'That wouldn't be in the Wilsons' criminal records,' Harry said sharply.

'My local library has *The Times* on microfilm. I use it a lot. I looked up the report of the trial. I thought you did very well under cross-examination, if I may say so.'

Harry Timberlake knew that Pegg was trying to be agreeable and was probably being sincere, but his manner put Harry's teeth on edge. Nevertheless, he admired Pegg's professionalism.

'That was smart work, Brian. I'll see that the Chief Super gets to know.'

'Thanks very much, guv.'

'One question,' Harry said.

Pegg knew the question and the answer. 'They were released a fortnight before Foulds was murdered.'

Although Harry Timberlake agreed with Shakespeare over 'First . . . let's kill all the lawyers', he was at odds with him over 'What's in a name?'. There's a lot in a name, Harry thought, as he drove to see the Wilson brothers. If Dr Frankenstein had been called Dr Bing, his creature somehow wouldn't have seemed so frightening. In fact you couldn't imagine anyone named Dr Bing actually making a monster from spare human parts filched from a graveyard. And if anyone introduced himself as Mr Angel, it wouldn't have the same effect on innocent virgins as if he said, 'My name is Count Dracula.' And would Hitler have been taken seriously in his early days if he'd kept the name Schickelgruber? Harry asked himself. For that matter, maybe a rose would smell as sweet if it were called a *krankheit* flower, but who would give his wife a bunch of *krankheit* flowers as a peace offering, and what young woman would want to be called a typical English *krankheit* flower?

So Harry Timberlake thought that the Wilson brothers' bland-sounding name was quite unsuitable. They should have been called something like Ripper, Lyncher or Crusher, for they were two of the most vicious and cruel criminals Harry had ever come across.

Lennie and Billie Wilson had moved to Harry Timberlake's patch because the terraced house where they used to live in east London had been demolished as unfit for human habitation and replaced by a high-rise block whose façade was already crumbling beneath the obscene grafitti and vandalism of its discontented tenants. Terrace Gardens Square, the Wilson's current address, was another example of an inappropriate name. It consisted of four-storey Victorian houses which had once been stately and well-preserved middle-class homes occupied by single families, but were now little more than decaying ruins swarming like ants' nests with nameless transients, most of them immigrants with skins of all shades from Arabian light brown to Ethiopian black. Harry was sure that most of them must be regretting ever leaving home.

As he drove into the square, his ears were assaulted by three different sets of reggae music bellowing out from ghetto-blasters. He found a parking space between an overflowing skip and an abandoned car that had been so efficiently stripped that he couldn't tell what make it was. There were two other wrecks in the square which the council hadn't bothered to remove yet. Harry got out of his car and made his way to the pavement through a barrier of bursting black rubbish bags which were being investigated by a couple of wary cats.

The Wilsons were living in a typically dilapidated house with broken steps up from the pavement and a peeling front door that looked as if it had been broken open a couple of times. It was unlocked. The entrance hall smelled of stale cabbage and urine.

The door to the Wilson's ground-floor flat was opened by Lennie, the elder brother. He looked at Harry Timberlake without surprise but with hate in his eyes. 'What do you want?'

'A word.' Harry walked past Lennie into the small hallway. 'Mind if I come in?' he asked from inside the flat. 'Thanks.'

The flat had been found for the Wilsons by the probation service, which did its best in difficult circumstances. The living room was dingy and plainly furnished, although there were one or two personal possessions to give the place something of a feeling of a home. Most prominent was a silver-framed photograph of Wilson *père*, who had a shaven head and a build like a Sumo wrestler. He was a well-known tearaway in his time. The photograph was old, but the scars on his face were still clearly visible. He had died in prison of syphilis, which was a fitting end for him. He was a great admirer of Al Capone, who died in the same way.

Billie Wilson was seated at the small table, doing a jigsaw puzzle. He looked up as Harry entered, but his gaze was vacant. Almost immediately he returned to his puzzle, his brow furrowing with concentration.

Harry sat down and studied the brothers in turn, trying to discover what prison had done to them. Lennie was wearing a T-shirt and jeans. He looked as hard as a sack of pebbles. For eight years he had worked hard at weight-lifting and body-building and now he had the dangerous physical presence of a caged wild animal. He was not the sort of man to turn your back on. What

105

prison had done to his mind Harry couldn't tell – at least, not yet.

Billie was puffy-faced and flabby; his general air of dissipation was emphasised by his prison pallor. Harry suspected that he'd had an easy time of it in prison: he had been a hardened and aggressive homosexual from the age of fourteen. He would have found many lovers inside.

Billie ignored Harry Timberlake and remained absorbed in his jigsaw. With a sudden shock Harry noticed that he was ignoring the design and forcing into place pieces that didn't fit, ignoring buckling edges and pressing them home with white, fleshy fingers that must have been stronger than they looked. He mouthed words silently as he worked at the puzzle. Harry glanced at Lennie, who glared back, daring him to say anything. Tough as Lennie was, Harry found the silent, slug-like Billie much more frightening.

'You heard that Howard Foulds was murdered,' Harry said to Lennie. It was not a question.

'Who?'

'Come off it, Lennie. You of all people know who he was.'

'Maybe.'

'It was in all the national and local papers, and on television. Where were you that night?'

'I don't remember.' The answer was instantaneous. Then, 'I expect we was here, playing cards with friends. We're here most nights, me and Billie.' Harry was quite sure the Wilsons would be able to bring witnesses to back up an alibi, phoney or otherwise. Lennie went on, 'I'm glad somebody killed the shitbag, although it wasn't us.'

'Well, you would say that, wouldn't you? You also said you didn't kill Bootsie McCann.'

'Only in court. Like I told you at the time: we topped the toe-rag all right. He was definitely out of order. The body's under twelve feet of concrete out in Essex, by the way. But we was found not guilty. You can't touch us for it now.'

Billie raised his head from his puzzle. Unexpectedly, he looked and sounded quite normal. 'We offered the story of how we did it to the papers, but none of them wanted to buy it. Bastards,' he added automatically. The moment of lucidity passed as quickly as it had come. He forced another piece of the puzzle into the wrong place.

Harry rose slowly. 'I'll be seeing you both again.'

106

'Yeah?' said Lennie. 'You'd better make it soon. We won't be in this rathole for ever. We got plans.'

'I bet,' Harry said. 'But watch it. It doesn't matter where you go.' He looked Lennie straight in the eye. 'You're on my list, son.'

'Fuck off, filth,' Lennie spat out malevolently. 'I haven't forgotten I owe you one.' There was a hollow ring to the tough words, and Harry knew that prison had got to Lennie after all.

Billie looked up from his puzzle again. He grinned at Harry, naked madness in his eyes. He looked capable of anything.

Chapter 6

'I'm sorry,' said Harry Timberlake, sitting up in bed. 'I just don't know what's wrong.'

'Forget it,' Jenny Long told him. 'It happens.'

'Not to me,' he said. For the first time in his post-puberty life, he had failed to finish what he had started.

Jenny and he had spent a pleasant evening together, beginning with a visit to a Young Vic production of *Three Sisters*, to which she had managed to drag him despite all his ingenious and determined excuses for not going. Until now he had managed to avoid Russian drama which, as everyone knew, was sheer gloom, despondency and hopelessness. The idea of sitting through an entire evening of what he expected to be Chekhovian melancholia filled him with despair. In fact, the play was far from the heavy weather he'd expected. To his considerable astonishment he discovered that Chekhov was also a writer of perceptive, wry comedy. The pleasant surprise made him feel quite euphoric as they left the theatre.

Harry had prepared a cold meal for their return to his flat: avocado with prawns, roast beef and mixed green salad, cheese and biscuits, and strawberries and cream – simple as usual, but very pleasant. While they ate, slowly and sensually, Harry played tapes he'd copied from two of his precious early English true-jazz records. The first was Jack Hylton's 'Grievin' for You' with Jack Jackson on trumpet and 'Poggie' Pogson on clarinet and alto; the second 'Clarinet Marmalade' with the extraordinary pianist Fred Elizalde, a Spanish-American Cambridge undergraduate. Harry listened to them without any exaggerated head-shaking, finger-snapping or foot-tapping.

Jenny assured him that she enjoyed the records and, on an evening when Harry actually enjoyed Chekhov, she may well

108

have been telling the truth. Between them they drank a bottle of Muscadet and one of Moulin à Vent. By the time they got to the last half of the second bottle they were already lying on the settee half undressed and very aroused.

However, Harry was feeling more than sexual excitement; he was conscious of a warmth, a relaxed contentment at simply being with Jenny. Once again the thought of marriage went through his mind. He knew it wasn't just the physical attraction that prompted it; he was experienced enough to know that sexual compatibility alone was no basis for a lasting marriage. And if truth be told, good as she was, sex with her was not the best he had ever had. What was different about her was that he simply enjoyed being with her, talking to her, sharing old and new experiences with her.

Jenny moved closer to him and stroked him expertly, driving everything from his mind except sensuality. Wordlessly they got up from the settee and moved to the bedroom.

They always – nearly always – spent a long time caressing and stimulating each other before he entered her, and when she said, 'Oh, now!', he quickly moved on top of her, hard and erect. But as he moved to penetrate her he suddenly went flaccid. Her efforts to arouse him were ineffectual, and after a few moments of humiliatingly fruitless effort by both of them, he moved away to sit up beside her.

'I'm sorry,' he said. 'I just don't know what's wrong.'

'Forget it,' she replied. 'It happens.'

'Not to me,' he said.

'Too much wine, that's all.'

He shook his head. 'I've drunk more without that happening.'

Jenny remained silent for a moment. She knew this was true.

'Darling, sex is such a fragile, complex affair that it doesn't take a great deal to upset the delicate balance of things. The main thing is not to worry about it.'

He wasn't convinced. She tried again.

'It's probably this Foulds case. You've been working too long and too hard. It's on your mind all the time.'

'Okay. You're probably right.'

That night Harry Timberlake slept only fitfully, and in his long periods of wakefulness he felt both angry and frustrated. That he told himself he didn't know why he was feeling angry only

109

intensified his ill-humour, while the reason for his frustration was only too obvious. Beside him Jenny Long was sleeping as soundly as if she'd had a sleeping-pill sandwich. Unfortunately for Harry, her firm, shapely buttocks were pressed against his groin, and she was making tiny unconscious movements in her deep sleep. Despite his earlier failure, he had an erection that was positively painful. If he moved away from her, she made slight protesting sounds, and before long, when Harry himself briefly fell asleep, he found he had unconsciously moved back to his original position, pressed up against her back again. Several times he wa on the point of trying to make love to her – he knew she wouldn't mind in the least being woken that way – but fear of a second misfire stopped him. He knew that if he had a second failure so soon, he'd develop a complex that might be hell's own job to cure. He had a wretched night.

He got up early to make breakfast, feeling terrible. As usual when he slept with Jenny, he was naked, and he threw on a thin cotton dressing gown. As soon as the coffee percolated he took a cup to Jenny. She woke slowly and looked at him from half-closed eyes, then smiled at him languorously. She looked so incredibly seductive that the sudden rush of desire made him almost dizzy.

'I've brought you some coffee,' he said superfluously in a shaky voice. Her reply threw him even further off balance, for she said a word she rarely used.

'Fuck the coffee,' she said. 'Or better still . . .'

It was as if the previous night had been only a prelude to this occasion. It was brief, but a noisy, limbs-threshing, urgent success.

As they lay still getting their breath back, Jenny suddenly started giggling.

'What's so funny?' he asked her.

'I nearly said something stupid.'

'What?'

'There was no cock-up this time.' She giggled again, and after a moment he started chuckling, but his laughter was short-lived.

The trouble was, he couldn't forget why he'd suddenly become impotent the night before, and it was nothing to do with the Foulds case.

* * *

Timberlake arrived at the Terrace Vale nick half an hour before the daily conference of the AMIP team and the local detectives working on the Foulds case. He was in a fairly cheerful frame of mind. His morning success in bed was fresh in his memory, the night-time failure had almost completely faded. He felt physically beautifully relaxed.

He was surprised to see Sarah Lewis already at her desk, labouring away at her typewriter with two determined fingers. He thought she looked thinner than he remembered her, and there were traces of dark shadows under her eyes.

'Hello, Sarah,' he said. 'You're in early.'

She stopped hammering away at the machine, and pulled out the top copy and a carbon.

'Good morning, guv. I think I've done it.'

'Done what?'

'I've worked out a list of likely runners for the Phantom Flannelfoot stakes: possible – probable – target houses. That's if he's still operating.' She handed him the top copy of what she had been typing. There were ten names and addresses on the list.

'Remind me' – although he had no need of reminding – 'how you picked them.'

'Houses sold through estate agents within the past two years; all within our price range, between two hundred and three hundred grand. I plotted all his jobs on a map. He's quite methodical: he moves steadily east . . .'

'He might well be doing the same thing. Using a map, I mean.'

'Yes.' She indicated marks on her map. 'These ten houses are next along his line.'

'What about timing?' Harry asked. 'Is there any pattern there?'

'It's not as clear-cut as picking the targets, it's not like clock-work, but if you asked me to guess, I'd say that he'll do his next one any time now, within the next ten days or so.'

'Great,' said Harry. 'That's great work, Sarah.' He paused. 'I know you've worked hard. Don't overdo it.'

'No guv. So what's next?'

'Stakeouts of as many of the houses as we can. Have you seen DCI Greening this morning?'

'I don't think he's in yet.'

111

'Really,' Harry said, successfully keeping all irony out of his voice.

'You can get dressed now,' Ted Greening was told. He pulled up his shorts and reached for his trousers.

'Well, doc?' he asked.

The police surgeon who had certified Reg Barclay dead at the car park was seeing Greening as a private patient. This did not mean that Greening would actually pay him anything: the doctor was examining him as a favour. His attitude to a live patient was different from his usual manner when he was dealing with a corpse. The main difference was that he didn't try to be funny. At least, not at first.

'Roll up your sleeve,' he ordered, ignoring Greening's question. He rolled the cuff of a sphygmomanometer round Greening's bicep and squeezed the rubber bulb that inflated it, pressed his stethoscope against the big vein in the crook of his arm, then slowly let the air out again, relieving the pressure on the cuff as he watched the column of mercury in the instrument. He did the procedure four times as if he couldn't believe what he saw first time.

'I'm going to listen to your chest,' he announced, and proceeded to auscult Greening with the stethoscope, which looked as if it had been designed about the time of wax-cylinder phonographs. When he told the patient to take a deep breath, Greening burst into a fit of bubbly coughing.

As the doctor put down the stethoscope at last, he looked at Greening for a long moment before speaking. His words took Greening off balance.

'D'you know the best way to listen to a patient's chest?' he asked. 'Press your ear to it. Much better than using these things,' he said, indicating the stethoscope. 'When I was a houseman at hospital the senior gynaecologist never used one. Always pressed his ear against the women's tits. Had to use one eventually, though. He fell asleep twice on the chests of women who were lying down. He might have got away with it if he hadn't snored.' He laughed coarsely.

'Yeah, but what about me?' Greening asked.

The doctor was not to be rushed.

'How many cigarettes a day do you smoke?'

'Twenty, about.'

112

'*How* many?'

'Okay. Forty,' Greening said sourly.

'And how much do you drink? No, don't bother to lie. I can guess. Women? Don't bother to answer that either,' he added quickly.

'So what's the verdict?' Greening asked, a mirthless, forced smile on his face.

'You're a mess. Your lungs must be the colour of a kipper and half full of liquid: if your heart was a car it would never pass its MOT; and I hate to think what your liver and kidneys must be like. Don't bother to sign any organ donor cards. Your blood pressure has a good chance of getting into the *Guinness Book of Records*.'

'Yes, but—'

'It's my duty to tell you, but I know I might as well talk to the wall. If you can't give up smoking, at least try to cut it down, the same thing with drink, and avoid fatty foods as much as possible. The way you're going, you'll only draw your pension for about a couple of years.'

'Things'll be easier when I retire,' Greening said. 'Less pressure. But what about the pimple?' He gestured towards his groin. There was a thin film of perspiration on his forehead.

'Oh, that.' The doctor laughed. 'It's only a follicle of a pubic hair that's got blocked and is stopping the sebum coming out. That's what the lump is.'

'Is it serious?'

'It isn't herpes or the clap. It's a pimple, for God's sake. Kids have thousands of them on their faces. I'll get rid of it for you in about a minute.

Greening drove his five-year-old battered Marina to Terrace Vale in a mixed frame of mind. He was relieved that the pimple wasn't serious, but annoyed that he'd made something of a fool of himself with the doctor and exposed himself to his criticism. 'I'll outlive you; I'll see you buried, you bloody quack,' he muttered to himself. He jammed on the brakes of the car with unnecessary viciousness as he arrived at his parking space.

He took two paces towards the entrance to the station and changed his mind. His sudden turn meant that he nearly bumped into a man who was coming up behind him.

'Morning, sir,' the man said. 'I was just coming to see you.' Greening knew he had seen the man before but couldn't place him for the moment. 'Sergeant Perch, Wallsend. We met at the post mortem of my hit-and-run case, just before the post mortem on Howard Foulds.'

'You don't have to tell me: I remember you,' Greening lied smoothly. 'What's up?'

'Courtesy call, really. I'm making enquiries on your patch. I just found Lloyd – that was the victim – used to live in Terrace Vale. Bishop's Walk.'

'A right bloody hole. If the bishops had any sense they'd run, not walk.'

Perch laughed politely.

'I tell you what,' Greening said, as if he'd just discovered relativity, 'you can buy me a pint at the Mucky Duck. Black Swan,' he explained. 'It's just round the corner.' He started walking out of the yard. Perch shrugged and followed him reluctantly. It was no great trick to guess that Greening wasn't the sort of man who drank just one pint, and was an expert at not paying his fair share of any drinking. He shrugged again. He could probably wangle his expenses enough to cover it.

When Ted Greening finally turned up at the station he was in a good mood. That damned pimple was off his mind at last, and he'd managed to con the unfortunate Sergeant Perch into providing him with some free drinks – doubles. So he was having a happy half hour. Harry Timberlake recognised the signs and seized the opportunity to rush in before Greening's alcoholic euphoria lost the one-sided battle with his liver and took a plunge into sour-tasting depression.

To give him his due, Greening's reaction to Harry Timberlake's outline of the progress in the Phantom Flannelfoot case was one of genuine appreciation, and he even had a good word for Sarah Lewis. And when Harry asked for help with manpower for the stakeouts, he immediately promised his complete co-operation. Not that Greening would personally speak to senior officers or actually *do* anything, of course. Harry had the full picture, and he'd be in a far better position to explain the situation to the bosses. But Harry could tell them that he had Greening's permission and full support.

So what Greening's support and co-operation amounted to was no more than that he wouldn't actively try to scotch Harry's efforts. Still, it was as much as he could realistically expect, Harry thought. And by the time he'd got that much out of Greening, the first dark clouds of boozer's gloom were appearing on Greening's horizon. Harry decided to run for it before the sun went in.

Harry was on his way to see Superintendent Harkness to ask for some of the Terrace Vale detectives working with the AMIP team to be released to him when a uniformed constable brought him an envelope that had just been delivered by motorcycle courier. It was from Claud Salter: the full computer printout of the reports of all Howard Foulds's cases of the past two years. It was an intimidating list. Well, if Harry was going to ask Harkness for a favour at least he had a gift to offer.

'How did you get on with Bradford?' Harkness asked him.

Harry briefly contemplated making a funny remark, but changed his mind, largely because he couldn't think of one. 'He wasn't at all helpful. However . . .' Harry said, producing the computer printout from behind his back. 'A journalist friend got it for me.' He explained the promise he'd made. Harkness made no comment. He took the list and scanned it. 'That was resourceful of you.' He paused. 'What about the Wilson brothers? Have you seen them?'

'Yes, sir. But I don't think they're in the frame for the Foulds murder. After all, eight years is a long time to wait to kill somebody.'

'Prison can be a great forcing ground for hate,' Harkness reminded him. 'Brooding for eight years on Foulds's treatment of his brother could have made Lennie Wilson's desire for revenge turn into an irresistible obsession.'

'True. But I don't think that's the case with Lennie. He's a psychotic, all right; he has no sense of right and wrong, and definitely no empathy, no imagination. Otherwise he couldn't have done what he did to his victims, the torture and nasty killings. But even though I'm sure Lennie enjoyed the suffering he inflicted, it was always for profit, if I can put it that way. To get information . . . to punish . . . *pour encourager les autres*. But Foulds . . .' Harry shook his head. 'There was no dividend for Lennie in killing him.'

'I take it that Lennie Wilson's encounters with the law – the police and the courts – were all part of the game: you win some and lose some, no hard feelings?'

'That's about it, except for the no hard feelings.'

'What about the other brother, Billie?'

'He's a psychopath, a real nutter. If we ever nick him again he's a certainty for Broadmoor.'

Harkness paused. 'But you don't think that either or both of them had anything to do with Foulds's murder?'

'No, sir. If Lennie had done it, he would have shit all over the study and smashed things up as a gesture. As far as Billie's concerned, it's true there's the homosexuality he had in common with Foulds, but I'm sure that's only a coincidence. He wouldn't have been satisfied with a single blow with the axe; he'd have hacked him to pieces. All that aside, there are two more reasons for ruling out the Wilsons.'

'Which are?'

'First, it was such a clean murder. No one saw the murderer or murderers. They were in and out without leaving anything more than one hair, which may or may not be from the perpetrator. The Wilsons aren't that clever: brute force and ignorance is their style. Besides, if either of them had been about Elm Park Square that night, someone would have spotted them. They would have stood out like a couple of lighthouses in the Sahara. They look every inch a couple of villains. And second—'

'Howard Foulds would never have let either of them in while he was alone in the house,' Harkness broke in. 'Did you notice whether there is a spyhole in the front door?'

'No,' Harry confessed shamefacedly.

'There is,' Harkness told him. 'And even if somehow they'd got past the front door – which I can't imagine – he would never have sat down in his study and let one of them get behind him.'

'You took the words out of my mouth, sir,' Harry said wryly.

Later it occurred to Timberlake that Harkness had known from the outset that the Wilsons weren't credible suspects in the Foulds murder. He wanted Harry to give his report, not to learn something of the Wilsons, but of Harry himself.

'One other thing, sir.'

'Yes?'

Harry explained the developments in the Phantom Flannelfoot case and asked if some of the Terrace Vale detectives seconded to Harkness could be released.

Harkness pondered the problem. 'The best I can do is to let you have six back. Perhaps your uniformed section could help out.'

'I'm very grateful, sir. I'll inform Chief Inspector Greening.'

'Yes,' said Harkness. The one syllable had more layers of meaning than an onion has skins.

The uniformed section, with the best will in the world – which wasn't exactly heart-warming between uniformed and CID at the best of times – could manage to lend Harry only five constables for surveillance duty, and the concession came with a condition. It would mean overtime for the officers concerned, and overtime payments were a sensitive issue. Harry would have to get the uniformed Chief Inspector's agreement.

The uniformed Chief Inspector came to an immediate decision. It was that he couldn't make the decision; Harry would have to see the Chief Superintendent.

It was a conditioned reflex for Chief Superintendent Liversedge to vacillate when asked to give a ruling. He took longer than Terry Griffiths or Steve Davis to consider all the angles. It occurred to him that if Phantom Flannelfoot was caught he would be able to wangle some of the credit for himself. But on the other hand, if Harry Timberlake's scheme didn't work, whopping great overtime payments would cause some very nasty remarks from Them Upstairs.

Harry had a fair idea of what was going through Liversedge's mind.

'It'll be a very big feather in our caps if we get Flannelfoot,' he urged. 'And according to WPC Lewis, who's been doing the research, the chances are the next job will be within the next ten days.'

'How reliable do you think her research is?'

'Very,' said Harry with rather more firmness than he actually felt.

'Well,' said Liversedge, relieved to have managed to pass the buck, 'if that's your considered judgement . . .' He paused as another thought struck him. By the time the accounts showed up the overtime payments, he would have left Terrace Vale. His successor could dodge any flak the best way he could. 'If that's your considered judgement,' he repeated, 'go ahead.'

The man wasn't very interested in books, except for the do-it-yourself and how-to-make kinds. Something about this particular one attracted him, though. It was about the various attempts on

Hitler's life. One of the last, and the most famous one, was at Rastenburg, when a bomb planted by Count von Stauffenberg was inadvertently moved away at the last moment from where Hitler was standing. The bomb exploded, injuring Hitler but failing to kill him.

The man was much more interested in the first of the assassination attempts at the beginning of the war. A cabinetmaker named George Elser constructed a bomb and hid it in a pillar in the Munich beerhall, the Bürgerbräukeller, just behind where Hitler was due to make his annual speech commemorating the *putsch* of 1923. Hitler never failed to appear at this annual reunion with the Old Fighters. What the man found so fascinating was that the bomb had a clockwork timer which ticked away silently for two weeks before setting off the fuse at the precise moment that he had planned. The only trouble was that Hitler had one of his extraordinary premonitions and left the Bürgerbräu after speaking for only six minutes instead of his customary two hours.

The man read the passage again.

George Elser – that was a man to admire! A home-made timing mechanism that was accurate to a minute after two weeks. The man made up his mind then and there that his next execution would be by a bomb. He contemplated making a clockwork timer as Elser had done, but reluctantly abandoned the idea. It wasn't that the task was beyond him, far from it, but it would take him too long. He decided to take advantage of modern technology and use an electronic watch for a timer. No, not a watch – one of those pocket electronic devices that combined calculator, diary, address book and alarms all in one. Some of them had alarms that could be programmed to six months or a year ahead.

There was another version of this attempt. Elser, who had become involved with a group of Communists, was picked up at Dachau concentration camp (it had not yet acquired its full sinister reputation) by the Gestapo. He was offered his freedom if he would do what he was told.

He was taken to the Bürgerbräukeller by the Gestapo. The pillar where he placed a bomb on Gestapo orders was a wooden one, which is why the Gestapo picked a cabinetmaker for the task rather than an engineer. Elser could remove a panel and then replace it without leaving a trace. The explosive had an alarm

118

clock attached, but this was unconnected to the fuse. This could be set off only by an external power source.

Soon after Hitler finished his speech the bomb was exploded, killing and wounding a number of party members. Later Elser was arrested, when he 'confessed', implicating two British Army officers in the plot.

The Gestapo's idea was that the failed 'British' assassination attempt would bolster Hitler's popularity in Germany, which it did. At the same time, the fact that he had left the reunion early confirmed Hitler's own belief that Providence was watching over him and would make sure he achieved all he set out to do.

Whichever version was true, the man was inspired by the story, and he set to planning his own bomb with meticulous care. He would turn the possible myth of the accurate long-delay fuse into reality.

The man began to hum. He felt quite elated by the prospect of making something quite so elegant.

'We can't cover all the houses on your list. The best we can do is six teams of two officers each,' Harry Timberlake told Sarah. 'Superintendent Harkness is giving us back six CID men and the uniformed branch are finding another five. We're stretched to the limit with these two murders on our patch. That means a total of twelve including you.'

'It's better than a poke in the eye with a sharp stick,' Sarah replied.

'Actually, it's not as bad as it seems at first sight. All the ten families on your list aren't going to be out on the same night.'

'Three of them at least will be. They're away on holiday.'

'Okay. That leaves seven other houses for the remaining three teams. We'll give each team two addresses. If the family in the first house of their pair hasn't gone out, leaving the place empty, by ten o'clock, we can reckon they're in for the rest of the night and the team can go on to the alternative target.'

'Good-oh, guv.'

'So what I want is Flannelfoot's six most probable targets.'

'The first six on the list,' Sarah replied at once. 'I worked out the priorities when I made it up.'

It wasn't the first time that Sarah had surprised Harry Timberlake. 'How come?' he asked.

'I've been round and had a look at them all. The last one on the list, for example, is definitely an outsider. It's on a busy road, lots of activity, no front garden and a front door that's lit by a street lamp. Top of the list is in a quiet road with lots of trees that cut down the street lighting. The house has a driveway and the front door's in shadow from a big porch. And it's one where they're on holiday. If I was Flannelfoot, it's the one I'd go for. It's odds-on.'

Resisting the temptation to tell Sarah she should have said 'If I *were* Flannelfoot . . . ', Harry said, 'That one's yours, then.' Sarah felt a sudden surge of excitement. He went on: 'I've got an appointment at seven, so briefing'll have to be at half five, in the CID main office. The others have been warned. I'll give you all the pairings and targets then.'

When Harry Timberlake telephoned Mrs Foulds she didn't sound overjoyed to hear from him, but after all it was only midday and she'd hardly woken up properly. She said she'd see him at seven o'clock that evening. He assumed it wasn't an invitation to dinner.

A muscular Portuguese with forearms like a stoker's and a dark moustache opened the door to Harry. He recognised her as the maid because she was wearing a skirt. He later described her as looking just like Mike Tyson with tits, except for the moustache. Until now he hadn't realised how hard it was to get good domestic help. On the day of Foulds's murder, Mrs Sanders, the cleaner, had told him that there was a Dutch au pair in the household. He wondered what she was like. If the maid was anything to go by she could probably pass for the wrestler Ed 'Strangler' Lewis.

The maid showed him into a drawing room with all the elegance of someone directing traffic, and left him without a word.

The curtains in the room were half closed, although there were still a good couple of hours of daylight left. Small amber- and rose-coloured table lamps and one standard lamp were alight, filling the room with unexpected shapes and shadows. Harry had been in that room before, on the day that Howard Foulds's body had been discovered, but then the curtains had been drawn back and the room was flooded with sunlight. It looked very different now, slightly . . . *voluptuous* was the only word Harry could think of: the sort of room that is a natural setting for sexual adventures. Against one wall of the room was an enormous settee on which two couples could have fornicated simultaneously without getting in each other's way. Harry recalled that on his first visit he had noticed that the Fouldses had separate bedrooms. The thought had seemed without relevance then, but on reflection he decided that perhaps it wasn't so inconsequential after all.

Lucia Foulds made her entrance into the room as if she were coming on to a stage. To meet the detective investigating the murder of her husband, she had chosen a simple black dress which did the double duty of emphasising her status as a widow and emphasising her lush figure. It was the sort of dress that would attract improper advances to a weeping widow at her husband's graveside, and Mrs Foulds looked far from tearful. There was no argument that she was beautiful, but occasionally Harry thought he caught a glint of steely calculation about her. He found it hard to guess her age. In this light she looked thirty-five to forty, but how much of that was natural it was impossible to say. She reminded him of something he had read once about Marlene Dietrich. When she was in her sixties she was asked the secret of her always looking so young. 'Money,' she answered simply. If Lucia Foulds's attractiveness owed more to money than youth, it was money well spent, Harry conceded.

She seemed surprised by Harry's appearance, and he guessed that she had been expecting a television-style detective in torn jeans and training shoes. 'How do you do,' she said formally and sat at one end of the enormous settee. She indicated to him to sit facing her.

He began by asking all the standard questions, the same ones he had asked Mrs Sanders and he would ask the other employees: whether Howard Foulds had seemed worried before his murder, whether there had been any unusual phone calls or visitors, whether he had been acting at all strangely. At this last question Timberlake thought he noticed the hint of amusement on Mrs Foulds's face.

'My husband and I lived quite separate lives,' she said with wide-eyed frankness. 'He had his own friends and interests, I have mine.'

I bet, Harry thought.

'We frequently didn't see each other for days . . . a couple of weeks . . . at a time.'

121

'I see.' He suppressed the desire to comment 'Hardly seemed worth getting married, then.'

She took from an ornate-looking box on a small marble-topped table a strange cigarette: long, black and with a cardboard mouthpiece that was more than half the cigarette's length. She licked her lips before she put it into her mouth and waited for Harry to give her a light from a silver cigarette lighter that tried hard to look as if it had been made in Queen Anne's time. As he stood and held the flame to her cigarette she took his hand in both hers – just for a moment, but long enough to be noticeable.

Oh, no, Harry said to himself, that really is too corn*j*. He was disappointed in Lucia Foulds, who had seemed so sophisticated. At the same moment she looked up at him with violet eyes from under her long eyelashes, taking him by surprise. As suddenly as if she had thrown a switch, she exuded a heady sexuality. All at once her gesture didn't seem in the least corny, and briefly he found it easy to believe she had the sexual power to drive someone to kill. Almost before he formulated the thought, he recognised that no one would need to kill Lucia Foulds's husband. He was no obstacle to an affair with her: she was as available as a public phone box. However, the glimpse of her latent sexual power raised another possibility. True, she was abroad when her husband was killed, but she could have instigated his murder. To Harry's considerable chagrin, which he was unable to hide completely, she seemed to read his mind.

'Of course, although I was in Italy at the time, I must be a major suspect as I'm Howard's only relative,' she said. 'Most murders are family affairs, are they not? And then there's the inevitable question, *Cui bono*? It means—'

' "Who profits?" I know,' Harry finished for her.

'Well, not me,' she said equably. 'I've always had all the freedom I want, and I don't benefit financially a great deal from my husband's death. This is my house and I have my own money. More than Howard, actually. Inherited from my second husband,' she explained. 'I'll give instructions to my solicitor to confirm all this for you, if you like.'

'I don't think that will be necessary,' Harry said. He was sure she was telling the truth. It left one question unanswered. Mrs Foulds was ahead of him again.

'I suppose you're wondering why I married Howard. And for that matter, why he married me.'

'That's none of my business.'

'You must be curious,' she said mockingly.

'I can guess. It gave you both established and secure positions in society.' Lucia Foulds looked disconcerted for the first time during the interview.

Harry Timberlake understood the Fouldses' situation perfectly. Without a husband, such an attractive woman would have been a threat to other women, who would be wary of her. Social invitations would be few. However, as a married woman – despite the fact that her husband was frequently 'unavailable because of the demands of his profession' – she was acceptable. As far as other men were concerned, she was a far better proposition for an affair as a married woman: she was unlikely to make trouble with a lover's wife. And, Harry knew, many men enjoyed boffing a married woman because of the extra pleasure of putting one over another man, particularly one as well known as Howard Foulds QC. His reason for having an attractive, sexy wife was simple: it was an excellent cover for his peculiar habits.

Mrs Foulds recovered quickly. 'Well, I suppose that's the end of this interview.' Harry nodded. 'Since you're no longer on duty can I offer you a drink, or anything?'

The pause before 'or anything' was just perceptible. It should have been as corny as the hand-touching routine, but the hint of a smile and another direct look from those disturbing violet eyes turned on the full force of her sexuality again.

Harry felt desire rising swiftly. He was quite sure that she wouldn't cause him any trouble. For the moment he entirely forgot that her husband had been brutally murdered not long ago in the next room, and he hesitated for one long, painful moment. She moistened her lips. Harry was within a breath of responding to her invitation, then said, 'Nothing for me, thanks.'

She moved a little on the enormous settee, a small, subtle movement to a position that emphasised her desirability. There was more leg visible; her breasts were more prominent. 'Are you quite sure?' She wasn't used to having her offers turned down.

'Quite sure.'

He was certain now that there were a lot of men she could

persuade to kill her husband . . . if she wanted them to for secret reasons of her own.

'Bit of luck, us getting paired,' Greg Davidson said from his seat beside Sarah in her Fiesta. They were parked in The Meadow, Terrace Vale's poshest street, nearly opposite Number Seven, The Cedars, Sarah's banker for Phantom Flannelfoot's next target. Both their seats were pushed fully back and in the half-reclining position. Unless a passer-by peered inside he wouldn't notice that the car was occupied. At the same time Sarah and Greg could comfortably see out to keep observation.

'Uhuh,' she replied absently. Part of her mind agreed with Greg. She could have paired with Joe Simpson, for example. He was unhappily married and bored the ears off any captive audience with a droning litany of his spouse's faults. Most of Simpson's Terrace Vale colleagues thought his wife must be something of a saint not to have flattened him with a coal hammer long since.

Or she might have got PC Alec Anderson as a partner. Anderson was bearable, just, as a companion patrolling streets and parks in the open, as long as you kept upwind, but he was murder in a closed environment like a car. He was what is medically known as a secreter, which meant among other things that even before genetic fingerprinting you could tell his blood group from his sweat and saliva. More immediately, it meant that his sweat smelled like a gorilla's jockstrap. Like two gorillas.

That wasn't the worst. He was also a high-fibre addict, which made him into a walking gasworks. He often said, 'I fart a lot, but at least my farts don't smell.' When people told him his nose needed attention because they smelt like a fire in a chemical-warfare factory, he thought they were joking.

So, while Sarah subconsciously knew she could have done a lot worse than get Greg, the majority of her mind was concentrating on keeping The Cedars under close surveillance. It was that same concentration that made her a little slow to become aware that Greg had managed to slip his hand in her blouse and was gently squeezing her left breast. He was already inside her bra and fingering her nipple when Sarah sat up abruptly, freeing herself from Greg's hand.

'What're you doing?' she asked superfluously.

124

'It's all right, nobody can see us,' he said, totally misunderstanding her reaction.

'We're on a job,' Sarah hissed.

'That's the trouble, we're not, not these days,' Greg replied, trying to make a joke of it. 'On the job, I mean.'

'What's the matter with you? We're working!' Her Welsh accent was quite strong, betraying her tension.

'I'll tell you what's wrong with me,' Greg said sulkily. 'D'you realise that Westcliff was the last time we went to bed together?'

Sarah was a sensual young woman and she couldn't help but feel a stirring of sexual excitement at the evocation of their weekend at the hotel. It had been rather special.

'Ever since you got involved in this bloody Phantom Flannelfoot business I've hardly seen you,' Greg ploughed on, right into the quicksands. 'When I have you've been knackered and looking like—' He stopped, three words too late. The moment of warmth that Sarah had felt was swept away as if by a gust of cold wind.

'This bloody Phantom Flannelfoot business, as you call it, is the most important thing that's happened to me since I joined the force. It might be the most important thing that ever does. Christ, don't you understand what it might mean?'

'You're the most important thing that's happened to me,' Greg said in a small voice. 'And I've missed you like hell. I love you.'

Although the two things don't always go together, Sarah was a Celt and a sucker for romantic sentimentality. She melted. 'And I love you,' she said, believing it. 'But this simply isn't the moment.'

Greg immediately sensed her weakening. 'Oh, come on,' he said eagerly. 'Chummy isn't going to turn up this early, if he comes at all.'

The pendulum of Sarah's mood swung back violently to the other end of its travel. 'What are you suggesting? You fuck me on the back seat?'

It was worse than a slap in the face for Greg. Oddly enough, despite their intimacy and the fact that they worked in a pretty rough environment, that was a word they rarely, if ever, uttered even in their most passionate moments of lovemaking. They had other ways of turning each other on. Used angrily in their present situation, the four-letter word shocked Greg. He leaned back in his seat in morose silence.

125

Sarah had also surprised herself. She felt ashamed and was on the point of trying to make up again with Greg, but something stopped her.

They stayed on surveillance all night, hardly exchanging a word. Greg fell asleep a couple of times but Sarah remained wakeful through a night that turned out to be as uneventful as a rained-off cricket match. The monotony was broken only by a couple of visits from Harry Timberlake in his car and a few radio messages to check that the personal radios were still working.

At ten to six Sarah had to accept that Flannelfoot wouldn't put in an appearance this time. It was light, and people had begun to appear in the streets. She started the engine of the Fiesta, waking Greg.

She drove him back to the station section house. For the first time since they started going together, careless of being seen, she kissed him; but from a sense of guilt rather than from real warmth.

'Sorry, Greg, darling,' she said softly. 'When this is all over we—'

'Sure,' he said. He got out of the car and went into the section house. Sarah drove straight home, her mouth compressed into a thin line. She didn't know what the hell she was feeling about anything.

The one stroke of luck, or happy coincidence, that the AMIP and Terrace Vale teams were still hoping for eventually occurred through the unlikely medium of Professor Peter Mortimer. The pathologist was driving home from an autopsy in Paddington in his aged Rover 3-litre V8 when the engine cut out as if it had suffered a sudden heart attack. The Professor was some two hundred yards from Terrace Vale police station, so he decided to ask for assistance there rather than call out the AA or RAC. As he was a member of neither it was an easy choice.

'What can I do for you, Professor?' asked Sergeant Ramsden, who was at the front desk.

'I'm Professor Mortimer.'

'Yes, sir, I recognised you.'

'My engine is dead.'

'Do you suspect foul play?' Ramsden asked with a straight face.

Mortimer's brow furrowed. 'The engine of my *car*, I was driving along and it stopped for no reason at all.'

Ramsden was about to observe that it must have stopped for *some* reason, but resisted the temptation. Professor Mortimer was clearly not very strong on badinage. He contented himself with, 'What make and number, and where is it?'

Mortimer told him.

'I'll get one of the mechanics to have a look at it. Doc Martin is the very man. He was here when we were running those 3-litre Rovers.'

'The mechanic is a doctor?'

'A nickname, Professor. Like the boots.'

'Of course,' Mortimer replied, totally at a loss. Ramsden reflected that it must be a barrel of laughs working with Mortimer all day.

'Why don't you go down to the canteen and have a cup of tea while your car's being looked at? Downstairs and to your right.'

Harry Timberlake was in the canteen just starting a double serving of bacon and eggs. It was three o'clock in the afternoon but Harry's internal clock was operating on a different time zone. He had been up most of the night visiting the surveillance teams on the Phantom Flannelfoot operation and monitoring the radio traffic. He had gone to bed just before four o'clock, and slept fitfully, half expecting the phone to ring at any moment. Up again at seven thirty, he could manage only a couple of slices of toast and now he was feeling almost faint with hunger. Bacon and eggs he found acceptable at any time of the night or day, and a good source of quick energy.

For once Ted Greening was also in the canteen instead of in one of the local boozers. This was because he wanted to speak to Harry about the Foulds and Phantom Flannelfoot cases, and one or two minor enquiries that had been put on hold while the murder investigation was going on. Greening was drinking tea and eating two large, unhealthy cheese rolls.

Without a word Professor Mortimer sat down at their table. He had a cup of tea and a marzipan-covered pastry of a poisonous green colour. It didn't occur to him to ask whether the other men minded if he joined them, or that he would be anything other than welcome. The two detectives greeted him with outward civility.

127

Greening, who had drunk just the right amount of Scotch at his lunchtime session, was in one of his brief hail-fellow-well-met moods. Fatally, he jocularly asked Mortimer, 'Seen any good bodies recently, Professor?'

'As a matter of fact I had an interesting case only this afternoon.' Harry suppressed a groan; the phoney smile melted from Greening's face. 'Autopsy of a male body that had been buried near the Regent's Park Canal. Quite fascinating, the amount of saponification that had taken place.'

'Eh?' said Greening, unwisely.

'Saponification. The change of the fatty constituents of the body into more-or-less stable new compounds. The process is caused by the gradual hydrogenation of the fats already present in the body into higher fatty acids. The material resulting from saponification is called adipocere. It is a fatty-looking substance, naturally enough, varying in colour from white to yellowish-white . . .'

Harry looked at the fatty edges to his rashers of bacon and the yolks of the eggs and tried to shut his ears to the Professor's little dissertation. Greening grinned at him.

'The adipocere feels oily to the touch, melts like candlewax when it's heated, and burns with a slight flame,' Mortimer droned on. Police officers at adjoining tables started talking loudly to each other to drown out Mortimer's voice.

'Oh, yes. It has a slightly mouldy, cheesy odour,' he added.

Greening froze with his cheese roll halfway to his mouth.

'This particular body was almost completely converted into adipocere, which is fairly unusual. The face was still quite recognisable with the features virtually unchanged. Of course, you realise what my problem was?' When the two men stared at him, Mortimer shook his head faintly at such lack of elementary knowledge. 'Determining the length of time the body had been there. The factors affecting the formation of adipocere are, of course, most variable.'

'Of course,' Harry said gravely. Mortimer looked at him keenly, but Harry remained impassive.

'I suppose the layman would think it is easier to determine how long a body has been dead when it is well preserved, rather than when there is a considerable degree of putrefaction.' Two PCs and a WPC got up from the next table and stamped out, giving Mortimer angry stares to which he was quite oblivious.

'But the late Professor Glaister devised an excellent method during the Ruxton case in 1935, when a doctor in Lancaster murdered his wife and maid, cut them up and distributed the pieces around the countryside. Glaister was able to establish how long previously death had occurred by determining what generation of maggots were present on the various parts of the bodies.' There was a long silence.

Mortimer glanced around the canteen with a jaundiced eye. 'Is it always this busy?' he asked, and went on again without waiting for an answer. 'That's probably the reason for the food being so bad; the kitchen staff undertrained and overworked.' He studied his pastry. 'It doesn't only look like a gall-bladder, it probably tastes like one, too.'

Neither of the two detectives felt inclined to ask him why he'd bought it in the first place. Greening said daringly, 'They won't give you your money back now.' This seemed to make Mortimer come to a decision. He took a bite of the pastry, said 'Hmmm,' and grimaced. 'I thought so.'

Harry had been contemplating eating his last slice of fried bread, but abruptly pushed his plate away. Professor Mortimer continued chewing on his dubious pastry, his prominent Adam's apple bobbing up and down like a yo-yo. The detectives watched it, fascinated.

'It's these murder enquiries,' Greening said eventually.

'What about them?'

'It's why the canteen is so crowded. We've got two AMIP teams here, one for the Foulds murder, the other for the car-park job, and detectives from the Southington nick working on the DC Robson case.'

'Ah, yes,' Mortimer said, his face lighting up. 'That was the shotgun murder. I haven't seen injuries as serious as that for years, at least to the head, when a workman fell into an industrial food mixer. He was in there some time before anyone noticed. He was delivered to the morgue in three sacks. His name was Worthington, as I recall. Your man Robson was nearly as bad. At least four-fifths of the brain tissue was absent and the skull was quite fragmented. Most interesting, the amount of damage a shotgun can inflict at close quarters. Who identified the body, by the way?'

'I did,' said Harry Timberlake with an edge to his voice like broken glass. 'From his clothes and the effects in his pockets.'

'Yes. It was quite impossible to identify him from his face. The features were utterly destroyed. Could have been anyone.'

'I know,' Harry said through his teeth. It somehow seemed inadequate.

Mortimer turned to Greening, who had been silent for some time. The warm glow of the lunchtime Scotch was degenerating into a cold sweat. 'Are you all right?' he asked with curiosity but no compassion.

'Fine,' Greening replied. 'Why shouldn't I be?'

Mortimer didn't bother to answer that. Changing the subject without warning he asked, 'I take it you're working on the assumption that all these local murders are connected, probably committed by the same man?'

The two detectives stared at him.

'There's absolutely nothing in common between any of them, Professor,' Greening said with pitying superiority, getting a fraction of his own back.

'Hit-and-run car, an axe, a crossbow and a shotgun: all completely different methods,' Harry added.

'Oh, that,' said Mortimer. 'That's incidental.' His bland certainty took their breath away. 'There's one significant common factor. I should have thought it was obvious to you.' He made it sound like 'thought it was obvious *even* to you'.

Greening burped noisily. 'All the victims are dead. They've got that in common.'

Mortimer looked at Greening as if he were something very unpleasant preserved in a jar. The two men waited for him to speak.

'In all your experience, both of you, have you ever known four murders in such a short space of time and in a very small area?'

'You car's ready, Professor,' Sergeant Ramsden said from just behind Mortimer. 'It was the coil. There was a faulty connection of the main lead to the distributor. Doc Martin's fixed it for you. It's in the station yard.'

Mortimer got up. He turned to Harry and Greening. 'Obvious,' he repeated, tut-tutting. They could have strangled him. Mortimer walked past Ramsden without so much as a 'Thanks', then had a second thought and turned back. 'I hope he hasn't left any oil or grease on the steering wheel.'

The three policemen watched Mortimer's stooped, angular figure brush past men and women as if they weren't there, or at least, not to be considered.

'You've got to make allowances,' Harry said at last. 'He's not used to dealing with people who are alive and vertical.'

When Sergeant Ramsden had gone Greening said to Harry Timberlake, 'I've got a nasty feeling the old bastard might be right.'

'Jesus,' Harry said. 'If he is, it means a total rethink of the whole works, right from square one.'

Chapter 7

Ernie Birt was an unusual celebrity. He was a television comedy scriptwriter whose name was known to many members of the public. Asked if they could name any television comedy writers a few mature viewers might remember Galton and Simpson. As for modern writers, probably only two with a show currently on TV would mean anything to the viewing public, and Ernie Birt was the first of them.

He created *The Grundys*, a ghastly married couple who lived in an upper-middle-class area, much to the disgust of their neighbours. How the underprivileged, dole-supported Grundys managed to occupy a £250,000 house in a select area was never explained, and no one thought to ask.

Ernie Birt won his success by hard work rather than creative imagination, of which he had very little. What he did have was an enormous library of radio tapes, video cassettes and comedy books. His shows were all derivative, owing much to *Hancock*, *Bilko*, *George and Mildred*, *In Loving Memory* and *Steptoe and Son*, among many other shows.

Ernie also worked at making himself a Personality, a Character. He grew a soup-strainer moustache and had a pudding-basin haircut. He broadened his accent and loudly declared at every opportunity that southern beer was gnats' piss. Although he professed to shun personal publicity ('It's the programme that's important, not me'), there had been a host of articles in Sunday supplements and glossy magazines devoted to Ernie and his house-boat *Ilkley*, moored on the Thames near Royalty Embankment. ITV had done a programme on Ernie.

To read the articles on Ernie Birt and his home anyone would believe that he lived on black pudding and tripe while listening to brass band music; that his favourite occupation was raising

132

whippets. Deep down he nurtured a well-known secret desire to return to his northern roots . . . it said here. In fact his tastes were more like Noel Coward's. You couldn't have dragged Ernie away from south-west London and back to Hull with a Caterpillar tractor. In the meantime, he enjoyed to the full money, success, and an adequate supple of stage-struck young women.

This was all to the good, and Ernie's cup runneth over, figuratively and frequently literally as well. But as everyone knows, life can be a bastard. There was a big fat fly in the ointment of Ernie's contentment, although he wasn't aware of it yet. Despite affecting to despise public recognition and publicity, he actually loved them. So he was delighted when the popular Press and a TV programme magazine announced that Ernie Birt was going to New York on the 17th of next month to see the first showing of the US version of *The Grundys*, returning on the 11th of the following month to start work writing the next series.

The trouble with a story like that was it could be an open invitation to burglars, but it had been well publicised that Ernie Birt's houseboat was furnished with all the luxury of a Victorian workhouse. In this way, Ernie said, he wouldn't be distracted by material things while he was working. So it wasn't a very tempting target for a housebreaker.

However, very much more serious was the fact that the news provided invaluable information for anyone who planned to kill Ernie.

Which somebody did.

Despite having slept so little the previous night, Harry Timberlake couldn't get to sleep that same evening after the cosy chat with Professor Mortimer. He tried lying on his right side in bed, on his left, and sitting up, but he remained wakeful. A macho measure of Scotch didn't help. Perhaps he was in that paradoxical but not unfamiliar state of being too tired to sleep, he thought at first. No, it wasn't that. It was Mortimer's suggestion that the Terrace Vale murders and the ones in the adjoining areas were all connected. Harry was angry with himself for not having thought of it first, but there was more to it than that.

It was as if Mortimer had pulled back a curtain a few inches to give a glimpse of a new and unknown picture, a brief revelation that was tantalising because it promised so much more. Timberlake was now sure that there would be other common factors linking the four murders if he could only rip away the curtain that Mortimer had opened only a few inches, and see the entire picture. He couldn't go to Superintendent Harkness with only a second-hand version of Mortimer's theory: he had to find other links. If they existed . . .

His certainty waned. Maybe he merely wanted there to be something all the others had missed and only he could find.

He looked at the clock-radio beside the bed and thought that his eyes were playing him tricks: it showed 3.45 a.m. He had lookr d at it five minutes earlier when it was 1.35 a.m. He realised that he had fallen asleep after all, and turned to Jenny Long, lying beside him, to see whether she was sleeping or whether the light had woken her.

Then he remembered that he was alone. Jenny had been with him in a dream that was so vivid he found it difficult to accept that it was only a dream.

There had been something different about Jenny that he couldn't quite put his finger on, for all the dream's intense clarity. He felt that the difference was important if he could identify it, but the more he tried to recall the dream the more it receded from him.

Harry shrugged. Maybe it would come to him later; if it didn't, it couldn't be all that important, he told himself.

He couldn't have been more wrong.

He turned over and tried to go to sleep again when an entirely different thought exploded in his mind. While he had been dozing or sleeping his subconscious mind had been working on the problem of the missing connections without his being aware of it.

Now he *knew*.

'What d'you think, Ted?' Harry Timberlake asked Greening, trying to suppress any note of anxiety in his voice. Greening sat at his desk, looking like a three-day-old corpse. When others asked what he'd been doing, he answered shortly, 'Working.' There was an element, a very small element, of truth in this. The fright that the damned pimple had given him had long receded from his memory, and he had made up lost time with his prostitute informants. Not one of them had a whisper of information to give him, but he'd had a hell of a time – especially with Rita.

A couple of nights with her could be very debilitating indeed. He stifled a yawn.

Harry Timberlake, sitting on the other side of the desk, repeated his question. Harry Timberlake was aware of Greening's shortcomings but he still had some respect for his detective's gut feeling. He had just explained his theory of links between the four local murders, and what had seemed logical and factual in the early hours now seemed irrational and insubstantial.

Greening was avoiding Harry's eye, and Harry took this as an indication that Greening wasn't impressed. Harry was wrong on two counts. Greening's thief-taking flair was atrophied; his instincts were now all tuned to keeping him from making waves. He simply didn't know whether Harry's ideas were good or not. More importantly, he couldn't guess what Superintendent Harkness's reactions would be, and he didn't want to commit himself. These days Greening avoided having to make important decisions. All he wanted was peace and quiet until he drew his chief inspector's pension. Long since he had come to accept that he had as much chance of making superintendent before he retired as Colonel Gadaffi had of winning the Golda Meir Memorial Medal.

'Could be something in it,' he said neutrally. 'Depends.'

Harry got the message. He glanced at his watch. 'I'm just going to speak to Superintendent Harkness. D'you want to come with me?'

Before Harry had finished the question Greening knew what his answer was going to be. Nevertheless he paused, to give the impression he was pondering his response. 'No, better not,' he said at last. 'It's your show, Harry. I don't want to give the impression I'm trying to nick the credit for your idea.'

Or take the blame for it. Greening really was too transparent, Harry thought.

To Harry's relief, Harkness's attitude was quite different. When Harry explained Professor Mortimer's theory Harkness considered it for a moment and said, 'Why didn't we think of it?'

'We couldn't see the forest for the tree. We were concentrating on our one case and not seeing the whole picture. It was easier for Professor Mortimer to make the connection because he was involved with all four victims.'

Harkness looked dubious. 'It's an interesting theory, no doubt about that. Even so, on its own it's not a great deal to go on. It could be a coincidence, a statistical freak.'

Harry pressed on. 'Look, sir, it took nearly a hundred years before someone worked out that Jack the Ripper's victims lived close to each other and knew each other—'

'True,' Harkness interrupted. 'But the *modus operandi* was the same each time. In our cases they're all completely dissimilar. All the indications are that the four murders were committed by four different people.'

Harry shook his head. 'I believe that one man deliberately used four different methods to put us off the track. He was clever and inventive, but not clever enough.' Another thought struck him. 'Or maybe he was too clever, and that's betrayed him.'

'How?'

'Apart from them all being perpetrated in one small area, there are two other factors common to all the murders. First, they were all motiveless.'

'There must be motives, otherwise there wouldn't be any murders. I take it you're not considering them to be the work of a random killer, a psychopath?'

'I meant apparently motiveless. There are motives all right, but they're not obvious. In all four killings, no one has come up with a motive.'

'How do you know about the others?' Harkness asked sharply.

'I asked.'

'Indeed.'

'I asked the DI on Superintendent Ward's AMIP team about the car-park murder, and one of the Southington CID detectives making enquiries about DC Robson's murder. Then I rang Sergeant Perch at Wallsend about the hit-and-run killing. Perch was the officer we met at the post mortem on Mr Foulds,' Harry added, and paused for effect. 'Not the hint of a motive in any of them.'

'And the other factor?'

'All four enquiries haven't turned up one single lead. We haven't one single worthwhile clue from all the investigations with more than a hundred officers involved. Think about it for a moment, sir.' He ticked off his points on his fingers. 'Take a period of any fortnight in the year. How many sets of four murders would there be in one small area? Or take any four

136

murders anywhere at random, irrespective of time or place. How many groups of four would have no discernible motive between the four of them? And finally, pick any other four murders anywhere, at random. What are the chances that all four would fail to produce one single, solitary clue?'

'And these are the facts on which you are predicating the theory that "our" murders were committed by the same man?'

'I'd say it was very much odds-on, sir?'

This time Harkness thought for a long moment before speaking. Almost reluctantly he said, 'Yes . . . you may well be right. I'm not trying to diminish the value or originality of your deductions, but once again I don't see how we all failed to pick it up.'

'Because they were negative facts: things that aren't there, not things that are.' He smiled. 'Sherlock Holmes's dog that didn't bark in the night.'

Harkness sighed. 'If the other AMIP teams agree with your theory, it'll mean an entirely new approach to our enquiries. All four sets of reports and statements will have to be gone through to see if we can find something or someone that links all the victims.'

The immensity of the work which this represented loomed over Harry Timberlake like a great, black thunder cloud. If he was wrong and it all came to nothing, he might as well start looking for a job as a nightwatchman somewhere.

Superintendent Harkness, the three other AMIP superintendents and some of their officers met at Terrace Vale the next morning. Ted Greening had seen which way the cat had jumped and insinuated himself into the meeting to join the winning side. It took all his thick-skinned brass nerve to put in an appearance. He had kept away from Harkness as much as possible since the withering dressing down he had subjected him to; the scars still smarted. He hoped that Harkness had forgotten most of his transgressions and shortcomings by now. He thought that turning up at the meeting would make him look keen, and there was always the faint possibility that some of the credit for Harry Timberlake's idea might rub off on to him. He avoided Harkness's eye at first, glancing at him with furtive, sideways looks, but Harkness paid him no attention. Oddly enough Greening was disappointed; he found it rather humiliating.

Harkness briefly explained that Inspector Timberlake had proposed a new hypothesis which suggested that all four enquiries might be linked; and he let Harry take it from there.

Harry Timberlake was thrown a little off balance by Harkness's lukewarm attitude, so much in contrast to his encouraging response the previous day. Almost at once he guessed that Harkness was taking care not to provoke a reaction against his ideas by over-selling them.

At first Harry found it daunting to lecture Scotland Yard heavy brass and their cynical-looking subordinates on where they had all gone wrong, but his confidence grew when he saw he was gaining their interest. He was interrupted a couple of times with questions, neither of them hostile.

'Well, that's it,' Harry finished rather tamely. The room was silent and Harry felt himself growing cold. He thought he saw a flicker of a sarcastic smile on Ted Greening's face.

Both Harry and Greening had mistaken the mood of the meeting. In a small way – a very small way – it was the sort of silence that sometimes greets an exceptional stage performance before the audience gathers itself and breaks into enthusiastic applause. Senior CID officers aren't given to cheering a great deal, except at private drunken parties. In addition, one or two AMIP men were disgruntled that a local detective inspector had stumbled on a new line of enquiry that had occurred to none of them. However, the rest of them reluctantly took off their hats to him.

So Harry had no ovation. Instead there was an eventual observation in Superintendent Frank Ward's countryman's burr. 'Looks like we got to start all over again.'

Harry wouldn't have swapped it for three curtain calls.

The search for a common factor or factors in the enormous mass of information collected by the four teams of detectives and their aides were carried out by junior officers who had put all the statements, reports and lists on to computers.

While this tedious operation was being carried out, Harry worked on the list that had been supplied by his journalist friend Claud Salter of the cases Howard Foulds had defended during the past two years. Without a great deal of optimism he pursued his earlier idea that a victim of a crime might be sufficiently incensed to attack Foulds because the lawyer had succeeded in getting the aggressor off the charge. Harry's first theory, which once seemed an attractive possibility, now looked as good a bet as a sure-fire system for making a fortune at roulette. Still, it had to be followed up. As Harry studied the cases with increasing pessimism, he decided that there were two outside possibilities at best, maybe three if he stretched things a little.

The first two were criminals who had been dealt large doses of grievous bodily harm, needing an impressive total of surgical stitches, by Foulds's clients, who had nevertheless walked away from the Central Criminal Court with no new stain on their unpleasant characters. One of the victims was in jail and had been for some time before Foulds's killing; the other, a Marty Fish, had apparently kissed and made up with his attacker because he had since become a loyal member of his gang. This model of charity and forgiveness was quoted verbatim by a detective whom Timberlake spoke to about the case. 'Fair's fair. I was definitely out of order,' Marty Fish had declared to the detective, who added that Marty Fish was as thick as a bookie's wallet, and definitely wasn't pretending.

The third case, and the widest of outsiders, was a company secretary, Tom Rimmer, who was charged with fraud jointly with his employer, Salem Mahmet, to all accounts a wily wheeler-dealer of uncertain Middle Eastern origins. Their company had swindled gullible investors of nearly a million pounds. This money was invested in a Liechtenstein-registered company which rapidly went bankrupt. The million pounds had simply disappeared. The prosecution alleged that Mahmet and Rimmer owned the Liechtenstein company, arranged the bankruptcy and pocketed the cash. The financial secrecy laws in Liechtenstein, the prosecution pointed out, made the Swiss look like blabbermouths by comparison.

Foulds appeared for Mahmet, whose defence was that Rimmer ran the entire scam while Mahmet was abroad on other business. Mahmet knew nothing of the operation until the Serious Fraud Squad knocked on the door.

Reading between the lines, which wasn't difficult, Harry Timberlake came to the conclusion that Rimmer was set up from the start to take the blame for the fraud, and played no active part in it.

However, Foulds's cross-examination of the unhappy Rimmer

139

was directed at loading all the blame on to his frail shoulders alone. The lawyer's belligerent, clever questioning reduced Rimmer to incoherent self-contradiction. Although the jury didn't swallow the story that Rimmer was the principal in the swindle, by the time Foulds had finished with him they thought he was involved at least to some degree. They found him guilty of conspiracy to defraud. They also found Mahmet guilty, and the judge sentenced him to five years, which he was still serving.

The experienced judge was less impressed than the jury by Foulds's cross-examination of Rimmer, and clearly saw that he was very much a minor figure. He gave him a year, half of it suspended. With time off for good behaviour Rimmer served four months, but his career as a company secretary came to a halt as brutally as if he had run into a brick wall.

When Harry Timberlake found Rimmer he suddenly had doubts about his innocence after all. He had a large house in Hampstead with a Daimler V12 in the driveway. The door was opened by a maid who, if she couldn't be mistaken for Bo Derek, wasn't in the class of Mrs Foulds's Portuguese bruiser either.

The former company secretary was the unusual combination of being something of a wimp but largely self-confident with it. When Harry said he was investigating the murder of Howard Foulds, Rimmer said, 'I don't see how I can help you. The only time I ever met him was in court.'

'He gave you a pretty rough time, trying to blame you for everything.'

'He was a bit strong,' Rimmer admitted.

'Weren't you at all resentful?'

Either Rimmer was rather dim, or he was an excellent actor. 'He was only doing his job. Mahmet was the real nasty bit of work. Finished me as a company secretary. Only another crook would employ me after I came out of jail.'

Harry Timberlake took in the expensively furnished drawing room, with its french windows giving on to a spacious garden. 'You seem to have done quite well for yourself despite it all. How did you manage?'

'Sold my house and bought a launderette. Lived in the rooms above the shop. It did all right and I bought a second one six months later.' At last the penny dropped. It had taken so long that Harry Timberlake could well believe that Mahmet had managed to dupe Rimmer so thoroughly. He looked at Timberlake wide-eyed. 'Here, you don't think I had anything to do with Mr Foulds's murder?'

'No.' Harry replied truthfully. However, if Rimmer hadn't been actively involved in the fraud, as Harry believed, there was one great, glaring inconsistency. Pointedly glancing round the luxurious room he asked, 'All this and a Daimler on two launderettes?'

'Oh, no,' Rimmer replied artlessly. 'I had a jackpot on the pools.' Harry Timberlake looked disbelieving. 'I put an X in the box for no publicity,' Rimmer added. He smiled. 'You lose some, you win some.'

Harry got up. He was losing them all.

When he returned to Terrace Vale to make out his report he was surprised to see Sarah Lewis working at a computer.

'Aren't you on surveillance tonight?'

'Yes, guv. I thought I'd put in a couple of hours on the cross-checking.' In something between an excuse and an explanation she added, 'I was the first on the scene at the Foulds murder.'

'I hadn't forgotten. It's all very well being here, but make sure you get enough rest.'

'Okay, guv.'

'How're you managing on the stakeout?'

'Fair enough. I'm sure we'll get him,' she said confidently. He envied her.

The stakeouts for the Phantom Flannelfoot were being maintained at a cost in overtime that could eventually be justified only by Flannelfoot being caught. Sarah and Greg were still paired. In the hothouse of hours spent in the confines of a small car their relationship had deteriorated to the sort of condition that normally would take years of married resentment to achieve.

The trouble was that at Westcliff and in their other moments together Sarah had been overwhelmed by physical pleasure that totally switched off her critical faculties. She could only feel, not think. Now, with long hours with nothing to do but think, Sarah's suspicions that there was little real substance to Greg were becoming set in concrete. At a more basic level, spasms of cramp, a numb bum and the need to pee in the inadequate cover of a tree aggravated Sarah's peevishness.

Still, most abrasive marriages at least begin with love and hope; and when the relationship becomes overcast there are still a few sunny intervals. Sarah glanced at Greg. He noticed nothing: he was staring straight ahead, a sulky expression on his face. She had to admit to herself that he was good-looking, and he had his moments of indisputable charm. Most of all, he was very good in bed. At the thought, not for the first time she felt the warmth of desire spreading in her loins. She knew only too well how Greg felt: she was a sensual being herself. Maybe she was being too demanding, she told herself. Greg wasn't too bad, albeit childish sometimes, but most men are and no one's perfect. She was halfway to making up with Greg when he spoke, shattering the fragile moment.

'I've applied for another job,' he said.

'What?'

'Security guard in the head office of a bank.'

'What on earth for?'

'More money – much more money, eight thirty to five thirty, five days a week, no nights, longer holidays and better chances of promotion . . . That enough for starters?'

'But wouldn't it be deadly dull?'

'D'you call this sort of surveillance lively?'

'Don't you like being a policeman?'

'You must be joking.'

'At least it's a useful job, helping people.'

'Big deal.'

Sarah's mouth tightened into a thin line.

A car passed. Sarah noted down the number. Any car that passed two or three times, particularly if it was going slowly, would be suspect. She had a whole list of numbers, but they mainly belonged to residents of The Meadows.

Greg made a muffled sound. Sarah looked at him: his eyes were shut and his mouth slightly open. She dug him viciously in the ribs with her elbow. 'We're supposed to be keeping a lookout for anyone acting suspiciously near the house. So stay awake,' she hissed spitefully.

* * *

142

Considering the amount of material that the four teams had amassed in their enquiries, it was astonishing that there was little or nothing of value in it. A review of the house-to-house enquiries, interviews with friends, relations, business associates, former women friends and their husbands, shopkeepers and known enemies (if any) of the victims produced zero, zilch, *nada, rien, niente* or *nicht*. Or as Ted Greening put it, fuck-all. There was no visible link between any of the victims and their associates. As the officers ploughing through the reports and statements failed to unearth a suspicion of a clue, Harry Timberlake became increasingly depressed. A dozen times he turned over in his mind the hypothesis that the crimes were connected. It seemed logical enough and he still believed in it; but for the millionth time the facts didn't match the theory, like the case of the humming bird: the experts said that it was aero-dynamically impossible for the bird to fly; the bird hadn't heard of the theory and buzzed around busily far more expertly than any other feathered flyer. Harry wasn't sure what disheartened him the more: the fact that a killer (he refused to admit it was killers) was getting away with it, or that his career looked like taking a whack from which it would take years to recover, if at all. He saw Jenny a couple of times, briefly, but she couldn't jolt him out of his despondency. She was wise enough not to try using sex to take his mind off his problems; another failure, which was likely in the circumstances, would have only added to them and taken him a long time to get over.

Harkness was as disappointed as Harry with the lack of prog-ress with the cases, but showed he hadn't lost faith in the idea by saying, 'The next thing is for everyone to go back to their major witnesses and put a list of names to them: the victims and those close to them. See if any of the names strike a chord.'

Harry decided to start with Mrs Foulds. Whether this was because he wanted to see her again, or he wanted to get the hardest interview over first he couldn't be sure. When he went to see her – another 7 p.m. appointment – she appeared to be in an ambivalent frame of mind herself. At their first meeting, his reluctance to respond to her advances stimulated her. Now he had asked to see her again on what she took to be a flimsy excuse, she was cool and withdrawn. She didn't normally give men a second chance. However, without exactly being a bit of rough, Harry Timberlake was very different from nearly all the men of her circle. He was clearly physically tough and not easily disconcerted. And, of course, he was in a dirty, sleazy and sometimes dangerous profession. In short, he was a turn-on. Maybe she'd allow him a second chance after all.

'Will you tell me if any of these names means anything to you?' he asked. He slowly went through the list, beginning with the other victims, Titus Lloyd, Reginald Barclay and Geoffrey Robson, and going on to the people close to them. Mrs Foulds replied to each with a 'No'. When Harry had finished reading out the names she said gaily, 'I'm sorry. I don't think I've said "no" so many times before. It's not one of my favourite words.' She turned on the full force of the disturbing gaze of her violet eyes. Harry remained impassive.

'Are you sure you haven't heard any of the names before? Please think for a moment.'

There was no other word for it : she pouted. 'I've told you: I don't know any of them.' She hesitated. 'Except . . .'

'Yes?'

'Titus. I've heard that one before.'

'In what context?' Harry asked eagerly.

'Andronicus. *Titus Andronicus*: the play. You know. And there was that conspirator. Titus Oates.'

'Yes.' Harry Timberlake's disappointment showed on his face.

'I'm sorry I can't help you with the enquiry,' Lucia Foulds said. 'Let me get you a drink. I have the very thing to raise your spirits.'

'No thank you.'

'Oh, come on. You need to keep your pecker up.'

Harry was very formal. 'You're very kind, Mrs Foulds, but no. If you'll forgive me, I have other people to see.' He started to leave, but she rose from her place on the enormous settee and moved between him and the door without obviously making a deliberate gesture of it.

'One drink won't jeopardise your professional integrity. All work, and no play . . . Relax, Inspector.'

She smiled. She was standing quite close to him. Her perfume was heady and insistent; but more than that she had a powerful, indescribable aura of sexuality.

Oh, hell, Harry said to himself. Why not? They moved almost imperceptibly closer together. Then Harry noticed something. Lucia Foulds's smile had more than invitation and pleasure in it; there was a hint of triumph in it. Perhaps it was because she had scored a victory in her plan to seduce him. Less likely but still possible, it could be because she had something to hide and she felt that having him as a lover would affect his professional judgement, or at least give her a lever to put pressure on him. He was too much of a policeman to take the risk.

'Sorry, Mrs Foulds,' he said, and moved round her.

As the front door closed behind him, Lucia Foulds said distinctly, 'Shit.' She went over to a mirror and studied her face intently. What she saw apparently satisfied her; she smiled and gave a small shrug.

Driving away from the Foulds home Harry clashed the gears of his car, twice.

Interviews the next day with the other witnesses he had seen at the beginning of the enquiry – *Odd we call them witnesses when they haven't seen or heard anything*, Harry thought – were equally unhelpful. Major Broadbent, Secretary of the Double-V Club, scarcely remembered Harry Timberlake. Harry called on him late in the day, which was a mistake, because the gallant Major was at his best in the mornings when he was still partially sober. When Harry asked Broadbent if he recognised the names of any of the victims and witnesses on his list Broadbent confusedly thought Harry was asking him if they were members of the club. It took some time to unravel that particular tangle. The result was, as Harry expected, a big fat nothing.

Terry Luckwell, the sometime actor, remembered Harry all right: he nearly had kittens when he saw him standing on the doorstep. This time there was no woman hiding in the bedroom of the Rancliffe Gardens basement flat, but it smelled of powerful perfume and sweat. Luckwell was keen to co-operate, just to get Harry out of his hair, but he had nothing to contribute to the enquiry.

Harry interviewed Wayne Dysart, the lover – or maybe he was the ex-lover by now – of Mrs Barclay at the Stratford betting shop. Jocko and Miss Stoneface positively vibrated with curiosity as Harry retired into the rear office with Dysart and closed the door behind them. Jocko fabricated an excuse to enter the office

145

abruptly with an 'urgent' query, but he was disappointed. Harry and Dysart weren't saying anything; Dysart was reading the list of names. Jocko retired frustrated and baffled. Dysart had nothing to offer.

Mrs Dysart had not warmed to Harry Timberlake since their first meeting. Grudgingly she agreed to listen to Harry's list of names, but she hadn't heard of any of them. Harry now had to tread on eggshells placed on ice.

'When I was here before you mentioned a woman named Sandra,' he began. The effect was rather like applying a lighted match to the blue touch-paper. Mrs Dysart began to fizz and Harry stood clear. She erupted for a few moments, and then calmed down a little.

'Well?' she asked in a voice like a knife-edge being dragged across a plate.

'I wonder if you know her full name and address?'

'You bet I bloody know it, the scraggy bitch.' That was the second time Mrs Dysart had called her that. She had an obsession about weight.

'You've actually met her, have you?' asked Harry.

'Right. I took half my husband's washing and mending round to her place and dumped it on her. I told her, "You want half my husband, you can have half the work that goes with him." '

Harry couldn't help himself. 'How did she take it?'

'I didn't wait to find out. Next time my husband asked for a clean shirt, I told him where he could go and get it.' The way she pronounced the word 'husband' made Harry feel in need of anti-venom serum. 'Well, d'you want the scraggy bitch's address or don't you?' Harry wrote it in his pocketbook.

He could have asked Wayne Dysart for his mistress's name and address, but if either of them had anything to hide – which Harry thought unlikely, but even the most unlikely possibilities had to be followed up – he didn't want Dysart phoning Sandra to warn her he was coming.

Harry was curious to see Sandra Beckwith, 'the scraggy bitch'. As he drove to her address on the Balham–Clapham border, he tried to visualise the sort of woman who could settle for being one of the mistresses of the unlikeable and married Wayne Dysart, and what her home was like. He found she lived in a street of small terraced houses which were definitely moving up-market, if the

146

expensive cars parked in the street and the burglar alarm boxes on the house fronts were anything to go by.

The woman who opened the door was tall, nearly as tall as Harry himself. If anything she was on the skinny side of slender, but he wouldn't have called her scraggy. She had large, dark eyes, a very pale skin and long, straight hair hanging down her back. Harry was irresistibly reminded of one of Charles Addams's sinister cartoon characters, although there was nothing disquieting about the woman. She wore tight black trousers and a black jumper which made it clear that she wasn't wearing a bra. She had no great need of one.

'Ms Sandra Beckwith?' Harry asked politely, slurring over the 'Ms' so as not to commit himself. He held up his warrant card and announced his name. Sandra Beckwith took it from his hand and peered at it from close range.

'May I come in?'

'What's it about?'

'A routine enquiry. I think it'd be better if we went inside.' Sandra Beckwith hesitated, and Harry caught a faint, familiar smell from inside the house. 'I'm not from the Drugs Squad,' he said. The use of marijuana was the one subject on which he did not have a completely black-and-white, according-to-the-book attitude. He took a relaxed view of marijuana even though it was officially illegal. Why, he didn't know. Perhaps it was something to do with the fact that he'd never had any problems of violence with marijuana users, but users of alcohol had cost him a number of scars and bruises. Marijuana's problems were rarely with its users, but with its pushers. For all that, Harry himself couldn't understand his tolerant attitude towards that particular drug – and that one alone – and the people who indulged in it. He talked about it to Jenny one night without coming to any conclusion. Finally he just shrugged and said, 'Well, no man is all of a piece,' and left it at that.

Sandra studied him carefully for a moment before turning round and going into the house, leaving the door open for him. He followed her into a room where the smell of the drug was almost strong enough to put in a bottle. She turned on an extractor fan.

Nearly all the wall space was taken up by bookshelves. One section contained encyclopaedias and reference books; the remainder

147

were full of mainly paperbacks. Other books and magazines were strewn on tables and chairs. Harry glanced at some of them. They were a weird collection of saccharine romantic novels, true crime stories and garish detective stories. In the corner of the room was a word processor.

'You're a writer?' Harry asked.

'Now I know you're a detective,' Sandra Beckwith said ironically, with the faintest of slurs in her speech. 'Would you like a joint?' she asked.

'Don't push it,' Harry warned.

She collapsed into rather than sat down on a battered armchair, her long limbs sprawling anyhow like a set of knitting needles that had been thrown down carelessly. She pulled up her jumper in a totally non-sexual way and idly scratched her midriff before pulling it down again. Harry judged that she wasn't stoned enough to be confused, but enough to be a little unguarded in her answers to his questions.

'Yes, I'm a writer. Romances for middle-aged housewives, famous crimes and cops-and-robbers for the semi-illiterate. You name it, I'll write it.'

'Pornography?' he asked, without knowing why.

'When I'm shoved, if you'll excuse the expression. There's less call for it now, with all the videos of close-up boffing available. Trouble is, they're counter-productive.'

Harry was interested. 'How do you mean?'

'All the women in them have tits like watermelons and the men have great donkey-sized dongs. It makes the real thing with ordinary people a terrible anticlimax, or a come-down, in a manner of speaking. You can forget pornography. And if you're from the Obscene Publications Squad, you're wasting your time. There's nothing like that here. That's not my bag. Romances about good girls who don't lose it until their wedding night, that's my speciality: they're the ones that pay best.'

'Really.'

'Look at Barbara Cartland. Or not, according to taste. Now, to what do I owe the honour of this visit?'

'I believe you know a Mr Wayne Dysart?'

'I know *the* Wayne Dysart. There can't be more than one like that. When they made Wayne Dysart they broke the mould, thank Christ. Pity they didn't do it before they made him. So what's he done? Who's he killed?' Harry looked startled for a moment, but stoned or not, Sandra Beckwith noticed. 'I was only joking, Inspector whatever-your-name-is. Christ, he wouldn't swat a fly if he thought it was big enough to bite back. The man's a schmuck. A shitty schmuck,' she elaborated.

'I thought you were friends,' Harry said.

'Some hopes! He only wants one thing from me, and I only want one thing from him. It's a convenient arrangement: sex without commitment or phoney sentimentality. He's a schlemiel, but he serves. Quite well, actually.' She smiled wolfishly. 'You shocked, Inspector?'

'I'm a policeman,' he replied. Without going into too much detail he explained that in the course of his enquiries he was looking for a possible connection between a number of crimes.

'What has Wayne got to do with it?'

'He's friendly with a person closely involved with one of the crimes, and you're friendly with Mr Dysart. It's possible that you may see a connection that links those crimes.'

'Friendly's hardly the word, but let that pass. What crimes, for Chrissake? Not having a TV licence? Riding a bicycle without lights?'

'I'm afraid I can't tell you that at this stage. Will you have a look at this list of names and see if any of them mean anything to you, or you know any of them?'

Sandra Beckwith scrabbled around in a pile of magazines and found a pair of spectacles with extra-large lenses. When she put them on she looked like an Australian bush baby. He realised that her unfocused look was due to short sight and not what she was smoking. She took the list from Harry and read it carefully. She handed it back. 'Sorry.'

'You're sure?'

'Sure.'

'Thank you. I'm sorry to have troubled you.'

'No trouble.' Unexpectedly she asked 'You married, Harry?' She'd been alert enough to remember the name on his warrant card after all.

Surprised, he answered, 'No.'

'Pity. I only have affairs with married men. They're a lot less trouble. If they get to be a bore and won't go away, you can always threaten to tell the little woman.'

'But Mrs Dysart knows about you already.'

'That's why I've elbowed him. He's definitely ex now. Next thing he would've wanted to move in with me. God! Can you imagine it?'

Harry couldn't.

As he left, Sandra Beckwith said, 'Hey, Harry, if you ever get married, look me up.'

There was no answer to that.

When Harry Timberlake returned to Terrace Vale nick the first thing he did was to ask if any of the other detectives working on the case had come up with anything that suggested a connection between the murders. The look on Ted Greening's face told him everything before he spoke a word. 'Nothing so far, but it's early days. Cheer up,' Greening said hypocritically. Apart from anything else, it wasn't early days any more. They were running out of witnesses to see. Harry had only one more, Mrs Barclay.

He wasn't looking forward to calling on her. First of all, he was concerned about how she was coping with the loss of her husband. She was composed enough when he first saw her, but there could well have been a delayed reaction, and he didn't want to have to revive any hurt by asking questions about her husband. She had also broken up with Wayne Dysart, although whether this would accelerate or slow down her recovery he wouldn't care to speculate. More selfishly he was concerned for himself. She was his last chance to find the elusive link which would tie all the cases together. He didn't want to admit to himself that the reason the connection was elusive was because it didn't exist. He dared not think about the implications of that.

Mrs Barclay was managing well enough. She had lost some weight and looked pale, but her voice was steady and she showed no inclination towards self-pity.

When Harry explained the purpose of his visit, she was eager to co-operate. He read out the list of names to her.

'Stop!' she said when he mentioned Geoff Robson.

'You've heard the name Geoff Robson before?' Harry said excitedly.

'No, not him. The one before that.'

'Titus Lloyd?'

'That's it! I'm sure someone mentioned the name to me.'

'When did you hear it? What was the connection?'

She thought hard. 'I . . . I'm sorry; I can't remember. But I know the name Titus rings a bell . . .' She held her forehead in concentration. 'I think it was . . . Yes, it was my husband who mentioned the name . . .'

'Are you sure it was Titus Lloyd? You couldn't be mixing him up in your mind with Titus Oates? Practically everyone else I've spoken to mentioned him.'

'No. It was Reg, and he definitely spoke about Titus Oates— I mean Lloyd. I can't help thinking it was something quite important.'

Harry tried to suppress any feeling of excitement. Her slip of the tongue in saying Oates instead of Lloyd – if it was a slip of the tongue – meant it was all still very iffy. His voice was unemotional when he asked her, 'Will you try to recall the conversation? What it was about; you don't have to try to remember the exact words.'

After some thought she said, 'I'm sorry; it's gone.' She gave a wan smile, and sounded sad for the first time during the interview. 'I'm afraid I'm rather forgetful these days.'

'Don't worry about it,' Harry said encouragingly. 'If you don't think about it, it'll come back to you on its own. And when it does, give me a ring.' He fished out an official card with his number at the Terrace Vale nick, and scribbled his home number on it. 'At any time,' he said encouragingly.

As he left the house Harry was already silently praying that she'd remember and give them a breakthrough.

He wished he'd had more recent practice in praying.

Chapter 8

There was something odd about the noise of the engine as the van entered the driveway beside the house. She had heard the van arrive there a hundred times but this time there was something different. She went to the side window, pulled back the net curtain a couple of inches and looked out. The van was reversing into the driveway instead of coming straight in. Although the woman didn't know it, the man wasn't all that good a driver and he was taking great care over backing in.

The man got out of the van, went to the back and took out two plastic shopping bags. One was from a supermarket, the other from a garden centre. The woman was puzzled. She normally did all the shopping, and they had no garden, only a small, flagged courtyard at the back.

The man took the two bags straight up to his private workshop. He offered no explanation of what was in the bags, and the woman asked no questions. Even if the man had told her what was in them it would have meant nothing to her.

One contained sugar, the other fertiliser.

Uncertainty was growing among some of the officers at Terrace Vale nick. Harry Timberlake had begun by convincing himself that his theory of the four connected crimes and a single murderer had a solid foundation. Now, the edifice he had constructed seemed to have the stability of a house of cards, and the wind was rising. The small hope that Tina Barclay had given him was a very fragile prop.

Superintendent Harkness outwardly had the self-confidence and certainty of being in the right that equalled Margaret Thatcher's assurance about everything, and with greater cause; but privately he was feeling misgivings over the way things were going. He was asking himself whether the support he had given to Harry Timberlake was for operational reasons – because he believed in the force of Timberlake's hypothesis; or for personal reasons – because he admired the younger man and would like to have him in his AMIP team.

Sarah Lewis's doubts had steadily increased as uneventful nights of surveillance on the Phantom Flannelfoot operation had dragged past, and the presence of Greg Davidson in the car with her only aggravated her disquiet. They had got to the stage of having almost nothing to say to each other; their mutual resentment was almost palpable. It wasn't exactly armed conflict, but it was definitely sub-zero cold war between them. It was driving Sarah's morale right into the ground.

Greg had suggested that they ask to be given new partners, which struck Sarah as a good idea at first, before she realised that if they asked for a transfer it would give rise to all sorts of nudge-nudge, wink-wink suggestions at Terrace Vale. There was only one other experienced WPC on this operation, Cynthia Fenwick. She was marvellous at calming frightened children and comforting distraught women, but she weighed twelve stones and had all the sex appeal of Nora Batty on washing day. If she and her partner wanted to split up no one would give it a second thought. On the other hand, Sarah definitely deserved her nickname the Welsh Rarebit, and if she and her partner wanted to part company there would be rumours of everything from attempted rape – either way – to non-stop copulation. Sarah and Greg were definitely stuck with each other.

At three o'clock in the morning, with his brain even more sluggish than usual, Greg thoughtlessly said, 'God, I'm bored. Flannelfoot's not going to turn up. It's all a total waste of time. The whole thing's a stupid idea,' he added.

Sarah turned on him with suppressed fury. Her Welsh accent was thick enough to win a prize at an eisteddfod. 'You *want* it to fail, don't you! You bloody want it to fail!'

Greg remembered too late whose idea it was. 'I'm sorry, I didn't mean—' he began, but Sarah didn't let him finish.

'You can't bear the thought that I might be better than you at something! Just because you're bloody apathetic and a bloody bad policeman without any ambition, you want *me* to fail!'

It was Greg's turn to become angry. 'The only bloody reason you're so keen is to impress Inspector bloody Flash Harry Timberlake because you fancy him. Anybody can see it with half an eye.'

They were both shocked into silence: Greg because he had surprised himself with what he had said; Sarah because she suddenly wondered whether the part about fancying Harry was true without her having realised it. Once again Greg pressed his self-destruct button. 'And he fancies you all right. Have you had it off with him yet?'

Sarah was on the point of making a debating point by whacking Greg in the chops when a car came to a silent stop beside them. 'Everything okay?' Harry Timberlake asked quietly through the passenger window of his car.

'Fine, guv,' Sarah said in a slightly strangled voice that made Harry ask, 'You sure?'

'Absolutely.' Beside her Greg nodded vigorously.

'Well, good luck,' Harry said and moved off.

After a long, icy pause Greg said, 'Sorry. You know.'

Sarah made an indeterminate noise that might have been an acceptance of his grudging apology, or it might not. Her mind was very much on Harry Timberlake and what Greg had said.

It really was too easy. At first the man had been doubtful that Ernie Birt would fall for such an elementary trick. As he considered the problem, though, he concluded that there was no reason why Birt should be at all suspicious: he was going to make a perfectly normal request. Besides, he knew he looked harmless. After all, he'd managed to con Howard Foulds into letting him into his house by saying he'd important information to give him about the case in which he was defending. Had the man known more about Ernie Birt, he would have realised that he had a big psychological advantage on his side: Birt's vanity, his preoccupation with Me, Me, Me.

Normally the man never allowed his victims to see him before the moment when he killed them, but he didn't think Birt would recognise him. He was older, and he had grown a moustache since Birt gave him the motive.

Although the magazine and newspaper photographs had given him a good idea of the interior of Birt's houseboat, there may have been changes since they were taken, and there were other details he needed to know. He had to call on him.

The man walked slowly along the gangplank, keeping his eyes open. He was particularly interested to see how the door to the cabin was secured.

He knocked on the door. Ernie Birt opened it. He was dressed with planned casualness, and sported a couple of days' designer stubble, although this scruffy habit had long since gone out of fashion. Clearly unimpressed by his visitor, Birt grumpily said, 'Yes?'

'Do forgive me for interrupting you,' the man said deferentially. He always spoke deferentially, when he said anything at all. 'I'm a great admirer of your work, and I wondered if you had an autographed photograph you could give me.' As Birt's jaw dropped a little, the man added, 'I'd be glad to pay for it, of course.'

Very, very few people ask television comedy writers, even Personalities, for an autograph, except at events like charity football matches and book signings. For someone to ask for a photograph – a signed photograph – was unheard of. Ernie Birt's ego found this irresistible.

'Pay for it? There's no call for that, lad,' he said, going all jocular. 'You'd better come in.'

He led the way into the main room, or cabin, which was surprisingly spacious. It appeared that Birt had made no changes in the furnishings since the last two illustrated magazine articles had been published. He was too busy going to a filing cabinet for a photograph to notice how keenly the man was inspecting the room. Almost immediately the man saw what he was looking for, and his spirits rose.

Ernie Birt kept his body between the open cabinet drawer and the man so that he wouldn't see a small stack of 10 x 8 photographs. He'd had them produced to give to fans who asked for them, but this was his first request.

'Ah, I thought so,' he said. 'I knew I had one somewhere. Don't really go in for that sort of thing myself, but my agent made me get my picture took to give to the Yanks.'

'Are you sure you can spare it?' the man asked.

'I'll manage,' Birt said, with what passed for a smile. He went to his desk, pick up a felt-tipped pen and prepared to write. 'What's your name?'

'Joseph.'

Birt scrawled, With best wishes to Joseph, Sincerely, and added a flowing signature that was a dead giveaway to his character.

The man accepted it with well-judged gratitude, and half-backed away to the door as if taking leave of minor royalty. Ernie was not anxious to see such a devoted fan leave so quickly. He wanted his ego massaged a little more while the going was good.

'Which one of my shows did you reckon was the best?' he asked with transparently thin casualness.

'I really couldn't say.' The man hadn't seen any of them; but he was quick-witted. 'Which one of Charlie Chaplin's films was the best?' he asked, fearing that he'd overdone it.

'Happen you're right,' Ernie replied, remembering a little late to sound northern. The man escaped, leaving a trail of thanks behind him.

As he walked along Royalty Embankment to where he had parked his van, the man contemplated throwing the photograph into the Thames. He changed his mind, and began to chuckle. He hardly ever chuckled, and it was a bizarre sound. It would be amusing to put the photograph of his latest victim with the hand-written 'sincerely' dedication on his wall with those of his other victims. He chuckled again.

For the first time in a long while Harry Timberlake was at peace with the world. He was sitting up in bed with his arm round Jenny Long, whose body smelt deliciously of Badedas bath essence and her mouth of his favourite wine.

'The advertisement got it wrong,' he said.

'What?'

' "Things happen after a Badedas bath." They happened before.'

'No reason why they shouldn't happen after, as well,' she said.

'In a minute. I've still got half a glass of wine.'

'Oh, God,' Jenny groaned. 'That puts me in my place: I come second to half a glass of wine.'

'Well, it is Moulin à Vent,' Harry said, keeping a straight face.

'Pig.'

'I've been called that before.'

'Not, I hope, in bed with a naked woman.'

Harry pretended to think hard. 'No, I don't think so.' She jabbed him hard in the ribs. He gasped. 'Christ, you've got sharp elbows for a nicely rounded female.'

They continued to chat in an inconsequential fashion, with an intimacy that was companionable as well as sexual. Yet the intimacy was mainly on the surface. For all their closeness, they were not as they were before with each other. There was a faint but unmistakable undertone of disharmony now; something was missing, or perhaps something new had intruded into their relationship, causing a barely perceptible sense of unease or reticence.

'It's been a long time since we were together like this,' she said after a while.

'Yes. I'm sorry. It's been this blasted Foulds case. And the others.

'What others?' she asked, and he explained.

'You should ease off. You're working too hard,' Jenny said later. 'And that's a professional opinion.'

'It goes with the territory. What do you do if there's an emergency and half a dozen people come in with serious injuries? Do you say you're working too hard and ease off, or get on with it?'

'It's not the same. I don't mean to sound pompous, but I am trying to save lives.'

'So am I. There's a murderer who's killed four people walking around somewhere, and for all I know he's planning to kill some more. Anyway, it's my job.'

'Mine's not much better,' she admitted ruefully. She paused again. Something was on her mind. 'Harry . . . darling . . . What are we going to do?'

'About what?' But he knew what she meant.

'It's not very satisfactory, is it? Meeting at odd times at short notice when our jobs let us. We hardly get a chance to talk, or to go out with each other. You might just as well be married to someone else for all the life we have together. Sure, we go to bed and it's marvellous, but there should be more to it than that. The trouble is that we have no real commitment to each other.'

'I love you,' he said, as if that alone was a commitment.

'And I love you,' she replied. 'You're marvellous to me,

157

thoughtful and kind and loving.' The unsaid 'But . . .' hung heavily in the air.

Not long ago he had asked Jenny to marry him and was disappointed when she hadn't heard him. But now . . . He didn't understand why he simply couldn't bring himself to say, 'Darling, move in. Let's live together.'

'You're right,' he said eventually. 'We have to sort this out.'

Jenny managed to smile. 'Yes, sure,' she said. Well, if Harry wouldn't suggest that she move in, she would have to do it herself. She decided to cheat a little, if it could be called cheating. She caressed him, and when he began to respond she said, 'Harry, why don't we—'

The phone rang.

Jenny swore silently.

Harry picked up the phone. 'Hello?'

'Inspector Timberlake? This is Tina Barclay. I know it's late, but you said to call you at any time.'

'It's perfectly all right, Mrs Barclay.'

'You see, I've just remembered what my husband said about Titus Lloyd.'

'Titus Lloyd was the foreman of a jury when Reg Barclay was one of the jurors at the Old Bailey,' Harry Timberlake said to Superintendent Harkness with a considerable degree of satisfaction. 'His wife rang me last night to tell me. I knew there was a connection.'

'Don't go galloping away like that. Only two of the victims are linked.'

'Yes, sir. But I'm sure we'll find other connections now.'

'Hmmm. Did she recall whose trial it was?'

'No. As you know, the usual practice at the Bailey is for juries to stay together during their service and do more than one trial. All she could remember was that one of the trials was a big one – manslaughter, or murder.'

'When?'

'About seven or eight years ago.'

'I'm not too sure what sort of records they keep at the Bailey, but they should be able to trace Lloyd and Barclay. When we know what trials they were on, we'll see what other leads that gives us. If any.'

Sarah Lewis was aware that her attitude towards Greg Davidson was beginning to change again. It was not in her nature to harbour grudges for a long time: she was not a brooder. Now, instead of actively resenting him, to her own considerable surprise she was developing a sort of indifference towards him; she was just tolerating him. The trouble was that her original assessment of him was right: his good looks and sometime charm disguised – at least for a while – that there was no great substance to him. It was true there had been times when they were in each other's arms that she could not recall any of the other men she had made love with. This was not because there had been so many that they became confused in her memory – on the contrary. It was as if her sexual life had begun only with Greg, and she had to admit to herself that he had excited her as nobody else had done. He was good. She gave him a surreptitious look as he sat beside her in the car. She silently sighed; it was a pity.

Greg was continuing to act as Sarah's partner in the belief that if they were together long enough their relationship would return to what it was. He enjoyed sex with her. For him, too, Westcliff had been something special. The difference between Greg and Sarah was that he didn't need anything more to their relationship than satisfactory sex, and he didn't realise that she wanted more. Greg managed to be both thick and shallow at the same time.

Sarah stirred in her seat and cleared her throat. 'Greg?'

'Yeah?' He waited expectantly for the first words of a reconciliation.

'What about you noting down some car numbers for a change?'

'Okay.' He took the pad from her. He sat up. 'I thought you said the people at The Cedars were away.'

'They are.'

'A light's just gone on upstairs. You can see it through that gap between the curtains. Either they're back or someone's got into the house.'

Sarah glanced at her watch. 'That's the time switch that turns the lights on and off. D'you mean you haven't noticed it before?'

The darkness hid Greg's embarrassment. 'Of course I have. I just didn't realise what time it was,' he said lamely. He continued writing down numbers for a while.

Shortly after the light went out again in The Cedars, Greg sat

159

up excitedly. He nudged Sarah. 'Hey, look at him, over there.'

A man in dark clothes was giving a perfect display of 'acting in a suspicious manner'. He was walking slowly along the pavement with an exaggerated nonchalance that was totally unconvincing, and looking round to see if he was observed. Sarah's blood raced. 'Get right down,' she said urgently, and they both slid down further in their seats.

The man drew level with the entrance to The Cedars, looked down the driveway towards the house, and walked on. He gave another look over his shoulder, wheeled round, and darted into the driveway and out of sight.

'Come on!' Greg said. 'It's Flannelfoot. Let's get him!'

'Hang on!' Sarah said sharply. 'Wait till he comes out with the stuff and then we'll nick him.'

Greg opened the passenger door of the car. 'He might get away through the back entrance. Let's have him while we can.'

'No! The back entrance leads out on to this road—' Sarah began, but Greg was already out of the car. She made a grab for his arm, too late. Silently cursing, she got out of the car herself, snatching up a flashlight. Although Greg had a flying start on her, he had to go round the car, while she was on the side nearer the house. She was only a couple of paces behind him as he ran across the road. At least he had the nous not to make a noise.

They ran into the driveway. A few yards inside she stopped and said in a normal voice, 'Greg.'

He turned. The suspect was standing next to the row of bushes between the house and the pavement. He was peeing.

When he saw two police officers approaching him, the man tried to stop, but he couldn't. 'I'm sorry, I couldn't wait,' he said apologetically. He continued to spray the privet. Anxiously he put away his penis a little too soon and made a dark dribble down his trouser leg.

'I had to go,' he said.

Sarah and Greg, who had relieved themselves a number of times in the inadequate shelter of a roadside tree during their surveillance, were not ready to cast the first stone.

As a matter of form they made him turn out his pockets. He had a couple of keys on him, both Yale, but nothing to fit the security locks on the front door and back doors of the house.

'I just couldn't wait,' the man repeated plaintively.

'Oh, go on, piss off,' Greg said. It wasn't the happiest of remarks.

Back in the car Sarah breathed heavily and stared fixedly straight ahead as if she was trying to shatter the windscreen by psychokinesis.

'Sorry. I—' Greg began. Sarah chopped him off short with words like a butcher's cleaver.

'Don't say anything! Don't say a bloody word!'

'Eh? I only—'

'You brainless, stupid . . .' She paused as she ran a whole string of swearwords through her mind, trying to decide on the worst one to call him. 'If bloody Flannelfoot's about somewhere, if he's been keeping the bloody house under observation himself, you've bloody scared him off. You've bloody blown it, you . . . you . . .' Her accent was thick again, and her anger was increased by her inability to be less repetitive and more articulate. 'Now just *shut up*!'

'I'm sorry. I just thought—'

'You didn't bloody think at all! If you don't want this torch shoved down your bloody throat, don't say another single fucking word!'

She'd said That Word again. And felt much better for it. Greg lapsed into sulky, shamefaced silence.

The man finished the last of the rice pudding and put his spoon down carefully on the plate. 'Very nice,' he said. The woman said mechanically, 'It was always one of your favourites.'

He looked at his electronic watch. He had two minutes left.

He got up from the table and went up the stairs to his workroom. He unlocked the door and entered. He went straight to his latest piece of work on the bench, the device to set off the detonator of the bomb to kill Ernie Birt. It was of simple design: the man had gone for simplicity because the simpler it was, the less chance there was of anything going wrong. It was just an added precaution; he didn't make mistakes.

The apparatus consisted of a spring-operated hammer with a firing pin, held in the cocked position by a small iron bolt. This bolt was the operating plunger of a solenoid, an electromagnetic coil. It was connected to a small nine-volt battery and an electronic calculator which included a clock, alarm and other

161

functions the man didn't need. Directly beneath the hammer with its firing pin was a used shotgun cartridge, embedded in a heavy-duty container constructed of the steel he used to make boilers for working steam engines. Inside the container was the home-made explosive. The man knew that the more tightly the explosive was packed and contained, the more powerful the blast would be.

He looked at his watch again, and compared it with the clock on the detonating mechanism.

Twenty seconds.

It was a handsome piece of work, well up to the man's superlative standards of construction. Briefly he felt depressed to think that in performing its function the device would be destroyed in the massive explosion; then he consoled himself with the thought of what that explosion would achieve.

Five seconds . . . four . . . three . . . two . . . one . . .

With the speed of light the alarm switched on the battery. The iron bolt was instantaneously drawn into the coil, releasing the spring-loaded hammer. It smashed down on to the shotgun cartridge.

The man nodded with satisfaction. This was the third test he had given the mechanism, setting it for longer periods each time. The next time it operated it would be with a live shotgun cartridge and real explosive, not a dummy package. He would have preferred an all-electronic detonator to set off the explosive, but for that he would have needed a special commercial detonator. Wryly he reflected that only terrorists had the expertise to acquire them illegally.

He picked up the device and carefully locked it away in a cupboard. It was an unnecessary precaution: he always locked the door of the room anyway. But the man didn't take chances, and didn't make mistakes. He went over to the wallboard where the photographs and newspaper cuttings were displayed. Ernie Birt smirked back at him obliviously from the signed photograph. The man studied a magazine picture of the cabin of Birt's houseboat, although he had no need to. It was exactly as he remembered it. He knew exactly where he was going to place the bomb for maximum effect.

He began to whistle.

* * *

162

Harry parked his Citroën in Terrace Vale yard and entered the station by the back door. Sergeant Ramsden, at his usual place near the counter, heard the door open and turned. 'Morning, Harry,' he said. 'Something's up.'

'What sort of something? Good or bad?' Harry asked.

'Heavy. Harkness got here early, called in the other AMIP superintendents from Southington and Wallsend, with about half their teams. They got here about an hour ago, stayed for half an hour and then pushed off again. Harkness has been trying to get hold of you. Where were you?'

'Enquiries,' Harry said laconically, giving the old and tried, classic response. 'Jogging on the common, as a matter of fact.'

'Well, you'd better get up there in case he wants you to take over command.'

'Ho. Ho. Ho,' said Harry, ponderously, but his pulse had quickened.

'Ah, there you are, Timberlake,' Harkness said as he entered the room. 'Come in, sit down.' Superintendent Ward was with him. Two of the AMIP detective inspectors were also in the room, but they said nothing all the time Harry Timberlake was there. They stared at him with a marked lack of friendliness when Harkness wasn't looking at them. On the surface Harkness was as impassive as ever, but Timberlake sensed an undercurrent of excitement in the older man. 'HOLMES and Records have come up with some information about Titus Lloyd, Reginald Barclay and DC Robson.' HOLMES was the acronym of the Scotland Yard computer known as Home Office Large Major Enquiries System.

'And Foulds?' Harry asked.

'That's a bit of a facer,' Ward said genially. 'He don't fit. At least, not altogether. Do, and don't.'

'Do you remember the Roy Pocock case?'

'Vaguely,' Harry said. 'It was a long time ago—'

'Ten years,' Harkness interjected.

'But there were some repercussions not all that long ago, weren't there, sir?'

'Yes.' Harkness briefly outlined the case. Ten years previously Roy Pocock, a small-time criminal of limited intelligence with a long record, was convicted of murder in the course of armed robbery, and was sentenced to life with a minimum recommendation

163

of eighteen years. Pocock vehemently protested his innocence, despite having made a confession. He admitted that he'd made the statement, but said he was 'confused and tired', and confessed just for peace and quiet. There was a short-lived 'Roy Pocock is innocent' campaign that came to nothing. He died in prison five years later.

'I remember something else about the case,' Ward rumbled. 'There was talk of attempted jury nobbling. Some of the jurors complained they was followed home when they left the court at night. Got some funny phone calls.'

Harkness nodded. 'You're right, and it could be significant.' He went on with his explanation, largely for Harry Timberlake's benefit. 'Two years ago another criminal, Cliff Soames, confessed to the murder for which Pocock was convicted. Pocock, whom Soames resembled, was not on the robbery, Soames said.

'Titus Lloyd was the foreman of the jury that convicted Pocock.

'Reg Barclay was a member of that jury.

'Geoff Robson, then a uniformed officer, took down Pocock's statement.'

'And Howard Foulds?' Harry asked again.

'He's the puzzle,' Harkness admitted. 'He *defended* Pocock. Lloyd, Barclay and Robson could all well be revenge killings, but not Foulds.'

'If it's two years since Pocock was proved to be wrongly convicted, why wait that long before doing anything about it?'

'Throw us off the track?' Ward rumbled. 'There's been a lot of that in these cases.'

'There is another element,' Harkness went on. 'It's like the Wilson brothers, Billie and Lennie. Pocock had a brother who was in prison himself until six months ago, and a younger one who hasn't had time yet to accumulate any serious convictions. According to the local collator, he appears to be rather more intelligent than the other members of the family, although that's hardly a great qualification.'

'Bit of a coincidence, isn't it sir? The Wilsons, and now the Pococks?'

'Not really. The Wilsons and the Pococks are criminal families. Prison is an occupational hazard with them. The Pococks in particular. They've spent more time inside than out.'

Harry nodded. 'So what now, sir?'

164

Harkness considered him for a long moment. 'It was your suggestions that opened up this line of enquiry. I take it you'd like to follow it up?'

'Definitely, sir. Definitely.'

'The elder Pocock brother is Keith, the younger one is Paul. They both live with their parents. Get their files from the CRO, then go to interview them.'

'Right,' Harry said. 'Thanks very much, sir.'

'When you go to see them take one of your officers with you. Not that the Pococks are likely to be violent, or at least, I don't think so, but I want someone to be able to corroborate your evidence of what they said, if it should come to court eventually.'

Harry Timberlake left Harkness's office as eagerly as a shark that has scented blood in the water, and uncaring of the nasty looks the AMIP detectives gave him. He felt the thrill of knowing that he was closing on his quarry.

In his workroom the man was packing his home-made explosive into its container. As he worked he was being ultra-careful, but his hand was steady. He was certain that he would never be suspected. Even if the police were clever enough, or lucky enough, to make the connection between the murders, there would be absolutely no reason to suspect *him*. He gave his weird chuckle again.

Harry studied the Pococks' criminal records with care and interest, and supplemented the information in the files by phoning the detective inspector at the area where they lived.

There were four surviving Pococks: father Horace, mother Ruby, née Crouch, and their sons Keith and Paul.

Horace was educated in criminal practices at a Borstal when he was just old enough to qualify for entry. He was not a brilliant student, for he grew up to become a low-life thief, specialising in thefts from working-class homes, particularly ones with elderly residents. He gained entry by posing as an inspector from the gas, electricity or water boards, occasionally as a council or social security official. The entries in Horace's record, bald and factual as they were, none the less revealed him to be a thick shit. Curiously, his conviction for this type of theft ended some ten or eleven years previously. Subsequent form was confined to petty offences like committing a

165

nuisance in public, creating a disturbance and insulting behaviour.

Keith, like his wrongly convicted dead brother Roy, was a couple of steps up from his father in the criminal league table. At least he was a burglar. But when Harry went through his file his heart sank. Like his parents, he had a long string of convictions. His record matched his father's in being studded with little gems like driving while disqualified, drunk and disorderly, using foul and abusive language, and one of assaulting a police officer.

Keith's major form, however, was for burglary. He picked houses which had an alleyway at the bottom of the garden. He broke into the gate or door and then through the back door or window of the house. Although most people's front doors are secure enough, their back doors are often protected by cheap locks and the window locks could be forced by anyone with a Boy Scout penknife. When Keith Pocock broke in, his method was unvarying: he used a jemmy in a characteristic way that was as good as chalking his signature on the door.

What Harry Timberlake found so depressing was the pettiness of Keith's crimes, which always followed the same pattern, and their lack of invention. He simply didn't have the mental equipment to plan four different murders. He was strictly a one-idea man. Nor was there any hint of violence in his burglaries. Once he had been arrested when he was caught by a couple of pensioners. The husband threatened him with an ancient cricket bat while the wife dialled 999. The possibility of Keith's committing one premeditated murder, let alone four, was something less than the chance of a rabbit hunting foxes.

Ruby Crouch/Pocock's record was the most interesting one. It went back to 1943, when she had her first conviction for soliciting before progressing to being sentenced for being a common prostitute. Afterwards she was in and out of the courts more often than the ushers, mainly on charges associated with prostitution.

When she married Horace Pocock, Ruby changed almost overnight. She gave up being a whore – or at least, she continued her old trade much more discreetly. She was hardly a model citizen, though. Like an ageing actress who can't give up the stage, Ruby continued to appear in magistrates' courts. Apart from offences like drunk and disorderly, breaches of the peace and insulting behaviour, she faced one serious charge: knowingly handling stolen property. Incomprehensibly, she got away lightly with a twelve-month suspended sentence. All this matched up with what the local DI told Harry when he brought him up to date on the Pococks.

Ruby Pocock had become a successful, astute fence. 'If you can get the cow for anything, good luck to you,' the DI said. 'It'll be as good as a month's leave to get her off our patch. But watch her, she's as crafty as a wog politician,' he said, with a fine disregard for the Race Relations Act. 'She's one of the richest and slippiest fences this side of the river. She must be coining it. The Bank of England could open a branch just for her.'

Although Horace, now retired from active thieving, was nominally the head of the family, there was no doubt that Ruby ran things as autocratically as Joseph Stalin, or even Margaret Thatcher. According to the date of his last conviction, Keith was still a busy tea-leaf, presumably selling his swag to the family firm and so cutting out the middleman.

No, Harry couldn't persuade himself that the Pococks were involved in murder. Still, as with the Wilsons, nothing could be taken for granted. So Harry Timberlake, accompanied by Detective Constable Darren Webb, set off for the Pococks' home in Streatham, which was really a cut above their social standing. As he drove, Harry explained to Webb the Pococks' involvement in the Foulds case.

'Looks like they're the best suspects in the other cases—' Webb ventured.

'The only suspects we've got for the moment,' Harry interrupted gloomily. He said nothing about their criminal records, which were practically character references in the present case.

'But I don't see how the Foulds murder fits the pattern,' Webb pressed on.

'It doesn't. At least, not that we can see. Now, when we get there, you keep your eyes and ears open and your mouth shut.'

'Right, guv,' Webb said with a slightly injured air.

'And as soon as we walk out of the place, write up your notes of what was said. I want it all down while it's fresh in your mind.'

The Pocock clan – 'family' was too cosy a word to describe the ill-favoured quartet – lived in a flat above Pococks' Antiques, which barely troubled to look legitimate. Behind the filthy shop window were Penguin paperbacks which originally cost 6d., some with one or both covers missing, one-handed clocks with broken springs, watches with no works at all, chipped Woolworth's cups and saucers, white metal cutlery in all shades from green to black, broken-backed chairs, perilously tilted tables, a couple of hopelessly sagging beds, jewellery with paste stones, a couple of typewriters that were probably quite valuable as museum antiques, paraffin stoves and lamps, and a whole selection of nameless junk, all overlaid with a thick layer of dust and flavoured with an aroma of damp graves.

The odour was not noticeable in the Pococks' flat above the shop, mainly because the place smelt of fried fish. The living room, for want of a better word, was furnished with fittings that were barely too good for the shop, which wasn't saying much. When Harry and Webb arrived, Horace Pocock was seated in an uncomfortable-looking armchair with a cloth cover whose original colour it was impossible to guess. He was a short, fat man with a full-moon face. His features were unremarkable – currant-sized eyes, squishy nose, loose lips and disappearing chin – except for his bristly eyebrows, which met above his nose like two furry caterpillars colliding head-on. Most people who spoke to Horace couldn't stop staring at the tangled black bushes which marked the lower boundary of his narrow brow. While he was a practising thief it had never seemed to occur to Horace that his was a face that people didn't forget. When victims of his thefts reported that the 'official' who had robbed them had eyebrows like a set of boot brushes, the police sighed, 'Oh, him again,' and went round to Horace Pocock, who always strenuously claimed to be the victim of mistaken identity. It was Ruby who eventually persuaded Horace to let other people do the nicking and make a profit from them with fencing.

Harry looked at Horace, who avoided his eye. A brown, crescent-shaped cigarette was stuck to his lower lip. Although a thin wisp of smoke testified that the cigarette was alight, it never grew any shorter. From time to time Horace was racked by a smoker's hawking cough, which failed to dislodge the cigarette.

Harry turned to Ruby Pocock. She was as thin as a dipstick and had a face like a piranha. Her scrawniness wasn't disguised by her floral cotton dress which outdid Joseph's coat for colour

and a drooping brown cardigan that was several sizes too large
for her. It was obvious that Ruby had never been pretty, not
even as a baby. When Harry Timberlake looked at her he found
it astonishing that she had ever picked up any clients when she was
a whore. But, he told himself, some men had extraordinary sexual
tastes. Besides, Ruby had operated in wartime, during the black-
out. By the time punters got her into the light it was too late to
change their minds and ask for their money back. He bet most of
them closed their eyes and thought of Betty Grable.

Keith Pocock, the elder surviving brother, was tall and gan-
gling like his mother, whom he resembled. There was nothing
about him to suggest that Horace was his father. When Harry
questioned Keith he answered without looking up. All the time
the detectives were there he concentrated on dismantling an old
carriage clock and carefully putting the parts into small dishes on a
tin tray. Harry wondered why a man capable of such delicate work
should brutalise his way into a house with a jemmy. Perhaps there
was more to Keith Pocock than appeared on the surface.

The one joker in the pack was Paul. He sat silently watching
Harry with bright, intelligent eyes. Beside him, Harry noticed was
a copy of Bertrand Russell's *An Enquiry into Meaning and Truth*.
He had not the slightest resemblance to his brother or his parents.
Because of his relative youth Ruby must have had him when she
was at the limit of childbearing age. If Horace wasn't the father
– which seemed highly likely – then, Harry speculated, who on
earth could possibly have managed to impregnate Ruby. Maybe a
Neapolitan sailor who'd been on a single-handed round-the-world
cruise without touching port; or someone who met her on the first
day of his release from a fifteen-year jail sentence.

The interview was a waste of time. Only two people talked
at any length, Harry Timberlake and Ruby Pocock. Darren
Webb took Harry's orders literally and remained completely
stumm. Ruby made a pretence of deferring to Horace that was
as convincing as a moneylender's smile. 'I don't think Dad would
agree to that, would you, Dad?'; 'Dad always takes care of that,
don't you, Dad?'; 'I expect Dad would want to see our solicitor
abut that, wouldn't you, Dad?' To which Horace gave the royal
assent with a nod, a grunt or a cough.

It became increasingly improbable that any of the Pococks
had killed Howard Foulds or any of the other victims, but Harry

pressed on with his questioning, hoping against hope. The only reservation he had about their innocence concerned Ruby. She had the nerve to plan the murders and reputedly had the money to pay someone else to do them. But who could she trust? Fences don't have friends. And then there was the enigmatic Paul.

Harry left the Pococks in a mood of depression that was even blacker than his earlier one when there were no leads at all and Tina Barclay had yet to come up with the Titus Lloyd connection. After the disappointments of the Wilson brothers and the ex-company secretary Rimmer, the Pococks had been his one realistic hope of finding a suspect and it had been crushed. Hope unfulfilled was worse than no hope at all.

When Harry Timberlake returned to Terrace Vale, Ted Greening was waiting to greet him. 'Old Liverish wants to see you,' he said with a smile that had the hint of an unpleasant quality about it.

'What does the Chief Super want? Any idea?' Harry asked.

'Not the faintest,' Greening said blandly. He was lying.

Since Chief Superintendent Liversedge had been told that he would soon be moving to Traffic Planning at Scotland Yard, he had become a lot less twitchy and less ready to dodge anything that smelled like responsibility. Like an outgoing government, he was content to leave the mess for the successor. But as soon as Harry Timberlake entered the Chief Superintendent's office he could see that he had become jittery once again. Liversedge couldn't meet Timberlake's eye. Like many uncertain men in positions of authority, he blustered when he felt uneasy.

'It's got to stop!' he said loudly.

Harry's heart fell like a lift with a broken cable. 'What's that, sir?' he asked politely, although from the moment he heard that Liversedge wanted to see him Harry Timberlake had had a pretty good idea what to expect.

'This surveillance in the Phantom Flannelfoot case.' He pronounced the name as if he had a nasty taste in his mouth. Liversedge put his hand to his lips with what was meant to look like a casual, unthinking gesture and directed his breath to his nose. It smelt sour. Bloody stomach playing up again, he thought. Christ, I wish I was out of here already. The nasty taste in his mouth was both literal and metaphorical.

'The overtime costs . . .' He indicated a computer printout

on his desk. 'They're monstrous. Call the operation off at once. Today.'

Harry Timberlake tried wheedling, flattery and argument – all useless against Liversedge's closed-mind obstinacy. When Harry pointed out that catching Phantom Flannelfoot would be an unanswerable way to justify the expense, Liversedge was unimpressed and muttered something about throwing good money after bad. The remark wasn't only unoriginal, it was bloody illogical, Harry thought.

'I don't know why I agreed to the plan in the first place,' Liversedge said unwisely.

'To get a result, sir,' Harry said forcibly.

'I'm afraid you made a serious error of judgement in being taken in by that WPC's theory.'

'With respect, sir, I don't think we were.' *We were*, he had said. *You wanted your fair share of the glory, you can have your fair share of the shit,* Harry signalled, as plainly as if he'd used semaphore. 'I'm sure she'd be proved right with a little more time.'

He tried again to get Liversedge to change his decision, but his heart wasn't in it. The Chief Superintendent's mind was ossified, his decisions warped by chicken-heartedness. Harry Timberlake, being Harry Timberlake, couldn't resist one last dig before leaving Liversedge's office.

'D'you know yet when you'll be leaving for Scotland Yard, sir?' he asked with insolent politeness. Liversedge was unsure quite how to take it. There was something of Superintendent Harkness's armour-piercing gaze in Harry Timberlake's look which put Liversedge on the defensive despite the superior fire-power of his rank.

'Quite soon now,' he said, ignoring any implications in the question.

Harry smiled and nodded. It was more eloquent than saying 'That's good.' He closed the door behind him with an exaggerated care which managed to emphasise his lack of respect.

Harry was as disappointed for Sarah's sake as for his own, perhaps even more so. After all, it was her idea and hard work that was being junked, while he still had the Foulds murder to work on. She took the news surprisingly well, considering the

171

crushing letdown it was to her. She proved her resilience by recovering quickly and saying, 'No reason why I shouldn't put in a bit of unpaid overtime and keep my eye on that place, is there, guv?'

'Would it make any difference if I said there was?'

'Not much,' she said with a smile. 'I'd just watch my step a bit, that's all.'

Harry grinned back at her. 'You'll do, Sarah,' he said. She felt as if she'd just been given a medal.

It began with a telephone call. In this modern world many unpleasant things do. There was nothing obviously ominous about Jenny Long's call to Harry, no suggestion of '. . . or else'. She simply made a date to come and see him at his flat. The way his luck had been running he should have suspected something, but all the psychological blows he'd had recently had blunted his sensibilities. Besides, he had no reason to be alarmed: Jenny had never caused him any problems.

'Okay,' he said. 'Nine o'clock?'

'Fine.' She paused. 'We've got to talk,' she said.

Still not alerted, he asked, 'What about?'

'Us.' It was like the crack of a sniper's rifle. She fired off a further hostile fusillade. 'We've got to decide once and for all where we're going.' It was too late for Harry to duck by saying that he'd just remembered a previous appointment. Not that it would have changed anything: she'd get him the next time anyway.

The rest of the day was taken up mainly by routine work: writing reports on the Foulds case, phoning the local CID at the Pococks' area, and conferring with junior detectives about other Terrace Vale cases. They seemed trifling compared with his major affairs, even though they had passed the points test of being worth investigating. When he went to the canteen for a coffee or meal with colleagues he was abstracted and had little to say. He was preoccupied with trying to analyse his feelings for Jenny. He could understand her wanting to formalise their relationship although he no longer felt any great need for it himself. He had retreated from the brink of asking Jenny to marry him, by chance rather than conscious choice. Now he was content to take every meeting with her as a single, self-contained incident without thinking too much of the future, about their future. What had brought about this change in him he had no idea.

He didn't know what the hell he wanted. The idea of living with Jenny, married or not, had its considerable advantages, but he knew instinctively that it would have its disadvantages, too, some of them probably serious. On the other hand, if Jenny insisted on a living-in commitment or nothing, the idea of breaking up with her badly disturbed him, almost enough to make him forget the substantial advantages of being free again. Almost, but not quite.

'I don't know what the bloody hell to do,' he thought.

'About what, guv?' Sarah Lewis, back in uniform, was taking a seat next to him in the canteen. He realised he must have spoken out loud.

'About talking to myself,' Harry replied at once.

She smiled appreciatively at his quick reaction. They both unaccountably felt a sense of friendship that went beyond their professional association, and each knew that the other was aware of it.

'Problems?' Sarah prompted him.

Harry nodded. 'Personal ones.' Despite the rapport that had suddenly developed between them, he was surprised at himself for telling her even that much.

'Join the club,' Sarah said ruefully. By not adding 'guv' she kept the conversation friendly and informal. Ironically, their new understanding didn't go deep enough for them to realise that Harry's problem was that he didn't want to make a commitment and Sarah's was that she did. They sighed simultaneously, looked surprised, then laughed.

Sarah rose. 'I'm off now to get a couple of hours' kip before I put in some unpaid overtime.'

'You're not going out on your own?'

She shook her head. 'PC Davidson offered to partner me again.'

'Good for him,' Harry said, unaware of the situation.

Sarah kept a straight face. When she told Greg that the surveillance had been officially called off she had added in angry disappointment, 'I suppose you're happy now.' Secretly Greg *was* pleased: he believed it was her obsession with the Phantom Flannelfoot operation that had caused Sarah to start acting weirdly – as he saw it – towards him. Now maybe she'd come to her senses. Good-looking, sexy and sometimes charming as he was, there were times when it seemed his IQ had difficulty getting into double figures.

'Anyway, I'm going on stakeout on my own time,' she had told him.

'I'll come with you,' he had said without thinking. A great happy smile spread over Sarah's face and quite impulsively she had kissed him, regretting it instantly in case it gave Greg the wrong idea about her feelings for him. Which it had done, of course.

'I'm sorry, what did you say?' she asked Harry.

'I said, "Good luck, and thanks again." ' He resolved to drive round and make a couple of calls on her during the night if he could sort out things with Jenny in time. He sighed. Fat chance.

The block of flats where Harry Timberlake lived was not in the more fashionable Old Town part of Clapham, although creeping gentrification was lapping at its borders. In front of the flats was a narrow private roadway divided from the pavement by a low wooden fence and a row of small plane trees. There were gaps in the fence for residents' cars to drive from the roadway on to the private ground.

Harry Timberlake got home at five to nine. There was no light in his flat so Jenny hadn't arrived early. He put his car in its garage and walked along the private pathway towards the main entrance of his block.

He was halfway to the main door when he lost his balance and stumbled to his knees. Then he realised dimly that he had an agonising pain at the back of his head. On all fours, he stared at the ground but the gravel pathway was blurred in his vision; he blinked, trying to focus his eyes. Another searing pain seemed to split his skull, then something scraped past his left ear and he felt a numbing blow to his shoulder. A further thump in the ribs momentarily knocked the breath out of him.

Dimly he realised he was being attacked. Still on his hands and knees, his head hanging, he could make out two pairs of feet in dirty training shoes, but he couldn't raise his head enough to see who his attackers were.

As another blow hit him, the terrifying thought flashed into his mind that they meant to kill him.

Chapter 9

Everything was going black when there was a sudden blinding light and a roaring noise that was familiar, although in his dazed state he couldn't place it for the moment. There was a strange, shrill sound which seemed to come from a great distance before he realised it was one of his attackers screaming. The two pairs of feet disappeared from his field of view. An iron bar clattered to the ground beside him with a noise like a great bell falling from a steeple. The blinding light gradually faded, and Harry gratefully closed his eyes.

When he opened them again he found he was sitting with his back to the wall of the flats. Jenny was leaning over him. Two flat-cap policemen from a patrol car were with her. A beat policeman from a panda car, his personal radio squawking incomprehensibly, was leaning against Jenny's Metro, its headlights and engine now switched off.

Harry had the worst headache he'd ever known, much worse than he would have thought possible. It was almost unbearable. He closed his eyes for a few seconds. There was something sticky on the back of his head and neck. Gingerly he put his hand there. It came away covered in blood.

'You all right?' the beat policeman asked cheerfully. He meant well.

'I'm bloody marvellous,' Harry said painfully, speaking with as much sarcasm as he could manage. 'What d'you think?' He turned to Jenny. 'What happened?'

'When I came round the corner I saw two men beating you up so I drove right in and into the one with the iron bar.'

'What happened to the bar?' Harry asked thickly. His voice sounded strange to him.

Jenny indicated the weapon lying near Harry. One of the men from the patrol car bent down to pick it up.

175

'Watch it!' Harry cried out. Talking sent spears of pain through his head and set little lights dancing in front of his eyes. 'Be careful how you pick it up,' he said more quietly. 'There may be finger-prints on it.' The policeman put on a driving glove and took the bar between forefinger and thumb at the very end, where there were bloodstains.

Jenny spoke again. 'I think I hit that one too hard and broke his leg.'

'It wasn't too hard,' Harry said.

'The other man helped him on to a motorbike and they drove off.'

'Did you get the number?' the irrepressible beat policeman asked her. Jenny knifed him several times with a look.

A rhythmical noise which Harry thought originated in his head he now identified as the two-note honking of an ambulance as it pulled up in the roadway in front of him, its twin blue flashing lamps adding to the stroboscopic effect of the police car's own lights.

'I'm taking you to the hospital,' Jenny said.

'You're bloody not,' Harry said with an incautious emphasis that made his head ring. He decided to show them that he was well enough to recover at home. Using the wall as a support he levered himself to his feet. He took one pace forward and pitched on to his face. At least, he would have done if the ambulancemen hadn't caught him. They were philosophical about it: they were used to dealing with big brave men who didn't need their help, thank you. As they shovelled him into the ambulance, Harry said to Jenny, 'Pity I'm not an American private eye.'

She looked at him with concern. 'Why's that, Harry?' she humoured him.

'If I was Sam Spade or Philip Marlowe all I'd need would be a coupla slugs of rye and a wisecrack and I'd be up and running.' Then he passed out.

He was conscious when they got to the hospital. Before the casualty officer gave him an injection to make him sleep, Harry phoned the Clapham detectives and told them that the major suspects for the attack were the Wilson brothers and the Pocock brothers. The thought persisted in Harry's aching head that the attack on him might mean he was getting close to a solution to the Foulds case, perhaps closer than he knew himself.

Next morning in hospital Harry felt well enough to speak to the Clapham CID on the phone. They told him that all local hospitals had been circularised the previous evening with the request that any cases of broken or seriously injured legs that could have been caused by a car be reported to them, but so far they'd had no luck. The detectives who were calling on the Wilsons and the Pococks that morning hadn't returned yet.

As soon as Jenny told him that his skull hadn't been fractured and the brain scan had shown no sign of any cerebral haemorrhage, Harry decided that one night in a hospital bed was enough. He was anxious to get back to Terrace Vale so he wouldn't miss any possible developments in either the Foulds or the Phantom Flannelfoot cases. Apart from that, he feared that Jenny might well take advantage of his being semi-captive in the single-bed room at the end of the ward that she had wangled for him. It was the perfect opportunity for her to have the delayed talk about their future. He still didn't know what he really wanted, and equivocating in any confrontation with her would be nearly as bad as making the wrong decision – whatever that was.

Jenny sat on his bed while he gingerly dressed in the clean clothes she had picked up in his flat. He took care not to move his head more than was absolutely necessary. His skull felt as if it was full of scrap iron and broken bottles. Without warning she said, 'I shan't be able to see you next week.' He wondered if that meant she was going out with someone else, and he didn't know how he felt about it. Before he could make up his mind she added, 'I'm on nights.'

'I'll come and see you after work. We can have a meal in your canteen.'

She smiled. 'I'd like that.' It seemed a long time since he'd seen her smile as warmly.

Just before he left his room he had a disappointing call from the Clapham CID. The Wilsons and Pococks were all in the clear. None of them had an injured leg, and their fingerprints, which were on record of course, didn't match the clear prints on the iron bar. In fiction detectives sometimes get an answer within hours as to whose fingerprints were found at the scene of the crime. It's not as easy as that. Scotland Yard has the prints of a couple of million people on file. Although there are short cuts to checking by eliminating certain groups of prints, matching unknown prints

177

is still a dauntingly long and tedious task. As far as identifying Harry's attackers by fingerprints was concerned, once again it was Square One time.

When Harry got back to Terrace Vale, Harkness sent for him to ask how he was. Ted Greening went through the big-smile, back-slapping routine of being concerned, but his mind was somewhere else. Harry Timberlake had the impression that Greening's principal reaction was relief that he hadn't been the one to be clobbered. Other detectives gave him a wave and a couple of cheery words.

All this was to be expected. Harry was surprised, though, by a visit from Sarah Lewis on her day off to see if he was all right. Ostensibly her reason for coming in was to bring him a report on her surveillance at The Cedars, but it was a routine matter that could have waited another day, or two or three. Harry was moved, and pleased, by her genuine interest; and he appreciated her discretion in disguising her real reason for appearing at the nick. If the CID men thought there was anything going on between him and Sarah they would have ribbed him rotten with sexual double-talk. More serious would have been that some of them would have been certain that Harry was showing favouritism to his girlfriend.

Sarah was well aware of this, and when she cooked up the idea of taking in the report it was to hide from the other detectives – and Harry – how concerned about him she was. The thought hit her that maybe she was trying to hide it from herself as well.

For want of anything better – or too suggestive – to say he asked her, 'Did you have a good rest this morning?' He was going to say 'Did you have a good lie-in?' but this might have had a nudge-nudge, wink-wink element about it. He remembered his journalist friend telling him that sub-editors on his paper were given a formal instruction not to put the word 'bed' in a headline. The paper said it was impossible to use 'bed' without making a *double entendre*.

'Yes thanks, guv.' She emphasised the 'guv'. 'I'll be fit for the stakeout tonight.'

'How long do you want to keep it up?'

'As long as it takes. Or till he's moved out of our patch.' She looked as determined as a Welsh front-row forward but, Harry thought, rather more attractive.

178

'I'll try to get round tonight – unless I get clobbered again,' he said wryly. He was going to be clobbered all right, in a way he least expected.

'This is my last night,' Greg Davidson said, breaking a long, cold silence. 'I've had it. I don't know why I agreed to come in the first place.' Sarah knew, but she said nothing. She just settled more comfortably into the seat of the Fiesta. It had dawned on Greg at last that she wasn't going to change her mind about him. It was over between them. She was grateful to Greg for coming on surveillance with her, but that was all she had for him: gratitude. It made him feel old.

'I don't know how you don't get bored out of your skull yourself,' Greg grumbled on.

That's your trouble, Sarah thought. You simply don't understand that I like being a copper. I like being a thief-taker. It's a useful job, for God's sake, better than being stuck in an office, and I like it.

Greg nearly said something to Sarah which would have passed for a witticism with him: as far as he was concerned she was called the Welsh Rarebit because it was very rare he got a bit. Fortunately for him he kept his mouth shut, otherwise he might have had the humiliation of having to walk home.

A silver 700-series BMW drove up The Meadows at a reasonable speed. Sarah noted down the number. It was a personalised one and seemed familiar. She flicked through the list of numbers she had made during the past few nights. She was right: it had passed along the road two nights previously. That was normal enough, but something about the particular car gave her a pricking in the thumbs.

'You see that BMW?' she asked Greg.

'Of course. Why?' He wasn't really interested.

'It came along a couple of nights ago.'

'So? Lots of cars have come past every night. People do, you know,' he said nastily.

'There was something . . .' She let it lie.

'Woman's intuition?' Greg said with a barely concealed sneer. Once again Sarah could have hit him. She couldn't believe that he didn't realise how much this operation meant to her.

'If you don't think it's kosher, get a vehicle number check.'

'How do I get that, you great galah?' Sarah exploded. She didn't know what a galah was, exactly, but she'd heard an Australian use the word and it definitely didn't sound complimentary. 'We don't have personal radios with us, and even if we did we couldn't ask for a licence check because we're not on official duty.'

'Well, I didn't see anything wrong with the car,' Greg grumbled. 'Anyway, tea-leaves don't go out thieving in 700-series BMWs.'

'Phantom Flannelfoot isn't your average burglar,' Sarah said sharply.

Greg didn't argue. He wondered if he could talk Sarah into packing up early. It should be obvious by now, even to her, that the whole thing was a total washout.

Sarah's feeling that there was something not quite right about the car hardened into certainty, but the more she tried to identify it, the more she felt as if she were beating her head against a wall.

Harry Timberlake shut his garage door and turned the key in the lock with his left hand. In his right was a policeman's truncheon, unobtrusively held down by the side of his leg. There was always the slight possibility that the two attackers might try again if they had something against him personally.

He walked steadily, his senses keen, towards the main door to the flats. He unlocked it, again with his left hand. There was no one in the well-lit vestibule. He opened the door to the lift, leant in and pressed the button for the second floor. He pulled his arm away quickly before the doors closed and the lift started on its journey empty.

Harry silently ran up the stairs, arriving at his floor at the same time as the rather weary lift. There was no one waiting for him. Why do people secretly think I'm paranoid? he said to himself with a wry smile.

Harry was glad to be home in his flat, not because he had been frightened on his way in, but because he felt tireder than he cared to admit to anyone and his head was starting up its big-drum concerto again. He went to the bathroom and found himself a couple of paracetamol tablets. The way he'd been eating recently, aspirin would probably make his stomach play up.

He picked up his bottle of malt whisky – one of his judicious extravagances – but put it down again almost at once. He remembered he'd promised to look in on Sarah Lewis during the night and he never, never drank within eight hours of driving. He wondered if she understood why he didn't offer to partner her himself – it would be more a case of her partnering him in view of their ranks – or to do a turn of surveillance. Apart from having a much greater workload than Sarah, Harry didn't want to take any credit from her if she struck lucky and caught Phantom Flannelfoot. If he was with her at the scene of an arrest, people would naturally think that he was the prime mover in the operation. Generals get the credit for winning battles, not the poor sods who have to dodge the bullets between long periods of boredom, he thought.

His headache had nearly gone and he felt hungry, yet disinclined to prepare a meal, peeling potatoes and cleaning vegetables. In the freezer his iron rations, as he called them – packets of ready-cooked meals which required only moments in the microwave oven – failed to tempt him. He decided on a couple of sandwiches: one of prawns which he had defrosted two nights before, the other of silverside and tomatoes.

He took the sandwiches into the living room and switched on the television, but there was nothing on any of the channels which interested him. It was the wrong night for the one police series which had any semblance of reality. He put on one of his very few classical recordings, a tape of the Brandenburg Concertos, beginning with the second in F Major. Harry had a great deal of admiration for Johann Sebastian for his extraordinary output; nearly 300 church cantatas, oratorios, preludes, fugues, concertos, works for the harpsichord and clavichord and goodness knows what else. And he fathered twenty children. Harry's appreciation of Bach's works was not for their quantity, but for their quality of imagination and mathematical precision.

The second Brandenburg Concerto is for solo flute, oboe, violin and trumpet. It has a brilliant and cruelly difficult high trumpet part, and as Harry listened to it, he wondered what the jazz cornettist and trumpeter 'Wild Bill' Davison would have made of it.

During the moment's silence between the second and third concertos Harry became instantly alert when he heard a faint noise at the front door. He let the tape run on, and got to his feet. He picked up the truncheon from the chair where he had thrown it

181

as he came in and silently moved to the door. He stood against the wall opposite the side where the door opened. He could feel the effect of the adrenalin pumping into his bloodstream. He raised the truncheon, but not high for a blow to the head, the easiest one for an experienced man to parry, but at his side, ready for the unexpected, bayonet-like thrust to the solar plexus, which didn't need to be as accurate as a head blow and was just as disabling.

There was a faint sound at the doorlock. Anyone who could pick that lock was obviously a professional – and a professional who wasn't coming to steal, not from a flat with lights on and music playing. Harry gripped the truncheon more firmly. Mounting anger was mingling with his other emotions: anger at the thought that someone would violate his home to attack him.

The lock clicked back.

The door opened slowly, hiding the intruder until the last moment.

Jenny Long entered, closing the door silently behind her. She turned, and saw Harry standing there, the truncheon still held ready in his hand. Her eyes widened and she fell back a pace, but she quickly recovered.

'I didn't expect you to greet me with that in your hand,' she said. 'As the actress said to the bishop.'

He put down his truncheon. 'I didn't think it was you. You said you were on nights this week.'

'I swapped duties with Tony – Dr Adams. It's his birthday or wedding anniversary, or something on Friday.' She paused. 'You don't look too pleased to see me.'

'I'm still in shock.' He smiled.

'I thought you'd be surprised,' Jenny said.

'Not surprised.' She looked at him quizzically. 'A.P. Herbert once wrote about the true meaning of surprise. The wife of an English professor came home and found her husband in bed with a neighbour. She said, "Well, I am surprised." He said, "No, you're not; you're shocked. We are surprised."'

'Ha, ha,' Jenny said. 'How do you feel?'

'Pretty good. A couple of aches and pains here and there, that's all.'

'We'll soon get rid of them. Or maybe give you a couple of new aches to take your mind off the old ones.'

Harry grinned. 'Have you eaten? Can I get you something first?'

'Just a drink. I ate at the hospital.' She took off her car coat. She was wearing a plain shirt and dark slacks. The top three buttons of the shirt were undone, and Harry felt the familiar surge of desire. Jenny looked at him and smiled.

Harry poured a whisky for her. 'Aren't you going to have one?' she asked.

He knew that if he drank any whisky it would mean he had given up the idea of going out to visit Sarah Lewis. Oh, well. Jenny planned to stay the night anyway, and to tell the truth, he was looking forward to it. He poured himself a large malt.

'Don't overdo it,' Jenny warned. 'We don't want any falling down on the job, do we?'

'You told me that alcohol in small doses is a vasodilator,' Harry said.

'Then drink up, and get dilating.'

Jenny was being unusually animated and provocative, Harry thought. 'What's got into you this evening?' he asked.

'You've got your tenses wrong, Inspector,' Jenny said. 'By the way, have you had your shower yet?' He shook his head. 'Nor have I. Let's save water and have one together.' She turned towards the bathroom, taking off her shirt as she went.

Sarah reached into the back of her Fiesta for her thermos of coffee, and stopped halfway. 'There's that BMW again,' she said.

'What?' Greg asked.

'The BMW. It's coming down the road.' Memory flooded back. 'I know what it is – I've seen that driver before. He was driving a big Merc the other time.'

'You sure?'

She snorted. Greg took it to mean that she was. He briefly considered the situation, and even he had to admit it was rather fishy. Sarah quivered with excitement. 'It's him! It's him! Look!'

The BMW reversed up the driveway of The Cedars, and stopped outside the garage – ready, Sarah guessed, for a quick getaway.

Sarah turned to Greg. 'Don't you move until I tell you!'

'Okay. Don't get excited,' Greg said in an unsteady voice. He might as well have told Niagara to stop flowing.

A man got out of the car. He was presentable-looking, and

probably in his mid-thirties. He took a large suitcase from the back seat of the car and walked up to the front door without a moment's hesitation.

'Cheeky sod,' Sarah breathed.

'I suppose it's not the owner come back?' Greg said dubiously.

Sarah's heart missed a beat, but she quickly recovered. 'If it's the owner, what was he doing driving a Merc past here the other night? And why hasn't he put the car in the garage?' she said. 'Right, we'll let him get inside, then I'll wait for him by the front door and nick him when he's least expecting it. You keep out of sight round the far side of the car and grab him if he gets away from me.'

The lights of the upper floor came on.

'He's taking a chance,' Greg said.

'No, it's the time switch. The crafty bastard's timed his job to coincide with the lights coming on, when the neighbours won't be suspicious. As long as he stays away from the windows he's all right.' She took a deep breath. 'Right, let's move.' She licked her lips, which had suddenly gone dry.

Jenny had always been good in bed. Very good, in fact, but not the best, as Harry sometimes reminded himself. The best had been Daisy Brown, the manageress of a Woolworth's store, who lived near the police section house in his early days as a policeman. She was ten years older than him. Nowadays Harry was inclined to believe that his own youthful virility at the time, together with the relative novelty for him of uninhibited sex, had much to do with Daisy Brown getting his personal Oscar for best performance. Nevertheless, there was no denying that Jenny Long was positively something special as a sexual artiste. She had the great advantage of being a handsome – not classically beautiful, her face was too strong for that – young woman of spirit and wit. She also had big tits.

On this particular evening she was even more exciting than usual. However, there was the faintest hint of something neurotic in her behaviour. Harry occasionally felt there was the slightest element of exaggeration in her movements, almost of desperation in the way she clutched him; just once in a while there was an overtone of unaccustomed shrillness in her cries. Or maybe it was him, his own nerves stretched, reading his own tension into her behaviour.

Eventually they both lay back on the bed, exhausted, sweaty and happy, although there was one thing that was niggling away at Harry.

'When we were in the other room,' Harry said, 'what gave you the idea to . . . you know.' At this stage in their relationship he didn't expect novelty, and he wondered whether she had been learning from someone else.

She smiled. 'One of the Indian doctors at the hospital has an old book on sex that's been doing the rounds.'

'In English?'

'Sanskrit.'

'I didn't know you spoke Sanskrit.'

'The pictures were in English. Some of the positions were quite impossible.'

'That one very nearly was. It might be all right for Indians, but I don't think I'd care to try it too often. It's likely to put my back out, if it doesn't actually break it.'

'You didn't complain at the time.'

'It didn't hurt then. It's like weeding the garden. You don't feel anything until afterwards.'

' "Weeding the garden . . ." God! You're so romantic.'

'You know what I mean.'

'Don't worry. When you've got your breath back I'll be the perfect little missionary's wife. Eyes closed and all. Now, what about a cup of tea?'

'Great idea. Thanks.'

'I meant you getting me one.'

Harry rolled his eyes dolefully and started to get out of bed. He groaned extravagantly. 'Oh, my back.'

'A cup of tea will do wonders for it, and that's a professional opinion, Chummy. Get moving.'

Sarah's heart was thumping so hard she could almost believe that anyone near her would hear it beating. She had been waiting for what seemed like ages in the shadow of the porchway of The Cedars for Phantom Flannelfoot to come out. Perhaps he'd got out the back way . . . No, of course he hadn't; she'd checked the house before and the only way out from the front or the back was along the driveway.

But he's been in there so long, she thought.

Sarah glanced at her watch and was astonished to find that she had been waiting for barely five minutes. There was a faint sound from within the house. Suddenly she felt an urgent desire to go to the loo. She resolutely fought the feeling, telling herself firmly that it was simply excitement and anyway she'd been only a couple of hours ago. Mercifully the desire passed.

The front door silently opened a few inches. She held her breath and pulled back further into the shadows. She could just make out the outline of a pale face. The burglar and the policewoman both stayed immobile for a long moment. Sarah prayed that Greg wouldn't give away his presence by coughing or making a careless movement.

At last the burglar was satisfied that the coast was clear. He came out, put down the suitcase which was obviously heavy now, and quietly shut the door behind him. He relocked the front door and picked up the suitcase. Now that he was handicapped by it, Sarah stepped up behind him and snapped a handcuff on his right wrist and snapped the other cuff on to her own left wrist.

'You're nicked, sunshine,' she said deliberately, with a note of triumph in her voice like a fanfare of trumpets. 'Greg! Greg!' she called. He came rushing out from behind the BMW and skidded to a halt in a small shower of gravel. 'It's all right, I've got him,' she said, forgetting in her excitement to say 'we'. She turned to the prisoner and, like a prima donna bursting into her big aria, she began the old refrain, 'You are not obliged to say anything, but anything you do say . . .'

By the nature of their profession, detectives are constantly exposed to the worst side of life and have to deal with the worst sort of people. It gives them a jaundiced view of humanity; it inevitably makes them suspicious and paranoid. It is a sort of unavoidable occupational sickness, like pitted blue scars on miners. Harry was very aware of this, and tried to eliminate unfair suspicions from his personal relationships. Nevertheless, as he lay back on his pillow with Jenny beside him, he couldn't rid himself of the idea that she had come to see him for more than to ask how he was, and to go to bed with him. He could think of two possible reasons for her unexpected visit.

First, she had used the key he had given her to call in without warning because she thought she might catch him with another

186

woman. Until now Jenny and he had considered themselves quite free, with no obligation of complete faithfulness to each other. It was that very freedom which helped keep him faithful to her. But now Jenny was checking up on him . . . perhaps. He wondered if he behaved in any way that would lead her to draw the (wrong) conclusion that there was another woman.

The second possible reason was that she wanted to have a talk 'about us . . . about where we're going'. She hadn't mentioned it so far during the evening, but she was shrewd enough to hold off until after they had made love and he had been softened up – in a manner of speaking. Harry considered this for a while before dismissing the idea as the product of a detective's nasty, sceptical mind.

Jenny lay looking up at the ceiling, her breasts rising and falling gently with her breathing. Harry studied her admiringly. She turned her head to look at him, and smiled. Then she did her favourite private gesture of tracing the line of his profile with one finger. It always made him feel sentimental and warm towards her.

'Darling,' she said, and then 'Darling' again.

Instantly Harry knew for an absolute certainty that she was going to bring up the subject of 'where we're going'. He still had no idea of what he wanted; all he could think of were the disadvantages of whatever decision he took.

Sometimes red comes up a dozen times running on the roulette wheel, or tossing a coin can give a dozen successive 'heads'. It was the sort of thing that happened to Harry right then. His luck was definitely on the upswing. The phone rang.

'Hello?' he said, trying to keep the relief from his voice. From the other end came a jumble of excited conversations, laughter and a few shouts. 'Hello!' he said again.

'Guv? We've got him! I nicked him redhanded coming out of that house with a suitcase of tom and silver, and copies of the doorkeys in his pocket!'

'That is bloody marvellous. Absolutely bloody fantastic! What a result for you! Congratulations!'

'He's started coughing the lot. We've got half a dozen pages of statement already. We've just broken for a meal. I couldn't phone you before.'

'No, all right. But who's "we"? Who took his statement?'

'I did. DC Webb was with me, but Chummy refused to talk to anyone else but me.'

'You've done it all by the book?'

'Absolutely, guv. Anyway, he didn't need any prompting. The problem was keeping up with him.'

'Okay, I'll be there right away. Congratulations again!' He was about to hang up when he remembered. 'Sarah! Get—Who's duty sergeant tonight?'

'Sergeant Andrews.'

'Get him to send a car for me right away.'

'Okay, guv.' She hung up.

'Who's Sarah?' asked Jenny, as casually as if she were asking the time.

'WPC Lewis. She's just made the arrest of the year. Of the past five years.' He started to get out of bed.

'Hooray for her,' Jenny said. 'So if she's made the arrest, what are you going to the station for?'

'Make sure everything's done properly. Half the CID teams this side of the river have been trying to feel this thief's collar for ages. God knows how many houses he's robbed. And a WPC, following her own instinct and working in her spare time, is the one who's nicked him. I'm sorry, darling, but I don't want any slip-ups with this one. I want him properly stitched up so he can't even wriggle.'

'Of course you must go. Besides, if that Ted Greening gets half a chance he'll try to steal the credit.' If there had been any sharpness in Jenny's manner, she had put it under control: she sounded understanding and sincere. Harry felt slightly sorry for Jenny because it was the second time she'd been cut off short. It deepened his feelings for her.

'Are you sure you don't mind?'

'Don't be silly. I know how important your work is to you.'

It didn't occur to him that she hadn't really answered his question. He leaned over the bed and kissed her. 'I can't say what time I'll be back.'

'I know you. If it's half as important as you say, it won't be till late.' She got out of bed. 'I'll go back to the hospital. It'll save us fighting for the bathroom tomorrow.' She glanced at the radio-alarm. 'This morning,' she corrected. 'Besides, you won't have to worry abut leaving the station too soon just because I'm on my own.'

Her smile was open and frank, without a hint of artifice. Harry looked at her. She was attractive, sexy, intelligent and understanding. He felt a thorough bastard for doubting her. But he still didn't know what he wanted.

Phantom Flannelfoot was Humphrey Court, an ex-public school-boy. He had left school before finishing his formal education there because of an incident involving a housemaster's wife – several incidents, to be accurate. However, he was at the school long enough to acquire its unmistakable manners and accent. They proved to be more valuable than formal qualifications.

Court became a salesman of new and used cars. It was a job which meant he was out a lot demonstrating Rollers, Bentleys, Mercs, Jags and BMWs to clients – they weren't called customers. Occasionally he showed off a Volvo for a client who wanted something for collecting the coals. His Park Lane firm didn't deal in Porsches: they were considered rather noisy and vulgar.

When Humphrey Court left the showroom to demonstrate a car he was able to take time to visit homes for sale. He always created an excellent impression with his public school accent, expensive suit and prestige cars. Getting his hands on the keys of the houses long enough to make impressions was child's play, he told Sarah.

Humphrey insisted on giving his statement to Sarah because he was something of a ladies' man, and he wanted to do her a good turn. Besides, he enjoyed talking to her. It was going to be a long time before he'd do much chatting to women.

When Harry Timberlake, still warm from the bed he had shared with Jenny Long, arrived at Terrace Vale police station the heady smell of success hung heavily in the air and a celebration was getting under way; but he refused the offer of a drink. After a few words with Sarah he carefully read through Humphrey Court's statement while she sat anxiously beside him. The statement was watertight, properly timed, initialled on every page, and signed and witnessed.

'Great,' said Harry. 'Now let me have a word with him.'

Humphrey was brought back from his cell to an interview room. Sarah was with Harry during this second interview; Sergeant Marwood, the charge officer, was also present as a back-up witness.

'I am Inspector Timberlake,' Harry introduced himself. 'I've read your signed statement. Is there anything you want to add to it, or change?'

'No thanks, old man.'

'So it is a full and accurate statement?'

'Yes. Can I go back to my cell now? Not that it's all that comfortable, but I'm tired.' He smiled wryly. 'It's been a fairly eventful night, one way and another. Oh, by the way: the BMW. Will you see it gets back to my people?'

'I'll take care of it personally,' Harry promised. 'There's one more matter. You wouldn't tell the other officers what you have done with the stolen property.'

'Ah, yes. I'm still thinking about that,' Humphrey Court replied genially. 'Maybe if the property was returned it could affect my sentence.'

'I'm afraid I can't comment on that,' Harry replied. He paused. 'A personal question.'

'Why?' Court said, guessing that was Harry's question. 'First time I did it for a lark, really, to see if I could get away with it. After that . . .' He shrugged. 'Selling cars isn't all that riveting. This provided a little excitement. Once I started . . . Now, can I go to bed?'

Before the night was over, Darren Webb and another detective constable returned from Court's house where they found his store of neatly ticketed duplicate doorkeys for his past and future robberies.

For a while after his arrest Humphrey Court would remain coy about what he had done with his loot. Eventually, under strong guard, he took Harry, Sarah and a couple of uniformed policemen to his cache, a railway-arch store which was an Aladdin's cave of every single valuable he had stolen. It looked like Sotheby's strongroom. Court simply hadn't known how to get rid of his loot. Although he met a number of people of dubious honesty in his normal job of flogging hyper-expensive cars, none of them was a fence as far as he knew.

It was a sensational coup for Sarah Lewis, and by extension Harry Timberlake, who was her guvnor and set up the operation. Not only was a badly wanted criminal arrested, but all the stolen property was recovered. Cataloguing the haul was a major job on its own. The operation gave rise to a whole series of side effects, sparking off long and acrimonious exchanges between some of the victims and their insurance companies. Eventually there were a few court cases, too, including criminal proceedings alleging false pretences. Items of property which owners thought had disappeared for ever suddenly surfaced again, revealing embarrassingly large discrepancies between the value claimed by the owners and the true value of the all-too-visible items.

Sarah was the object of intense media interest for a while, as was Harry, to a lesser degree. Greg Davidson managed to get his face in front of the cameras on a few occasions, too. Sarah handled herself very well.

The fact that Sarah had arrested Phantom Flannelfoot at night meant that the AMIP teams had left the Terrace Vale police station by the time she and Greg Davidson brought in the prisoner. As a result the small, impromptu celebration that began almost of its own accord was a purely Terrace Vale affair, and all the more enthusiastic for that reason. Nabbing Phantom Flannelfoot was a personal triumph for Sarah, of course, but Terrace Vale as a whole would be seen in the good light of reflected glory.

The uniformed branch had their share of the general euphoria, for Sarah was one of them, even though it was obvious she would soon become a CID officer.

Their celebration on the ground floor was a comparatively sober affair. Most of the toasts to Sarah were in slot-machine coffee and tea. There were muted congratulations for Greg, too; more than he merited. What the others took to be a becoming modesty in him was embarrassment, particularly when he caught Sarah's eye. Crass as he could be sometimes, he couldn't help feeling shamefaced when he remembered how he wanted to leave her on her own because he thought the entire operation was a waste of time. And then there was the occasion when he might have ruined everything by rushing in when Sarah told him to wait. He was only too aware of his own minor contribution – if it wasn't actually a negative one – to the success. Later he would begin to feel differently and he would persuade himself that he was an equal partner in the enterprise. Memory is a selective and elastic faculty. What he didn't realise now was that, although the others were being generous with their compliments, they knew Sarah really deserved all the credit.

191

The party was losing its momentum when Darren Webb came down to take Sarah upstairs to the CID, 'so we can give you three cheers'. Somehow Greg Davidson didn't get invited, and he didn't have quite thick enough a skin to invite himself.

The detectives had brought out their bottles and half-bottles of Scotch from bottom drawers and filing cabinets. Some of the men were drinking from coffee mugs and plastic cups; others were unblushingly swigging straight from the bottle. They were loud and lively, but no one was drunk. CID officers have to learn to drink and hold their liquor like junior officers in former Prussian regiments, because detectives get much of their information drinking with villains and figures on the fringes of the underworld.

Sarah walked in to the accompaniment of cheers and handclaps for the Welsh Rarebit. Someone had actually found a clean glass and four or five detectives poured tots of whisky from their bottles into it. Christ, I can't drink all that, Sarah thought. She took the glass and drank a little, trying to make it look like a big swallow. She kept the glass in her hand so no one could put any more whisky into it.

'We'll have a proper organised do later,' someone said as he clinked his mug against her glass. Sarah thought she couldn't wait.

She looked great. She should have been tired but she felt full of life; her eyes were large and brilliant. Yet, curiously, it might have seemed, none of the men made a pass at her. They were bawdy and ribald, but made no direct personal approaches. Visible beneath her attractiveness was an obvious reserve that discouraged any thought of suggestiveness. Some of the detectives came to her and kissed her on the cheek, a few gave her shoulder a friendly squeeze, but that was as far as it went. Then they returned to their own groups. For most of the detectives the celebration was as much an excuse to drink as much as possible as to congratulate Sarah.

Harry was one of the last to go to compliment her. Rather formally he shook her hand, which surprised rather than disappointed her.

Ted Greening was not at the station and no one had thought to call him with the news of the arrest, or more likely, those who had thought of it had quickly decided against it. At the time Sarah was bringing in Phantom Flannelfoot Greening was with Rita. She was

192

sick of the sight and smell of him because he was snoring noisily and dribbling on to one of her pink pillows. He stank of cheap whisky and cigarettes. Rita swore loudly at his unconscious form as she thought of all the trouble she would have getting rid of the stench.

Ironically, his excuse for going to see her was to ask if she'd heard anything about the Phantom Flannelfoot robberies. This sex session was going to be extremely expensive for Greening – not financially, he never paid a whore – but because, of all the documents referring to Humphrey Court's arrest, charge and statement, not one had Ted Greening's name on it. He simply wasn't officially associated with the successful operation, although he lobbied hard to persuade people that he was involved from day one. He didn't have much luck.

At the party Harry Timberlake moved away from the desk where he was sitting. 'I'm off,' he said to the room in general. There was a chorus of 'Goodnight guv' from the detectives, who then went back to their tall-story exchanges. Harry moved over to Sarah.

'I want to get in early so I can be the one to tell Old Liver— the Chief Superintendent,' he corrected quickly, but not quickly enough. 'I'm looking forward to seeing his face when I remind him of all he said about the operation being a bad idea and a waste of time.'

'But it's Sunday tomorrow,' she reminded him.

'I'd forgotten. Never mind. I'll phone him and get him to come in. This is important enough.'

Sarah's smile was a rare delight. He went on, 'I'll see if I can get him to make up the overtime pay you missed.'

'I don't mind, guv. I didn't do it for that.'

'I know. All the more reason for getting it. What duty are you on tomorrow?'

'Afternoon shift.'

'Good oh. So you won't have to lose an hour's sleep.' She looked at him in puzzlement. 'Now you've reminded me, don't forget the clocks go on tonight.'

She smiled ruefully. 'My turn: I'd forgotten.'

'I'm not surprised.' He squeezed her arm. 'Bloody marvellous. I can't tell you how pleased and proud of you I am.' He turned away before she could say anything.

193

After a moment Sarah's feet touched the floor again and she glanced round the room. No one was paying her any attention, so she slipped out to follow Harry Timberlake. He had just got to his upturned shoebox of an office when she called out 'Guv!' He gestured to her to enter.

'Yes, Sarah?' he said.

She remained silent, not sure herself why she had followed him. They stood looking at each other, neither knowing what to say, but knowing there was something. He noticed the nearly full glass of whisky she was still holding. Rather lamely he said, 'You going to be all right to drive home?'

'Oh, sure. I've only had a sip. I couldn't stop them filling it up.'

He took the glass from her and poured the whisky into the pot of a sad-looking cheese plant. 'Maybe that'll buck it up a bit.' He put the glass down on the desk.

'Thanks.' She moved closer as if to take the glass, but went right up to him and kissed him full on the lips. He froze in surprise, then responded, his mouth opening wide as hers did. She put her arm round his neck and he pulled her closer to him. They remained like this for a few seconds or for an age, oblivious of where they were, before they broke away. They looked wide-eyed at each other. They were both violently aware of the implications of that kiss of invitation and acceptance. Once more, time both raced and stood still.

At last Sarah turned and walked quickly away from the office. Her pace was slightly unsteady and she brushed against the door as she went out, but she hardly felt the contact.

Harry stood staring at the empty doorway before he came to his senses in his turn. He switched off the lights and went downstairs to arrange transport home. There was no sign of Sarah.

As usual, the man's planning had been meticulous, with every detail checked and double-checked: he never made mistakes. Nevertheless, this time there were unavoidable risks, there were circumstances that could not be foreseen. As he set out on this operation the man was aware that never before had he been in such danger of being caught. For the first time in his life he almost decided to abandon a carefully prepared plan. But, he told himself, this one would be a really spectacular killing, a highly dramatic one fitting for a public figure like Ernie Birt. All the man had to do was keep his eyes and ears open and his wits about him. It would be a pity not to go through with such an elegant, dazzling plan.

He was unaware that there had been a fundamental change in his character since he began his campaign. At first his motive had been only vengeance, retribution. He had a strong sense of justice in what he was doing: there was no pleasure in it. Now he was enjoying the operation for itself. He was admiring his own cleverness and ingenuity.

It was 4 a.m. and low tide. Careful as ever in his preparations, the man had looked up the tide tables in *Whitaker's Almanack*. Ernie Birt's houseboat was well below the level of Chelsea Embankment, making it difficult for anyone to see the man from the pavement. His only danger came from people in neighbouring houseboats, but no lights were showing and he was certain that everyone in them was asleep.

He padded silently along the gangplank on to the deck. He knew the gangplank didn't creak; he'd tested it when he visited the houseboat quite openly in daylight.

Fate gave the man a hand. A converted canal longboat put-puttered fussily upstream. People who live on the river aren't woken by the sound of passing boats any more than railside dwellers are woken by trains. The noise of the longboat's engine and the slap-slap of its wake against the hulls of the houseboats covered any small sound the man might make.

This stroke of luck meant nothing to him. It didn't occur to him that fate was on his side. By now he was again totally self-confident in the certainty that what he was doing was right and justified.

In his left hand the man carried a roughly cubic object, about eighteen inches square. His right hand was jammed into his jacket pocket, where he clutched a set of picklocks.

The man had been astounded when he saw them on show in a shop window in central London. He had gone to visit a specialist model shop near a mainline station. Almost next door was this shop selling picklocks and a book showing how to use them on padlocks and other locks. There were a number of roughly printed publications on even more illegal crafts. At that time the man had no firm plan for Ernie Birt, or anyone else for that matter, but he felt sure that the book and the picklocks might prove useful one day. He bought them, still strongly disapproving of the shop that sold them.

Later he congratulated himself on his foresight when he visited Ernie Birt's houseboat. He acquired a padlock of the same make and model as the one on the door of the houseboat and in his workroom he practised picking it until he could eventually do it in a matter of seconds, blindfolded. The dark would cause him no difficulty.

The man arrived on the deck unobserved and put down the object he was carrying. In a matter of seconds he had the padlock unfastened. He picked up the odd cube-shaped article and entered the boat. Less than a minute later he came out again, still carrying the cube. He locked the front door behind him and walked quickly but steadily back along the gangplank. He hummed cheerfully all the way back to his van, parked anonymously among a streetful of vehicles half a mile away.

Chapter 10

When Harry got back to his flat he found that Jenny hadn't made the bed for once. He guessed that she wanted him to be reminded of their time together earlier that night. She needn't have worried. There was nothing about that night he was going to forget.

He was woken by someone ringing the doorbell just after eight o'clock. He struggled out of bed and dragged on his dressing gown. He peered through the judas window in the front door. A man he didn't know was there. Harry put the chain on the door and turned th security lock. 'Yes?' he said through the partly open door. The man produced a warrant card.

'DI Harvey, Clapham Central. We spoke on the phone.'

Harry let him in. He made coffee while they talked.

'We've nicked the pair that mugged you the other night,' Detective Inspector Harvey told him. 'The Yard came up with a match for the fingerprints on the bar. One of a pair of cousins. They've got lots of form.'

'I told you: I shan't be able to identify them. I didn't see their faces.'

'They don't know that. And there was your friend, Doctor What's-her-name. Anyway, we shan't need either of you. When we walked in and told them about the dabs on the bar they were so flabbergasted they coughed the lot.'

'Did one of them have an injured leg?'

'Oh, yes. He'd put a rough splint on it, but the small bone was broken. We took his trousers to see if the paint marks on them match up to your friend's car. Just in case.'

'Did they say why?' Harry asked, in the faint hope there might be some connection with the Foulds cases.

DI Harvey looked at him in surprise. 'Robbery. What else?'

Harry nodded. 'The brief's going to get them to plead guilty to GBH, alternatively actual bodily harm,' Harvey went on.

'What?!'

'We said we thought the Crown Prosecution Service would go for attempted murder. Their brief probably told them they'd be better off pleading guilty so—'

'So all the details of what they did to me don't have to come out in court,' Harry finished for him. 'Yes, I know.'

'And the brief'll say they're very sorry they were naughty and it was all because they came from broken homes.'

'Which undoubtedly they broke up,' Harry said. 'Sugar?'

The official celebration party for Sarah Lewis and Greg Davidson was held in a private room over Terrace Vale's local pub. The experienced landlord cleared the room of all movable breakables in preparation.

By now Greg had managed to persuade himself that he played a significant part in Phantom Flannelfoot's capture. At the same time, off duty, he was well on the way to seducing a sexy but rather daft schoolteacher. He was feeling rather pleased with himself these days.

The balloon of his self-esteem as far as the arrest was concerned soon became leaky. All the congratulations were for Sarah, who looked as captivating as Cinderella at five to midnight. At least, Harry thought so. Harry finally deflated Greg's balloon when he overheard him rabbiting on to a newly arrived WPC about his major part in the collar. He took Greg to one side and gave him The Look.

'Listen, sonny. It was WPC Lewis's idea from day one. Her research, her determination and her collar. You were lucky to be there when it happened. So a little less of the trumpet voluntary.'

Greg opened and shut his mouth like a guppy, then nodded, and moved away.

The party developed in much the same way as do all these parties for members of closed, largely male societies – police, armed forces, firemen, engine drivers, you name it. Alcohol encourages the emergence of standard types. There was the boozer, Ted Greening, who had put his tenner into the kitty with considerable reluctance, and now was set on drinking more than his money's-worth; the charmer, Greg, was chatting up a barmaid with macho suggestiveness; the dirty storyteller was entertaining a guffawing group in a corner; the belligerent lager lout was a couple of drinks short of picking a fight with someone; the bathroom baritone was limbering up his voice . . . Drinks began to be spilled, and the noise, already at a level to make spoken conversation impossible, was increasing as if someone was slowly opening the throttles of Concorde.

One noticeable absentee, although no one really noticed his absence, was Chief Superintendent Liversedge. He was an expert at passing the buck, getting out from under, and of flannel and flimflam. However, the meeting when he came in to hear Harry Timberlake report Sarah Lewis's capture of Phantom Flannelfoot had been one of Old Liverish's most embarrassing quarters of an hour. He was sure that Harry had recounted the whole story to the entire CID personnel, and he couldn't bring himself to face them while knowing they were laughing at him whenever he turned his back.

He was wrong on two accounts. Harry, who had a strong sense of professional propriety, had kept the details of the senior man's humiliation to himself. And even if he had spread the story, most of the detectives would have had a grudging respect for Liversedge for turning up and brazenly outfacing them. But Liversedge, once a gutsy officer, had long since lost that sort of bottle.

Greening, a glass as firmly in his hand as if it were glued there, came over to Harry. He was still walking straight; he hadn't had his ten quid's-worth yet.

'The Welsh Rarebit looks very tasty,' Greening said. 'I wouldn't mind giving her one.'

Harry's expression didn't change. 'I didn't think she was your type,' he said, but Greening was beyond irony.

'If they've got one, they're my type.' He grinned nastily. 'What about you, Harry? Don't you fancy her yourself? Or have you already given her one? Or two?' He revealed another facet of his character when he added, 'You must be in with a chance. She'll reckon she owes you.'

Harry bit his tongue. Keeping his voice level, he said, 'You know the old saying about your own doorstep.'

'I wasn't talking about shitting,' Greening said with a Peter Lorre smile.

'You're a card,' Harry said. He was proud of the fact that he hadn't kicked Greening in the balls. He smiled and left to get a drink to take the taste out of his mouth.

Sarah went through the motions of accepting congratulations all over again but the novelty had worn off. Now she was conscious of jealousy from some of her colleagues. She was in the position of a footballer who has come on first time at a Cup Final and scored the winning goal. The team were delighted to win, but some of the players were secretly resentful that they owed their victory to the inexperienced newcomer. What galled some of them even more was that they couldn't put her success down to beginner's luck. Inspiration, hard work and persistence had won the day for her. So Sarah soon began to find she was enjoying this party less than the earlier impromptu one where the congratulations were entirely spontaneous. She was also disappointed that she'd barely managed to have more than a few words with Harry all evening.

Harry, too, was disappointed, but he was uncertain what approach to adopt with Sarah, and uncertain how she would react to him. In fact, Harry had hardly seen Sarah since the night of Humphrey Court's arrest. They had passed each other a couple of times in the station, and once she had come to his office with a report. They were strange encounters of slightly exaggerated formality yet with no apparent awkwardness between them. At least, on the surface. As far as he was concerned, he had been very aware of his own recurring physical reaction when he thought of that kiss. He wondered if it was the same with her, or whether the kiss had been a fleeting impulse without significance.

Eventually Sarah managed to get over to Harry. 'How are you getting home, guv?'

'I don't know. I hadn't thought. You?'

'I've got a minicab coming in half an hour.'

He didn't let her make all the running. 'Could you give me a lift?'

'Where d'you live?'

'Clapham.'

'Fine. That's on my way.' She lived in Ealing, which was at least 135 degrees from Clapham, but no one was counting.

Harry thought for a moment. He said to her quietly, 'I'll go back to my office now. When your minicab turns up, come to the nick and get the driver to ask for me. I'll tell the desk I'm expecting him. That way we won't leave here together.' Already there was a complicity between them: an offer had been made and accepted. The rest was a formality.

She nodded. 'I'll see you later.'

The arrival of Sarah's minicab triggered off half a dozen vigorous offers from detectives to see her home. With a few smiles and some fancy footwork she avoided them all without any broken bones or perforated egos.

She kept out of sight in the back of the cab while the driver went to fetch Harry Timberlake at the station. No one saw them leave together. They stayed in opposite corners of the back seat and said practically nothing to each other throughout the journey to Clapham.

When they got to Harry's flat he said casually, 'Thanks for the lift.' Then, as an apparent afterthought, 'Oh, would you like a coffee before you go home?'

Sarah pretended to consider the offer. 'Yes, why not?'

'We'll let the cab go,' Harry said to Sarah, but for the benefit of the driver. 'I've got my car here. I can either drive you home myself or ring for another minicab.' He turned to the driver. 'How much do we owe you?'

The driver told him, looking at Harry knowingly. He'd played the non-speaking role in this same old comedy more times than he could remember. Any lingering doubts he may have had about Harry's and Sarah's intentions were blown away when Harry over-tipped him. In this situation it was a dead giveaway.

Next morning Harry woke to the sound of coffee percolating. Through the open doors of the bedroom and kitchen he could see Sarah pouring orange juice into glasses as the percolator gave its last gurgles. She turned her head and saw him sitting up in bed. 'Stay there,' she called out. She poured out the coffee. 'Milk? Sugar?'

'Plain black.'

'Good. Me, too.' She put the glasses and cups on a tray and brought them into the bedroom. She was wearing his pyjama jacket, unbuttoned. To his surprise, Harry thought she looked sexier than she did naked. He was even more surprised to find that last night's exorbitant sex hadn't drained him after all. Sarah leaned across Harry to put his orange juice and coffee on the small table at his side. Her body pressed against his. He took a deep breath.

Sarah dropped the pyjama jacket beside the bed and got in to sit beside him. Harry was having a confused morning. He now thought she looked sexier without the jacket after all.

'God, what a night,' he said with a certain fervour.

'Mmmm,' Sarah agreed.

The events of the previous night were clear in his mind and reliving them aroused him. With Sarah there had been the added stimulation of discovery, which began for him as soon as he closed the front door behind them, and – remembering Jenny's last surprise visit – put on the security chain.

Everything Sarah did was fresh and unexpected to some degree – the way she undressed and helped him to undress, the things she said. There was more excitement in simply seeing this new body with its different shapes and curves. When he touched her skin, it had an unfamiliar texture, and there were subtle but unmistakable differences in her secret places.

Harry was almost unbearably excited by the time they began to make love after a long period of caressing and mutual discovery. When Sarah began to sigh and moan with enormous pleasure, he had to stop thrusting. 'Don't move; for God's sake don't move!' he whispered urgently. She had enough awareness and just enough willpower to remain almost motionless beneath him. At last he was able to start again.

The mechanics of sex are basically simple. Yet for both of them this was so different from their immediately previous experiences. The rhythms, the sighs and the cries – Sarah's seductive cries of delight were nearly enough on their own to make Harry lose his self-control – were new and so all the more exciting. But there was more to it than sheer sensuality for Harry. There was affection – no, much more than that. Resolute as Sarah was when she was being a policewoman, now there was a conscious vulnerability about her; a waif-like, gamine quality that aroused a tenderness that equalled desire in its effect on him.

Sarah's sexual pleasure was heightened because she not only wanted Harry and had done for longer than she had realised, but she also respected and admired him. These were two emotions she had never felt for Greg, and the difference it made to her enjoyment of him was enormous: she couldn't have enough of

Harry. Yet there was a bizarre element in her relationship with him. Despite their ultimate intimacy, she simply couldn't call him by his name. When they spoke she didn't say his name, or call him 'darling' – such a devalued word, it seemed to her – even in their most uninhibited moments.

'I'm on duty this afternoon,' Sarah said, as she finished her coffee.

'Great. Then there's no need for us to get up for a while.'

'I think I'll ask Sergeant Ramsden to put me in a panda,' Sarah said. 'I won't be fit for much walking.'

'Perhaps you'd better lie down for a while,' Harry suggested.

'That's just what I was thinking.' Unaccountably she thought of Greg, to his disadvantage. It made her recollect something. She turned to Harry, 'Oh, by the way, d'you know what a galah is?'

'That's what the Aussies call a pink cocky.' Her mouth fell open. He went on, 'To be exact, it's a rose-breasted cockatoo.'

'Serves me right for asking,' she said.

The telephone rang. Harry was certain it was Jenny. He picked it up.

'Inspector Timberlake?' A man's voice.

'Yes?'

'Superintendent Harkness. There's been an important development. Come and see me when you get in.'

'Right, sir.'

'What was that about?' Sarah asked.

Harry told her. He started to get out of bed, but Sarah put her hand on his arm to stop him. She turned over on her stomach, raised her bottom a little and wiggled it provocatively. 'Do you have to leave right away?' she said with a mock sultry voice, spoiling the effect by giggling.

'I suppose ten minutes one way or the other won't matter,' Harry said reflectively.

'If it's only going to be ten minutes, don't bother. And it'll be one way, not the other.'

'You talked me into it, you silver-tongued temptress,' Harry said. They both laughed and put their arms round each other.

Later Harry was lying on his side, looking down at Sarah, when suddenly a thought came to him that stunned him.

It must have showed on his face. 'God, are you all right?' Sarah asked.

'Fine. Just a spasm of cramp,' he lied, recovering with difficulty. His memory had gone back to the night after the meeting in the canteen with Professor Mortimer. He had woken in the middle of the night and turned to look at Jenny Long, to see if she were sleeping or had been woken by the light. Then he had realised that he was alone. Jenny had been with him in a dream that was so vivid that he could scarcely believe it was a dream. But that wasn't what had so shaken him. In that dream there had been something different about Jenny that he couldn't identify at the time. Now he knew.

Jenny had been a brunette, instead of her natural blonde colour. A brunette, like Sarah. In fact she had looked a great deal like Sarah. In his half-sleeping, half-waking state he had just assumed that he had been dreaming about Jenny.

'The case has become rather more serious than we first realised,' Harkness told Harry. The Superintendent had a single sheet of computer printout before him on his otherwise clear desk, the battered pale oak piece of furniture which was the best Terrace Vale storeroom had to offer. Somehow Harnkess gave it style.

'When we got the full list of jurors, witnesses and others involved in the Pocock trial, we ran the names through HOLMES. The computer produced some disquieting facts.' He referred to the printout.

'Peter Longford, juror, was stabbed to death in Leeds, where he had moved from London. It was believed that he was a victim of a mugger who was disturbed before he stole anything. The crime was unsolved.' Harry felt his pulse quicken.

'Trevor Naismith, juror, was killed by potassium cyanide poisoning. The cyanide was injected into the bottle of milk left at the door of his flat in St Albans. The murderer used a fine hypodermic syringe. The major suspect was the husband of Naismith's mistress. The crime was unsolved.

'Simon Porter, a witness to identification of Pocock at the trial, disappeared from a night cross-Channel ferry. The coroner's jury returned an open verdict. It's an unhappy compensation for you, but these other crimes completely substantiate your hypothesis of connected murders. Not – as you know – that I doubted it anyway.'

'On the surface it looks as if the Pococks are involved after all,' Harry said hesitantly.

204

Harkness nodded. 'I already have officers checking on all known associates of the Pococks, including criminals with records of violence who were in prison at the same time as Roy Pocock before he died, and with other members of the family. Other officers are interviewing the more likely professional killers.' He paused. 'You said "on the surface".'

'From what I saw of the Pococks, only the mother has the strength of character – of bad character – to plan and set up something like this.'

'Could she have arranged the murders?'

Harry nodded decisively. Harkness went on, 'There were three women on the jury and another three women prosecution witnesses. There's no record of anything happening to them.'

'I don't think that strengthens the suspicions against Mrs Pocock, sir. She's definitely not the type to have fellow-feelings for her own sex. If anything, I'd say she'd be more prejudiced against them.'

'Mmmm,' Harkness said neutrally. 'What about the other son, Paul?'

'He's the one enigma. Intelligent, and silent. But my feeling is he had nothing to do with the Foulds killing. He could hardly have known his brother Roy, and I don't see that family talking him into doing anything he didn't want to do – not even his mother.'

'The rest of my officers are visiting witnesses outside London to warn them to be vigilant.'

'The judge?'

'He's dead. Oh, not suspiciously. He died in bed of a heart attack on holiday in Tunisia.' He coughed delicately. 'He had a young companion on holiday with him.'

'Is there anything you'd like me to do, sir?'

'Yes. There are five jurors left. One of them lives in south-west London and the other in Kent. The other three live locally.' He ticked off three names on the sheet and passed it to Harry. 'I want you to visit them and warn them of the situation as diplomatically as you can without alarming them.' Harry smiled wryly, and Harkness smiled back. 'Alarming them unduly,' he amended.

'Police protection – at least for the time being?'

'I've seen Chief Superintendent Liversedge. We're trying to

muster the manpower. Perhaps we can borrow some men from the other AMIP teams. In the meantime . . .'

'Don't talk to strangers and lock your door,' Harry said. He got up to go out and give the jurors the good news.

The first of Harry Timberlake's three jurors was a Mr Lincoln Edwards, who lived in a small, end-of-terrace house in Avondale Gardens, Northwell, which was the next area to Terrace Vale to the north-east. After the drab decay of Terrace Gardens Square, Avondale Gardens was as colourful as a seed catalogue. The windowframes and front doors of all the houses were painted in strong colours from fire-engine red to emerald green. No house's colour scheme matched that of its neighbour, but the general effect was cheerful. Unusually for the area, the pavements were clean and unlittered: a state which owed more to the residents than to the local council, Harry guessed. All the parked cars seemed to be in running order.

After Harry had knocked twice at Lincoln Edwards's home without getting an answer, the front door of the neighbouring house opened. The doorframe was filled by the colossal form of a black man dressed in flowing African robes. His shaven head shone like polished ebony.

'If you're looking for Lincoln he's not at home. He's in hospital,' he said with a pure BBC-Oxbridge accent. Harry thought, Oh, my God. The killer's got another one.

'D'you know what's wrong with him?' Harry asked. 'Did he have . . . an accident?' The black man shook his head, which gave off unexpected gleams of reflected light. 'What hospital is he in?'

'Probably St William's. That's where they take people from round here. The ones that can't argue,' he added cryptically.

'Thanks,' said Harry, turning to go.

'You're a policeman, aren't you?' the man asked without emphasis.

'That's right.' Harry smiled. 'I didn't know it was so easy to tell.'

'If you're black and live round here you learn quickly.' There was no animosity in his tone. It was a flat statement. There was no answer to that remark that wouldn't start a debate, so Harry left it.

'Anyway, it's just a routine enquiry. Mr Edwards isn't in any trouble.'

'If he's in St William's, he is, man. Anyone walks away from there under their own power, they run up a flag.'

Harry checked his move towards his car. 'A purely unofficial question. D'you mind telling me what you do?'

'I am the Black Hellhound.' He gave a terrifying scowl, and a deep rumbling growl came from somewhere inside his massive chest. His shoulders lifted and his arms began to rise from his sides. Two enormous forearms like small tree-trunks emerged from the sleeves of his robe. Hands like mechanical diggers clawed the air. Harry fell back a pace.

'I'm evil, man,' the Black Hellhound said. He started to return to his normal self. 'I'm a wrestler. My real name's Basil Pink.' He gave a full piano-keyboard smile, revealing teeth that looked as if they could crack beef bones. 'Didn't seem quite appropriate for my image, somehow.' The smile broadened irresistibly. Harry smiled back. He guessed that most people smiled at Basil Pink.

As soon as Harry Timberlake saw St William's Hospital he knew what the big man had meant about only patients who couldn't argue being brought there. The building looked like one of Blake's dark Satanic mills. It was the sort of place that is always in gloomy shadow even on the sunniest days. The main hall was crowded and chaotic with outpatients and visitors, most of whom had small children with them.

Harry approached the reception desk, an island of calm and order in the turbulent human sea, without a great deal of hope of getting any easy co-operation, but this was one of his days for surprises.

'Good afternoon. Do you have a patient here named Lincoln Edwards, of Avondale Gardens, Northwell?'

'Are you a relation?' the young woman behind the desk asked him.

'Police,' said Harry, showing his warrant card. 'It's only a routine matter. Mr Edwards isn't in any sort of trouble.' Unless you count being a potential murder victim as trouble, Harry thought.

'One moment, please, Inspector.' She operated the keyboard of a computer, and after a moment told him, 'Lister Ward. Second floor, to your right as you leave the lift. Speak to the sister there.'

'Can you tell me what's wrong with him?' Harry asked, but the receptionist had already turned to an Indian girl who looked too young to know the facts of life, much less to practise them. She was heavily pregnant and accompanied by two small, impeccably dressed children of about two and four years of age who stared up unwaveringly at Harry with enormous, prune-dark eyes. He found it mildly uncomfortable. Harry was about to repeat the question to the receptionist when he guessed that she had deliberately become involved with the Indian girl to avoid answering him. He shrugged. The sister would tell him.

Lister Ward was at the end of a long corridor with a linoleum-covered floor. The linoleum was polished but worn and cracked; it would probably shake the last breath of life out of any patient wheeled along it on a trolley. The government-green plaster on the walls was flaking. Harry wouldn't have been surprised if Lister himself had been a student at the hospital, and the surgeons still operated in pus-encrusted frock coats. It was the sort of place where the ear clinic would be named the Van Gogh Ward. He couldn't help comparing St William's with St Lawrence's, where Jenny Long worked. They were a few miles and a century apart.

Sister Oona Kennedy was small, slight and bird-like, with a prominent nose and bright, boot-button eyes. She had an accent as Irish as Paddy's pig.

'You'll be the one enquiring about Mr Edwards,' she greeted him without preamble. 'Reception phoned,' she added in answer to his unspoken question.

Something's up, Harry thought. 'Can I see him, please?'

'Doctor'll be here in a moment,' Sister Kennedy said as if Harry hadn't spoken. 'Ah, here he is.'

A young man with a heavy beard that failed to conceal his thoroughly unpleasant skin came up behind Harry Timberlake. He wore a rumpled and none-too-clean white coat with a stethoscope hanging out of a pocket. Harry disliked him on sight and felt sure the feeling was reciprocated.

'Dr Jones,' he announced himself with a gust of bad breath. 'I'm the medical registrar here.' He didn't offer to shake hands and didn't add anything polite and civilised like 'Can I help you?'

'Inspector Timberlake, Terrace Vale. I'm making enquiries – routine enquiries – about one of your patients, Mr Lincoln Edwards. Can you tell me what's wrong with him, please?'

'He's dead,' Dr Jones said, not trying to be funny. 'He died yesterday.'

'What was the cause of death?'

'A combination of a heart attack and a stroke.'

'I see.' Harry paused, thinking how best to phrase the next question. 'Was it . . . unexpected?'

'Hardly. He'd had three previous heart attacks and a stroke.'

'No question of the diagnosis, then,' Harry said, trying to sound offhand. Dr Jones looked at him as if he'd just made a bad smell.

'None,' he said in a voice like a coffin lid being nailed down.

As Harry made his way along the cheerless corridors to the exit, he speculated that the hospital was still functioning only because it had been officially listed as an ancient monument. When he got to his car parked near the entrance he noticed something that had escaped him when he arrived. In the hundred-yard-long parade of shops opposite St William's Hospital there were three undertakers.

'It figures,' Harry said to himself. He debated with himself whether to visit the second ex-juror on his list or to call it a day and call the nick from home.

'Oh, sod it,' he said out loud, which meant that he had decided to visit the ex-juror, Victor Prendergast. Well, at least it wasn't far: Vicarage Lane, Terrace Vale.

It was Harry's day for surprises, all right.

Vicarage Lane had the same design of houses as Terrace Gardens Square, the home of the repulsive Wilson brothers, but the physical decay and social decline were not yet as advanced. As Harry Timberlake drove slowly down the street, he noticed that the front doors had only two or three bell-pushes instead of the great accordion-keyboards of buttons in Terrace Gardens Square.

Number Thirty-one was a semi-detached house which looked as if it was being kept together by the ivy which covered most of the building. But the windows and the curtains behind them were clean, the short gravel driveway raked, and the four steps leading to the front door had been washed and swept. To Harry's surprise there was only one bell-push, and it had no nameplate beside it. When he rang, the bell sent back a jangling echo from the interior.

The door was opened cautiously by a woman wearing a faded, flower-patterned dress and a pink cotton pinafore, thick stockings and highly polished lace-up shoes. She had the sort of featureless face that defeats police artists and photo-fits. Harry estimated her to be in her mid-sixties. In fact she was ten years younger. She had the look of someone who lived in a permanent overcast and never got into the first three of anything.

'Good afternoon,' Harry said. 'Is Mr Prendergast at home?'

'I'm Mrs Prendergast.' The woman's voice matched her appearance. 'What's it about?'

'Detective Inspector Timberlake, Terrace—' Harry began, producing his warrant card. Before he could say anything more the woman came to agitated life.

'What's he done?' she said in a suddenly shrill voice.

'Nothing. It's just a routine matter. May I come in?'

She stepped back, opening the door barely wide enough for Harry to enter. She shepherded him into the front room, which was crowded with heavy, old-fashioned furniture that was probably expensive when it was new. Everything had been polished until it shone. Harry didn't think the room was used a great deal.

'Why do you want to see Mr Prendergast?' the woman said, calmer now.

'As I said, it's a personal matter relating to a routine enquiry.'

'He's not in.'

'When will he be back?'

'I don't know. Probably not tonight.'

The impression was growing in Harry that there was something strange about this house, this island of one-family, shabby gentility in a rising sea of urban decay. The ambience was definitely spooky. Behind Mrs Prendergast's façade of depressed anonymity was something secret, an old skeleton at the back of a dark cupboard. His feeling had no logical basis, and Harry tried to resist it as being the result of overwork and anxiety about this case. And yet . . .

Mrs Prendergast had hardly finished speaking when the sound of footsteps and the brief whirr of an electric drill came from a room upstairs. She involuntarily looked up, then at Harry, guilt painted all over her face. It should have been easy for her to find an explanation for the sounds, but she remained silent as she clearly struggled for words.

210

Harry's instincts exploded into certainty. *What's going on here?* he asked himself. He brushed past Mrs Prendergast and went to the stairs in the hall. 'Hello?' he called.

A door at the head of the stairs opened and a man came out. He left the door half open behind him. Harry moved up the stairs slowly, so as not to alarm him, but also warily for his own protection against any surprises.

The man was an old thirty-five with an oddly large, pallid face that went ill with his spare build and slightly rounded shoulders. His thinning hair was carefully plastered across his pate in a vain attempt to disguise his baldness. He was dressed in grey trousers, a white shirt and blue cardigan. Despite his premature ageing, he looked young to be Mrs Prendergast's husband.

'Mr Prendergast? Mr Victor Prendergast?' Harry asked.

The man nodded.

Harry continued his slow progress up the stairs, with what he hoped was a friendly smile on his face. Despite the smile, the hairs on the back of his neck were sticking up – not with fear, but with a hunter's instinct. He reached for his warrant card and started the ritual of identifying himself just as part of the room became visible through the half-open door. As soon as Harry said 'Detective Inspector . . .' the man closed the door behind him.

Too late.

Harry reached the landing. Keeping his voice under control he said, 'Shall we go in?' and without waiting for an answer, 'Thank you.' He moved towards the door.

The man made a half-hearted gesture to stop Harry, who ignored him and entered the room.

The first thing that struck Harry was the strange amber-golden light that suffused the room, the result of the late afternoon sunlight shining through orange-coloured coarse-weave curtains. The place was a beautifully fitted-out workroom with tools and delicate instruments ranged in racks with Guards-like precision. Beneath them were a couple of fixed drills and a small lathe. On the spotless workbench a number of parts of a model steam locomotive and a model World War I aircraft were covered with the sort of glass domes which used to protect railway-buffet sandwiches. The bench had a couple of fluorescent lamps, not alight, with integral magnifying glasses.

In one corner was a small desk with a typewriter. Above

the central heating radiator was a set of bookshelves carrying technical books and manuals. A superb model Halifax MkIII bomber – the version with the radial Hercules engines – hung from an almost invisible nylon thread attached to the centre light. The movement of the two men in the room caused tiny air eddies which made the aircraft turn gently as if at a pilot's command.

But it was the wallboard which Harry had glimpsed from the stairs that was the real focus of his attention. He had seen it for only a second before Prendergast had tried to keep it from view, but that was long enough.

There was a key in the door. Harry locked the door behind him and slipped the key into his pocket. Prendergast made no protest. He was strangely impassive. Harry skirted a half-sized bottled-gas heater on the polished wood floor and went to study the wallboard.

It carried a number of photographs, most of them taken from newspapers and magazines. The pictures had typewritten captions with the names of the subjects. Ernie Birt smirked at him from the large, signed photograph. Harry studied it, and the floridly written dedication. 'Joseph?' he asked.

'It's my first name, but I never use it,' Prendergast told him. 'Only she does.'

Near the centre of the board was a typewritten list of names. Harry recognised some of them: Titus Lloyd, Reginald Barclay, Trevor Naismith, Peter Longford, Lincoln Edwards, Ernie Birt. All jurors. J. Victor Prendergast was not on the list. Separated from these names and two others that meant nothing to him was another group. It was headed by Howard Foulds and included DC Geoffrey Robson and Simon Porter. Each person on the list who was dead had a thin line drawn through his name and a small cross beside it.

Harry turned slowly and looked at Prendergast.

'So it was you,' he said.

Conflicting emotions chased across Prendergast's face: fear – a little, not much – satisfaction, pride even, and something else Harry couldn't decipher.

'I don't know what you suspect me of, Inspector, but if I had done something wrong, you'd never prove anything. I don't make mistakes.' His words were braver than he sounded.

'Really, Mr Prendergast,' said Harry. He regarded Prendergast squarely and considered what approach to take with him. He decided to let Prendergast have it right between the eyes. 'Well, I suspect you of having committed a number of murders. Whether you made any mistakes or not, we'll see. First of all, there is the evidence of that wallboard and the list on it, and your connection with those people. That's the circumstantial evidence. At the scene of Howard Foulds's murder we found one hair. Genetic finger-printing will tell us with absolute certainty whether or not it was your hair. Then microscopic examination of the bolt which killed Reginald Barclay will establish whether or not it was turned on that lathe with your tools. They can match up the minutest grooves on the bolt with imperfections in the cutting edge of the tools, invisible under the strongest magnifying glass. That's material evidence. And I wonder if you threw away the shotgun, or whether we'll find it here somewhere.'

Prendergast looked like a doll with the sawdust running out. He sat down heavily. For a brief moment Harry almost felt sorry for him, but only almost.

'I'd like you to come to the police station with me and answer some questions to help us with our enquiries, sir,' Harry said formally. He began the standard caution. 'I must remind you that I suspect you of having committed a number of murders. You are not obliged to say anything, but anything you do say will be taken down and may be used in evidence.' He took out his pocketbook.

After a pause Prendergast said quietly, 'What led you to me?'

Harry noted that this was not necessarily an incriminating statement, as any competent lawyer would point out. It was the sort of remark any innocent man might make. Prendergast had his wits about him.

Harry knew he was at a crucial point in this first interview. How well the rest of the interview proceeded could all depend on what he said now and the effect it had on Prendergast.

'What led me to you? I'd rather leave that until we get to the station,' he said. The other man looked disappointed. With a flash of inspiration Harry added, 'I'll admit you were clever. Very clever. But let's say for now that you were too clever.'

Prendergast straightened up in his chair. Something like a smile appeared on his face.

'Now if you're ready, sir,' Harry said, deliberately being almost over-polite.

213

'Joseph?' came Mrs Prendergast's voice from downstairs. 'Is everything all right?'

'Yes, Mother,' Prendergast called out, rather petulantly.

Harry locked the workroom door behind them and kept the key. He took Prendergast down to the hall where his mother was waiting. She looked first at her son, and then at Harry. With a shock he knew without a doubt that she had been aware all along of her son's murderous activities.

He phoned Terrace Vale and asked for officers to be sent to the Prendergast home to make sure the workroom door stayed locked until J. Victor Prendergast's situation was resolved. The SOCOs would come and go through the place with their equipment, and take away all material evidence from the house.

Prendergast's chances of being released, Harry thought, were about as likely as finding a black gynaecologist in a South African hospital for Blankes.

Chapter 11

Experienced interrogators know that sometimes it isn't good technique to let a suspect talk just when he wants to. There comes a psychological moment when he will pour out everything the interrogator wants to know, and the trick is to recognise that moment. So, timing is everything. Trying to make him talk too soon can produce precisely the wrong effect and make the subject turn sulky and refuse to say anything for a long time. Leaving it too late can make him refuse to co-operate either from apathy or from sheer bloody-mindedness.

While Harry and Prendergast were waiting for the back-up to arrive, Prendergast made half-hearted attempts to start a conversation, but Harry remained monosyllabic; he stonewalled while remaining apparently deferential. On the drive to Terrace Vale he could feel that Prendergast's internal pressure to talk was mounting, but Harry sensed that the critical moment hadn't quite arrived.

Terrace Vale station was humming as if someone had won the pools jackpot and the Queen was coming to tea. Harry whisked Prendergast into an interview room, shielding him from all the excitement. Superintendent Harkness and Ward and a shorthand writer joined them there.

On some occasions an interrogator tries to create an intimacy with the suspect by being friendly and calling him by his Christian name – the technique of which Superintendent Frank Ward was a master. Instinctively, Harry knew that it would be a mistake to treat Prendergast like this. He had sensed that Prendergast was naturally reserved and to some degree was – paradoxically for a murderer – basically timid. At the same time he wanted to impress Harry, who encouraged the feeling. All his life Prendergast had been treated offhandedly; now Harry behaved towards him with respect and called him 'Mr Prendergast' and 'sir'.

The two senior officers were ready to intervene in the interrogation if Harry faltered, but he didn't put a foot wrong. He let Prendergast think he was controlling the interview and was demonstrating his own cleverness when it was really Harry's quiet, astute prompting which determined its direction.

Harry began by formally cautioning Prendergast again, this time in front of the witnesses. When he put his first question it had been carefully prepared.

'On the wallboard in your workroom is a list of names, all of people who were involved in the trial of Roy Pocock.'

'That's right.'

'Some of the names have a line through them and have a cross beside them. All these people have been killed.' He nearly said 'murdered', but checked in time. 'Do you want to say anything about that?'

Harry's timing was impeccable: Prendergast had a great deal to say. From the point of view of the perpetrator of the perfect murder that perfect murder still has one flaw. He can't tell anyone about it. But now Prendergast could talk about the murders and how clever he had been. He was positively simmering with eagerness to explain. For the moment he seemed to overlook the fact that he hadn't been clever enough not to get caught.

He took the detectives through the saga of his killings: how he had watched and followed his victims, how he procured the means for killing them. When it came down to it, Prendergast had managed to do nothing any man of determination and average intelligence could not have achieved.

He had one advantage: he had all the time he needed, for he didn't have to work for a living. His mother had a substantial private income from investments bought with the proceeds of a large insurance policy after her husband was killed in an industrial accident and the compensation paid by his employers. She gave Prendergast all the money he needed, and more. But he had no father: Prendergast was six when he died.

There was still one big question that remained untouched, the biggest one of all, but Harry didn't want to break the flow of Prendergast's long recital. As it ran its shocking course, Harry

216

grew increasingly aware that, although Prendergast was intellectually far superior to the average low-life violent criminal, he was definitely short of some marbles. He was a psychotic; he showed absolutely no remorse for his actions and could see nothing wrong with them. At last he said something that gave the detectives an insight into his mind. Quite casually Prendergast declared, 'I used a different method each time so you wouldn't realise, or at least, not until it was too late, that there was a connection between the executions.'

The word lay between them like an unexploded bomb.

'Executions?' Harry asked. It opened the door to the big question: 'Why?'

'You know I was on the Roy Pocock jury. Well, ever since the truth of his innocence came out I couldn't forgive myself for finding him guilty. I knew he was innocent. For a long time I couldn't sleep, until—' He stopped for a moment. 'I wanted to find him not guilty, you know, but all the others kept on at me.'

'Why did you think – know – he was innocent?' Harry asked.

'I could tell by looking at him,' Prendergast said simply. He paused. 'As I said, all the others kept on at me, saying I was stupid and wasting their time.' He wiped away flecks of spittle from the corner of his mouth. 'So, they had to be punished.'

'Killed,' said Harry. They'd got a full statement from Prendergast now, and he didn't have to be all that careful any more. Prendergast just shrugged.

Harkness made his first intervention. 'They had to be punished for finding an innocent man guilty?'

'Oh, that as well,' Prendergast said dismissively. 'But they made *me* feel guilty. For years it preyed on my mind more and more. I had this terrible weight of guilt, and all because of them.' He smiled; a small, gentle, awful smile. 'Until I decided to punish them and in that way get rid of my guilt.'

'How about the people you killed? Don't you feel any guilt about them?' Harkness asked. 'Or remorse?'

Prendergast looked at him in surprise. 'I told you: they had to be punished for what they did.' He frowned, and for a moment he was lost in his own labyrinthine thoughts. 'Besides, they forced me to make a mistake, and I don't make mistakes,' he added, still frowning. 'I don't make mistakes.'

'Two more things, Mr Prendergast,' Harry said. 'The women

217

on the jury. You took no action against them.' He couldn't bring himself to say 'punished' or 'executed'.

'Oh, women,' Prendergast answered contemptuously. 'They don't know what to think unless someone tells them. It wasn't their fault.'

Harry nodded. 'You've spoken about jurors, and witnesses whose evidence was faulty. What about Mr Foulds, who defended Roy Pocock?'

'I'm surprised that you didn't see why he had to be punished,' Prendergast said reproachfully.

'Tell me.'

'He defended Pocock, but he did it badly. If you ask me, he didn't believe in his own client's innocence. If Howard Foulds had carried out the defence properly, Pocock would have been acquitted. It stands to reason.'

'That was a fine piece of work,' Superintendent Harkness told Harry Timberlake. Which was about as much praise as he would give someone for winning World War III practically single-handed.

'I was just lucky I was the one to call on Prendergast,' Harry said uncomfortably.

'I meant the whole thing, from the original concept of a single murder to your interview with Prendergast. It was all very well done.'

Harry felt that any more modest disclaimers would risk sounding hypocritical, so he muttered, 'Thank you.'

They were in Harkness's office, with Superintendent Ward and his opposite number from the Southington area who had been leading the enquiry into DC Robson's murder. Since Prendergast's arrest, wires had been humming. Ward and the Southington superintendent were drinking whisky, Harkness was drinking Badoit, of which he always seemed to have a supply. Harry Timberlake would dearly have liked a whisky himself, but to his surprise Harkness's abstinence intimidated him. It wasn't the only reason he was drinking slot-machine coffee, though. An inconvenient thought was nagging at him like a forgotten name of someone he should know, and he wanted a clear head to deal with it.

Harkness looked at him closely. 'You don't seem completely satisfied with your success.'

Harry searched for the right words. 'Prendergast's attitude at the end: it wasn't right, somehow. It wasn't what it should be, given all the circumstances. I got a nasty feeling he was holding something back; there was something I missed.'

'His statement seemed comprehensive enough to me,' Harkness said. 'But you were the one having eye contact with him all the time and I could see you were studying him carefully. If your instinct tells you there's an important piece missing, you must go after it. Your instinct has been pretty accurate up to now.' Ward gave an 'Aaar' of agreement.

'It wasn't only Prendergast himself,' Harry said thoughtfully. He was thinking out loud to help get his ideas in order. 'It was his workroom. There was something I saw there that should have registered and didn't – I'm sure of it.'

'You'd better get back there, then,' Harkness said. 'If you get Prendergast out of his cell and start questioning him again, he'll guess you know he's holding something back and he'll become twice as secretive.'

'But why would he hold something back?' the other superintendent asked.

'Because he wants to prove that he's cleverer than the rest of us after all,' Harry said. He got up and started for the door.

Mrs Prendergast let Harry into the house. She was wearing a dressing gown that nineteenth-century missionaries might have found overly modest. Harry waited for her to ask about her son, but she said nothing. Before Harry could decide whether or not to offer any information, she turned and disappeared towards the back of the house.

'What a bloody pair,' Harry muttered.

The constable guarding the workroom let him in. Paradoxically the room seemed brighter by artificial light than in daytime. The orange-amber glow created by the curtains was replaced by the hard, bluish-white light of fluorescent tubes. Harry began his examination at the door. He was almost certain that the clue he was looking for was on the other side of the room, on the wallboard, but, for a reason that he only half understood, he wanted to leave it till last. As he studied the parts of models on the workbench, Harry marvelled at the quality of Prendergast's work, which somehow he could not dare to touch. The models must have needed inhuman patience and concentration.

219

There was nothing new that Harry needed to learn from the workbench and its contents. The long interview had given him sufficient insight into Prendergast's strange mind. He made his way round the room to the bookshelves over the radiator. There were books on model-making, reference books on aircraft, cars and locomotives, a thin book on picking locks, a couple of books on chemistry and several on electronics. They meant nothing to Harry.

He arrived in front of the wallboard. He looked at the type-written list of names.

The clue he had been looking for leapt off the paper at him.

The crosses beside the names of the victims had one line in blue, the other in red. Next to Ernie Birt's name was a blue diagonal. Harry was bewildered that he hadn't seen something so obvious on his first visit before the explanation came to him. The other occasion had been in the late afternoon when the orange-amber light had disguised the colour of the crosses, as yellow sodium-vapour street lights can make it impossible to make out the real colour of a dark car. When he had seen it before, the one stroke next to Birt's name had looked like an accidental mark.

It didn't take a genius to guess that a blue stroke meant that an attack had been planned or prepared, and the red stroke to form the cross signified that the coup had succeeded. Prendergast had been as fussily meticulous in his murdering as in his model-making. And it had given Harry a valuable clue: an attack on Birt had been planned . . . or perhaps it had already been put into action, and that accounted for Prendergast's secret satisfaction. Perhaps there was poison somewhere waiting for the unsuspecting Birt to take, as in the case of the unfortunate Trevor Naismith.

What had Prendergast planned for Birt?

Although time might be vital, Harry carefully went through the room again, but there was nothing he could see that gave him any indication of Prendergast's intentions. What he didn't know was that Prendergast, motivated by the same sense of self-preservation which had prompted him to throw the crossbow into the Thames, had destroyed the book on the assassination attempts on Hitler and the pamphlet for anarchists which gave instructions for making an explosive from fertiliser and sugar.

Harry sighed. He would have to tackle Prendergast again and hope to God that he didn't make any mistakes.

Prendergast was asleep in his cell when Harry returned to the station. Under the cell's harsh light that was never turned out, Prendergast's face had the unhealthy fish-belly pallor of a nightclub worker or a professional snooker player. Prendergast's long day, his interrogation, and the reaction of sudden release of nervous tension now that it was all over, had left him drained.

Harry woke him gently. Shock tactics, talking tough, threats or bullying would be counterproductive, Harry knew. If Prendergast had set in motion a plan to kill Birt, he would keep it secret at all costs, to score over Harry and the other detectives. No, guile was the only way. When Prendergast was thoroughly awake Harry asked him if he wanted a cup of cocoa. During his interview he had refused tea and coffee and asked for cocoa. The canteen had had to search the storeroom for some.

'No, thanks.' He paused and looked at Harry. 'Why did you wake me?'

'Have I played fair with you, Mr Prendergast?' It was a hypocritical question, for Harry meant to be as unfair as he could manage.

'Yes.'

'Then why haven't you played fair with me?'

'What do you mean?'

'I've been back to your workroom for another look round.'

Prendergast looked indignant. 'I hope you haven't been moving my things,' he said sharply. Apparently it didn't occur to him that he wouldn't see his workroom again for many years, if ever.

'No, of course not,' Harry said comfortingly. He paused. 'You didn't tell me about Ernie Birt.'

Prendergast looked cunning and frank at the same time. 'You didn't ask me.'

Harry managed a smile. 'True enough.' He paused again. 'He's the next one on your list, of course. I could tell from your board: you've already planned something for him.'

Prendergast smiled slyly. 'You could say that.' He was feeling superior, almost god-like. 'What time is it?'

'About a quarter to twelve.'

'Exactly?'

Harry studied his digital watch. 23.46.20. 'Eleven forty-six and . . . twenty seconds.'

Prendergast gave his weird little chuckle.

221

'You're too late.'

Alarmed, Harry asked, 'What d'you mean?'

'It'll go off before you get there.'

At first Harry didn't believe it, or didn't want to. 'You've planted a bomb?'

Another chuckle. 'That's right.'

Harry tried to sound unconcerned, but his voice betrayed the sudden strain he was feeling. 'And where, may I ask, Mr Prendergast, did you get the explosive?'

'I made it myself. Fertiliser and sugar, mainly. It's quite simple, really.' He smiled with satisfaction. 'I tested a little of it. Very effective.' An icy hand gripped Harry's heart. Prendergast went on, 'And even if you got there in time, which I doubt, you'd still have to find it.'

'What time is it set for?'

'Midnight exactly. To the second. Electronically timed.'

Without another word Harry raced out of the cell, rushing past the constable who was the custody officer. 'Bang him up!' Harry shouted over his shoulder. The constable pulled himself together and locked the cell door.

Harry rushed to the front desk where Sergeant Rumsden was doing a rare night duty. As he ran he took the list of addresses Superintendent Harkness had given him from his pocket and scanned it.

'Listen, Tony,' Harry said urgently, 'I've only got time to say this once. Prendergast's put a bomb on Ernie Birt's houseboat near Royalty Embankment. Here's the address.' He threw the sheet of paper on the counter. 'It's due to go off at midnight.'

Rumsden automatically looked at the clock. 'Christ,' he said.

'Have someone phone Birt to get him out of it, then they can get on to MP to have as many mobiles as they can raise to evacuate the area. You warn the bomb squad, and inform the local station so they can help the evacuation.'

'Right,' said Sergeant Rumsden, picking up the phone. 'Sarah!' he bellowed.

Sarah Lewis stuck her head round the door. 'Sarge?'

'Here, at the double.'

As she hurried to the counter Harry Timberlake said, 'I want a car with a siren.'

Rumsden reached for a set of keys from the board behind

222

him. 'Better take a patrol car. Hotel-Echo, it's in the yard. No: take Kilo-Whisky. It's got a motorway horn.' He threw over the keys. As Harry turned to go Rumsden added, 'Harry – Birt's houseboat, it's green and white and it's tied up almost directly opposite the King William pub. I saw it on telly.'

'Thanks,' Harry said over his shoulder.

'What's up, Sarge?' Sarah asked.

'Bomb scare. Now listen.' He began to give her instructions while he dialled a number on his own phone.

Harry lost five precious seconds trying to start Kilo-Whisky with too much choke, because the engine was still warm. He switched on the powerful siren, which sent the most God-awful banshee shriek echoing and re-echoing round the yard. He snapped on the radio, the flashing blue lamps, full headlights and the amber flashers. Anyone would have to be deaf, stupid and tunnel-vision blind not to be aware of the car a quarter of a mile away. Unfortunately, a lot of people were all three once they got behind a steering wheel, Harry knew. He felt a mounting rage against Prendergast, and was determined not to let him get the better of him. There had been nothing Harry could do to stop any of the previous murders, but he was not going to let that madman succeed with this one. It had become a personal thing, Harry knew, which was unprofessional, but to hell with that. Despite all the odds, he was going to beat the bastard.

23.48.11

He shot out of the yard leaving black tyre marks and a stench of burnt rubber behind him. He caught a glimpse of a pale, frightened face as the car hurtled through the gates, across the pavement and on to the roadway.

At the bottom of the street was a T-junction with the main road. There were two ways to get to the Royalty Embankment. Turning left would take him on to the shorter route, but some of the streets were narrow and full of parked cars. Going to the right would be longer, but the journey would be on wider roads with faster-moving traffic.

The traffic lights at the T-junction were at red as Harry Timberlake rushed towards them, but he kept his foot hard down on the accelerator until the last possible moment. The few drivers in the main road had heard Harry's arrival and were approaching warily. All except one driver, who doggedly insisted on his right to pass a green light and ploughed on.

Harry flashed across the front of the car, yanking the steering wheel to the right. The rear of the car broke away on a patch of oil, but he spun the wheel the other way and checked the skid. Behind him an ashen-faced driver stood on his brakes, then felt a metal-crunching thump as another driver, fascinated by the manoeuvre of Kilo-Whisky, saw the other car too late and ran into the back of it.

Harry kept the Rover in second gear for maximum acceleration and engine braking. He needed neither as he approached the big roundabout with the turnoff south: his flashing lights and howling siren carved a clear way through the fairly light traffic and he took the roundabout at something like 60 m.p.h., the Rover heeling over with a shriek of tortured tyres.

23.50.47

Kilo-Whisky plummeted on down towards the river through a twisting one-way system where fate gave Harry a hand by keeping all the lights on green. The radio crackled into life.

'Central to Kilo-Whisky.'

Harry pressed the transmit button. 'Kilo-Whisky. Over!'

'Message from O Division. Mr Birt has an ex-directory number and hasn't been contacted yet. Still trying.'

'Oh, shit!' Harry said before pressing the transmit button again. 'Roger.'

'Kilo-Whisky, other mobiles *en route* for Royalty Embankment. Proceed with caution.'

'Oh, yeah,' Harry said sarcastically to himself. 'Roger, out,' he said on the radio.

He gave a quick glance at the dashboard clock.

23.52.14

Just in time he looked up to be able to take a sliding turn to the left, and to the right again at a big cinema. As he turned into Southington Court Road, Harry took a chance and overtook a bus blind, a thing he had never done before and would never do again, if he lived long enough to have the opportunity. A motor coach was coming in the opposite direction. He steered for the gap between them and prayed.

There couldn't have been more than three inches clearance on either side. The palms of his hands felt damp.

As he roared past the large modern Southington police station, he wondered briefly if anyone had been looking out of the windows, and what they thought of him if they saw him. He didn't waste much time worrying about it and raced on towards Camel Alley with its still-open shops and pedestrians who walked on pavements and roadway indiscriminately.

The rev counter needle was in the red sector on the dial, and the scream of the protesting engine added to the fearsome din of the siren to blast a way through the traffic and pedestrians.

Then the unbelievable happened.

23.54.33

Despite the lights and the monstrous noise from Kilo-Whisky, a young couple, totally absorbed in each other, stepped off the pavement in front of Harry.

There was simply no room to stop.

Too late, the couple spun round, and in a second that was packed with movement and terror, their faces became white blobs of panic in the glare of the headlights. The boy tried to drag the girl across to the far side of the road, but she resisted and struggled to get back to the pavement. Between them they blocked the road.

It was a question of which one Harry was going to kill.

He heaved on the wheel. The girl's high-pitched scream cut through all other sounds. There was a sickening bump which Harry thought for a split second was the car hitting a body, but it was the Rover's front wheel hitting the kerb. The car mounted the pavement, lifting the nearside wheel off the ground, but as Harry swung the steering wheel the offside wheel, forced down hard as the car pitched, gave enough grip to straighten the car. Kilo-Whisky bucketed along the pavement – luckily free of pedestrians – for some fifty yards before Harry regained full control and put it back on the roadway again.

His throat was tight and he could feel his heart beating so fast he thought it would burst. He let the car slow down.

'Christ, is it worth it, just to beat Prendergast? he asked himself. I could have killed somebody back there. But he realised that the only justification for what he had done was to keep on going and be in time: there was Birt's life to consider as well.

23.56.29

He put his foot down hard on the accelerator again. He was

now in the residential area of Whitecliffe Gardens. Unaware of it, he raced past the small garden square where Prendergast had blown off most of Geoff Robson's head. He wasn't far from Royalty Embankment now. He didn't dare look at his watch again in case he found he was going to be too late. As long as he didn't know the time, he could believe that he would be there in time. He wished to God that his heart would slow down.

In the mirror Harry could see the reflection of another flashing blue light of a police car far behind him, or maybe it was the fire brigade or bomb squad. He couldn't hear its siren, though, and it dawned on him that the almost unbearable sound of his own siren was drowning out any others that might be in the vicinity. Proceed with caution be buggered.

23.58.01

He kept his foot hard down as he took the last left-hand bend on to Queen's Walk and Royalty Embankment. There was more traffic here and twice he went round the outside of a traffic bollard in the middle of the road. For once he got the car up into third gear and hurtled along the wrong side of the straight but narrow road at more than 70 m.p.h. before getting back to his own side. After what he had just been through it seemed unimportant.

23.58.44

In the distance Harry could see the bulk of the King William pub on his left. There was nothing coming in the opposite direction, so he drove diagonally across the road and stopped next to the entry to the towpath where a line of houseboats was moored. He left the lights of the car on, but switched off the siren. Now he heard a whole discordant chorus of sirens approaching, including the old-fashioned two-note sirens of fire engines, and flashing blue lights bounced back from the tops of buildings.

At last he dared look at his watch.

23.59.17

Less than one minute to get Birt and anyone else out of danger, if he could . . .

Harry leapt on to the towpath. The neatly lined-up houseboats had small signboards with their names on posts. Triple umbilical cords of water, electricity and telephone lines linked them to dry land. Harry hoped to God the craft were sturdy enough to protect the people in them if the bomb went off. At least there was no one on the towpath.

23.59.38

Where the fuck was Birt's boat?

With one eye on his watch so he could be ready to throw himself to the ground, Harry pounded along the towpath.

24.00.00

It all happened at once.

As his watch flicked over to 24.00.00, he saw the noticeboard, *Ilkley*.

There were two houseboats on either side, but where *Ilkley* should have been, there was nothing. Just dirty, black water with oil and rubbish bobbing gently on the surface. And no houseboat.

Harry stood there, frozen, uncomprehending. His first thought was that the bomb had gone off early and sunk Birt's houseboat, but he dismissed it almost before it was formulated. He would have heard the explosion, there would have been wreckage, and people about.

The noise and flashing lights began to rouse people and bring them to the scene from the large houses and expensive flats across the road. Policemen from the cars poured on to the towpath and milled about, uncertain what to do, adding to the general air of confusion.

A man wearing a striped dressing gown over what appeared to be a long nightshirt, and a pair of slippers with turned-up toes, appeared on the deck of the houseboat next to the empty space. He blinked some of the sleep from his eyes. Harry's immediate impression of him was that he was something of a prat.

'What's going on?' he asked.

'Where's Mr Birt's houseboat?' Harry asked sharply.

The man looked at him, at the empty space, and back at Harry again. 'It's not here,' he said. Harry could have taken him by the neck and shaken him.

'I know,' he said with monumental self-control. 'Do you know where it is?'

A dark young woman joined the man on the deck. If her clothes were anything to go by, she played centre-forward for Celtic.

'Who are you?' came a voice from behind Harry. It was a large police sergeant. Harry ignored him.

'Do you know where it is?' Harry asked the young woman.

'Just a moment, do you mind telling me who you are?' the sergeant persisted.

'Inspector Timberlake, Terrace Vale,' Harry said grittily. The sergeant retreated. Harry looked at the young woman.

'Mr Birt had it taken to Hunter's Boatyard, up towards Chiswick, yesterday. It needed some work on the hull.'

'Thanks. You wouldn't have the phone number, would you?'

'As a matter of fact we do have it. We took our own boat there a few months ago.'

'That's right,' the man said, anxious to make a contribution to the conversation.

'May I use your phone?'

The woman nodded and went back inside the boat, beckoning to Harry to follow her. After a moment's indecision, the man tailed on behind.

The interior of the boat could have been part of a luxury mews house, except for the floor which was gently curved and higher at one end than at the other. Harry thought he'd be seasick after living two days there.

The young woman pointed to the telephone, and looked up the number in an address book for him. Harry dialled, listened and finally put the phone down with some annoyance. 'Answering machine,' he said tersely. 'Do you have any idea what road you have to take for the yard?' he asked the young woman.

'Westfields Lane. It's off Brentford Cut. First on the left past the big hospital. I went there a couple of times while our boat was being repainted.'

'Brilliant. Thanks very much,' Harry said.

'What's all the fuss about?' the young woman asked.

'Sorry, no time,' he told her. He went out back on deck and signalled to the police sergeant, who had been joined by a senior fire officer. 'Where's the bomb planted?' he said, keeping his voice down so that the members of the public couldn't hear.

'On a houseboat, *Ilkley*, at Hunter's Boatyard, near Chiswick,' Harry told him. 'If there is a bomb.'

'Out of our area,' the fire officer said. 'I'll let the station know so they can inform the local brigade.'

Harry addressed the sergeant. 'You heard that. Hunter's Boatyard. Inform MP and make your own way there.'

He ran to his car and managed to get moving before the massive fire appliances started up and blocked most of the road. He was well on his way before the other policemen had got themselves organised to follow him.

31 mins. 00 secs to Zero

Harry drove fast, but not as excessively as he had done before. Rightly or wrongly, the extreme sense of urgency that he had been feeling since the moment he left Terrace Vale had all but evaporated. He had time to notice at last that the Rover's steering wheel was 45 degrees off centre when the car was going straight. Hitting the kerb had knocked Kilo-Whisky's tracking badly out of line.

He was trembling slightly from reaction after his hair-raising journey from Terrace Vale and the near miss of the couple in the roadway. The anticlimax of finding the mooring space empty had left him feeling flat. He was puzzled, too. He had heard no explosion, and there had been no news of one coming over the police radio. Yet from what he had seen of Prendergast and his work Harry could not believe that his device, whatever it was, didn't work. Prendergast was too precise and meticulous. So what could have happened . . .?

Maybe it was all a false alarm. Prendergast had been playing a nasty, twisted practical joke on him and there was no danger after all, Harry tried to convince himself. But he knew better.

He was soon to find out that terror and potential carnage was waiting for him at Hunter's Boatyard, more than even Prendergast could have conceived.

The noisy agitation of the police presence departed from the Royalty Embankment area to be replaced by a different sort of disturbance as the inhabitants buzzed around trying to find out what all the commotion had been about. It was the turn of people in Brentford and Chiswick to be roused by a whoop-whooping caravan of police cars and vans. Harry Timberlake had taken a flying start from the embankment and he maintained his lead over the others all the way to Hunter's Boatyard in Westfields Lane. It was a cul-de-sac which ended at the main gate and high wall of the boatyard. If the night watchman had been sleeping earlier, by the time the rest of the police and the fire brigade were driving down Westfields Lane no one within the vicinity who wasn't actually stone deaf or deceased was not awake. He opened the gates for the small army of police and firemen.

Ilkley was in the boatyard all right. It was drawn up out of the water, resting on a large wooden cradle under a tall three-sided shed. If there was a bomb aboard, due to go off at any moment, there was no possibility of getting the houseboat to a slightly less dangerous position in the middle of the river. Then Harry saw it.

24 mins. 05 secs.

On a sort of wharf beside Ernie Birt's houseboat was a large stockpile of bottled gas cylinders, the sort used for self-contained heaters and boat cooking stoves. Behind them was a large paint store.

'Jesus Christ!' somebody said. Harry looked round. A senior fire officer was staring at the wharf. 'Station Officer Bill Smedley. The sergeant said you were in charge.'

'Sort of. Harry Timberlake.'

'Well, Harry, if there's a bomb that sets this little lot off, half of London W5 will be a smoky hole in the ground.'

A uniformed police inspector walked up swiftly to Harry.

'Inspector Timberlake?'

'Yes.'

'I'm Inspector Puddefoot. What's the situation?'

Harry explained, and the fire officer added a few frightening grace notes. 'You'd better get everybody out of the area,' Harry concluded. 'Any sign of the bomb squad yet?'

'They're on their way. ETA in eleven minutes.' Puddefoot hurried off to organise his men into evacuating the area.

21 mins. 37 secs.

'D'you reckon there is a bomb on the boat?' the fire officer asked.

'Very probably. What I don't understand is why it hasn't gone off. It was timed for midnight.'

'Bad workmanship?'

'Not much chance of that, I'm afraid.' Harry bit his lip. 'If the sodding thing goes off while people are in the streets, moving away . . .'

'Don't,' said the fire officer.

It was nearly twelve years since Harry had given up smoking. He felt like a cigarette now. He and the fire officer backed off from the houseboat, Harry to wait for the bomb squad, Bill Smedley to arrange the setting up of appliances ready to tackle any fire a bomb might set off. Harry watched the well-organised, disciplined fire crews working fast but carefully.

'Think all that will do any good?' Harry asked.

'If that lot' – the fire officer indicated the gas cylinders – 'goes up, we'll never know. Unless you believe in an afterlife. But we can't just stand here, do nothing and hope for the best.'

'Thanks for the encouragement.' Harry looked at his watch. 'Where's the bloody bomb squad?' he asked, not expecting an answer.

The waiting was getting on Harry's nerves. He had an uncomfortable pricking of the thumbs that something was wrong and going to get worse. He left the houseboat and went looking for Inspector Puddefoot.

12 mins. 19 secs.

He found him in a sort of command headquarters, a large communications van. 'What's the news of the bomb squad?' Harry asked.

'They're not answering their R/T,' Puddefoot told him. Both men knew that there could be any one of three perfectly straightforward reasons for this: the bomb squad's receiver was on the blink; their transmitter was on the blink; or they were in one of the few blind spots for radio communications – for example, in a road tunnel or near another powerful transmitter. For all anyone could tell the squad's transport could come rolling down the road at any moment.

Nevertheless, Harry Timberlake got another nasty feeling that something was badly wrong. This was a night when everything was out of joint, when events seemed to have a malign illogicality about them. 'Don't forget Sod's Law,' Harry said morosely. ' "If things can go wrong, they will." '

'Don't worry,' Puddefoot said confidently. 'They'll be here any minute. Besides, we don't even know that there is a bomb. You said it was supposed to go off at midnight.' He looked at his watch. 'It's nearly ten to one.' Harry wasn't comforted. He returned to the wharf, where the firemen were finishing their preparations. The waiting seemed interminable.

6 mins. 19 secs.

'Well, we're as ready as we'll ever be,' Station Officer Smedley said. 'Look, why don't you get back a bit? If something does go up, there's no point in you going up with it. And I don't want to worry about seeing if you're all right.'

Harry didn't answer. He simply stared intently at *Ilkley* as if he could see through the hull to the bomb inside, wherever it was. Smedley was about to say something more when Inspector Puddefoot approached. Before Harry even saw his face he knew it was bad news.

'The bomb squad vehicle has been in a traffic accident and is out of action. They're sending another one, or getting the army squad in,' Puddefoot said.

'A right bloody *Walpurgisnacht*, all right,' Harry said bitterly.

'Huh?' said Smedley.

'Walpurgis night. When the witches meet the Devil and stir things up.' He thought hard, and took in a deep shuddering breath. 'I'm going to have a look for it.'

'You're not a bomb expert, are you?' Puddefoot asked.

'No. But I'm an expert on the man who made it. It might help me to find it quickly.

'Better wait for the bomb squad,' the fire officer said.

It was a tempting suggestion, but Harry forced himself to reject it. 'That could be too late,' he said reluctantly. Besides, there was still this personal thing between him and Prendergast. Maybe Prendergast would have the last laugh after all, when Harry was blown into small pieces. Still, Harry wouldn't know anything about it. He took another deep breath, and stepped on to the wharf with its deadly load of explosive tanks and highly inflammable material in the paint store.

3 mins. 50 secs.

He walked up the gangplank. The door to the cabin had its padlock on it. Harry called out to Smedley. 'You got a crowbar, or something, to break this lock?'

The other man came across and handed Harry his axe. Two blows sent the lock spinning across the deck. The noise of it hitting the decking made Harry jump. He hoped the fire officer hadn't noticed.

'No need for both of us to get blown up,' Harry said.

'This is my sort of job. I'll look around with you.'

'No you bloody won't. You stay put, ready in case . . . ' He left the rest unsaid and ended the conversation by entering the cabin.

Harry pressed the light switch.

Nothing.

Of course, he told himself, they haven't connected up the power from outside. He stuck his head out of the cabin. 'You got a big lamp?' Wordlessly, the fire officer passed him one and Harry went back inside.

He switched on the powerful lamp. His hand was trembling badly enough to make the beam of the lamp waver noticeably. Cold sweat stood out on his forehead. Although he knew it was only imagination he thought he could hear the ticking of the time fuse. He knew this was stupid because Prendergast had said that the timer was electronic.

2 mins. 42 secs.

Harry swung the lamp slowly. In turn it showed up bookshelves, a large filing cabinet, a desk with a word processor, a closed cupboard, a few chairs.

1 min. 11 secs.

Harry froze.

There was the terrifying sound of electronic bleeping.

Was it a sort of ten-second warning before the bomb exploded?

Harry jumped so badly he dropped the lamp. He bent down to grab it and whirled round. The beam was reflected back brilliantly by a battery alarm clock that was flashing as its alarm sounded.

He crossed the cabin floor and switched off the alarm. From outside he could hear policemen with loud hailers directing people away from their homes. He wished he could get the hell out of it with them.

0 min. 55 secs.

He checked. Something was wrong. He looked at the alarm clock and then at his watch. His heart pounded and he felt breathless. Everything had come to him in a flash. He knew now that there was a bomb, and he knew he had less than a minute to find it and disarm it.

He swung the light round the room again, more slowly. He had to guess right first time. His mind raced.

0 min. 50 secs.

The bookshelves? No: there wasn't room enough for a homemade bomb powerful enough to cause real damage.

0min. 45 secs.

The filing cabinet? Perhaps. But presumably Birt might use it, and would spot anything like a bomb that had been planted there. Prendergast wouldn't risk using that for a hiding place.

0 min. 40 secs.

The cupboard? Theoretically the best bet, yet somehow it seemed too obvious.

0 min. 35 secs.

Where was it hidden?

Wastepaper bin, desk, portable heater, word processor, photo-copier . . . Portable gas heater!

Prendergast had exactly the same model in his workroom even though he had central heating radiators in the room! It had to be that!

0 min. 30 secs.

Harry rushed over to the heater. Feverishly he tried to prop up the lamp while he took the back off the heater. He bent down. His heartbeats hammered in his ears.

0 min. 14 secs.

The back jammed . . . No, he was just being clumsy. Careful!

0 min. 9 secs.

The back came off.

0 min. 6 secs.

Inside was the gas bottle . . . and a shaped metal container, some sort of firing device, an electric calculator and a nine-volt battery with two wires attached.

The noise of heavy footsteps and the cell door being unlocked woke J. Victor Prendergast. He opened his eyes and was quickly alert this time when he saw Sergeant Rumsden and the custody officer beside his bed. Before he said anything he studied their faces to see if they gave any clue as to why they were there, but both men were as expressionless as professional poker players.

'What time is it?' Prendergast asked.

'Just gone two,' Rumsden said. His voice was as unrevealing as his face. 'Come with me, please.'

'Why?'

'All in good time,' Rumsden said.

Prendergast slowly got up from the bed. He started to straighten the blankets.

'Leave that,' Rumsden told him.

Prendergast led the way from his cell. He thought that the two policemen were being unnaturally restrained. He gave that small, gentle, awful smile again, hidden from his escort. He could guess why, all right. He knew what had happened. Inspector Timberlake had tried to find the bomb and had been too late. It had blown up in his face, in a manner of speaking.

They got to the interview room where he had given his statement earlier and went in.

'Sit down,' Rumsden said flatly. The constable stood with his back against the wall close to the door.

'What's all this about?' Prendergast asked.

'All in good time,' Rumsden said. 'What I can tell you is that we shall be bringing further charges against you.'

Prendergast's heart soared. Got him! He'd got Clever-clogs Timberlake after all! Who was having the last laugh now! Rumsden left the room, closing the door behind him. The constable was surprised to hear Prendergast humming to himself.

The door opened and Sergeant Rumsden came back in. There was someone behind him.

Prendergast's jaw dropped.

Harry Timberlake entered.

Prendergast saw something that made his head spin as if he'd taken a punch in the face.

Harry advanced to the centre of the room, and put on the table a half-size bottled-gas heater. *The* heater.

'You never make mistakes?' Harry asked, not really expecting an answer. 'Well, you made two this time.'

'I didn't! I couldn't have done!' Prendergast shouted. His voice sounded girlish and hysterical. He was staring disbelievingly at the heater. When Harry spoke and moved about Prendergast didn't take his eyes off it.

'Two mistakes,' Harry repeated. 'It didn't occur to you that Mr Birt might move his houseboat and wouldn't be on it when your bomb was due to go off.'

'I watched the boat for a fortnight!' Prendergast said, his voice still not fully under control. 'Every night he was there at midnight, working.'

'Not this time,' Harry said.

'I would have got him eventually,' Prendergast said defiantly. He paused. Still looking at the heater, he shook his head, totally

235

bewildered. 'But why . . . ? I tested the explosive and the detonator; I checked and rechecked . . .'

'When you set the timer, you set it for midnight, Greenwich Mean Time. You forgot that the clocks went on for British Summer Time in the interval before it was due to explode. Mistake number two,' Harry said. 'So, although it was due to go off at midnight GMT, that was one a.m. our time now. And that gave me long enough.' By about two seconds, Harry thought. He didn't give Prendergast the satisfaction of knowing how close a call it had been.

As Harry and Rumsden left the interview room the Sergeant asked Harry, 'How did you manage to guess that?'

'An alarm clock on the houseboat. It was an hour slow. Ernie Birt went away before the clocks went on an hour.'

It was broad daylight before Harry Timberlake was ready to leave the station. There had been a small celebration party, smaller than the first one for Sarah Lewis, largely because there were fewer policemen in the station and Harry was too physically and mentally exhausted to do much celebrating. He was aware that it would take only a couple of drinks to make him quite drunk, and he wanted to do his report before he went home.

He finished typing, read through the report, corrected a few typographical errors, and signed the copies. He stood up, conscious of all sorts of aches and pains. He stretched his arms, flexed his shoulders, and rubbed the back of his neck. The muscles there felt as if they had been riveted solid. He realised for the first time just how tensed up he had been on the houseboat.

Someone behind him coughed. It was Sarah Lewis.

'Hi,' she said.

'Hi, Sarah.'

'Glad you're back. I was a bit worried when the Sarge told me you'd gone out on a bomb scare.'

'Thanks.'

They exchanged a few more words, then Harry set off for home.

A large malt whisky, a long hot bath, followed by bacon and eggs that Jenny Long would have sternly disapproved of, combined to make Harry feel much more human. Luckily he had changed the sheets on his bed the previous night. It would make going to bed

236

that little bit more luxurious. A tape he had made of records by King Joe Oliver played in the background. It was a tape with two of King Oliver's most famous compositions on it, 'Dipper Mouth Blues' and 'Canal Street Blues'. Harry played it only on very special occasions. For once he actually contemplated taking the phone off the hook, but he knew he'd only worry about it and be unable to wind down completely.

Harry took the plates and tea things into the kitchen and put them on the draining board. Normally he didn't leave the washing-up, no matter how tired he was, but this was a very special occasion. As he came out of the kitchen into the main living room, he stopped dead.

Jenny Long was standing in the middle of the room, the key he had given her still in her hand.

'Hello, darling,' she said. 'I tried to get you at the nick last night, but they said you were out. I rang them again this morning and they told me the whole story of last night. That was bloody marvellous. I'm proud of you. Anyway, they said you'd gone home. So, here I am . . .'

'Why didn't you phone first?'

Jenny looked at him in surprise. Harry had sounded unusually ungracious, but she put it down to strain. 'I thought you might be asleep after last night, and I didn't want to risk waking you.' She smiled. 'So I decided to sneak in and give you a surprise. I didn't think you'd be behind the door holding that thing in your hand again.' She smiled wickedly.

Sarah Lewis walked in from the bathroom wearing a towel.

When the two women saw each other they stood like stone statues for a long moment. Harry was just as paralysed.

Jenny was the first one to recover. With considerable poise she said, 'I see the surprise is on the other foot in a manner of speaking.'

Sarah, who had matured enormously in the past few weeks, was almost equally self-assured. She said, 'Hello. My name's Sarah Lewis.'

'Jenny Long,' Jenny said automatically. 'Well, now.' She looked at Harry. 'Aren't you going to say anything?'

Harry desperately sought something witty and sophisticated to offer, but his mind had seized up. He would have been hard put to it to find an answer to 'good morning.'

Jenny broke the deadlock. With histrionic care she placed Harry's front door key on the table. 'I think you'd better make up your mind who you want to give this to,' she said.

According to Greek legend, Paris had to judge three women and award the winner with a golden apple. Paris had it easy, Harry reckoned.

Since he had slept with Sarah occasionally he had wondered which one of the two women he would pick if he were forced to make a choice – a purely hypothetical question, he had thought, which would never arise – and he hadn't been able to make up his mind. Now that hypothetical question had become very concrete indeed.

He looked at Jenny and Sarah and back again.

To his astonishment, he found that he had no hesitation at all now it had come to it.

He picked up the key and held it out.